Fist of Rage

Kisa Murrin

Kisa Murrin

PO Box 861

Winnemucca, Nevada 89446

Copyright © 2020 by Kisa Murrin

ISBN: 978-1-7367292-0-5

kisa.murrin@gmail.com

Editor – Cheree Castellanos

Cover and page art – Emily Swindle

Photographer – Monica Sartor

For my Mother

I wish you were here to see this

Acknowledgments

There are so many people that have helped me on this journey. First and foremost, I need to thank my family. My husband Ken, whose unwavering support kept me going. My kids, Aubree, Britnee, Journey and Jesse, their constant encouragement kept me motivated.

My sisters, Desirae and Corrisa, my brother Joe, thank you for believing in me and cheering me on.

My editor, Cheree Castellanos, without your support and guidance, none of this would be possible.

My cover designer and page artist, Emily Swindle, thank you for answering my constant questions and for making all the changes when I couldn't make up my mind.

Monica Sartor, thank you for taking my pictures and making me look beautiful. Thank you for picking up the phone every time I called with more questions and throwing out ideas to make scenes work better.

To all that read my rough drafts and offered critiques but also told me how much they loved what I put on paper, you all gave me the confidence to keep going! Ericka Adams, Nichole Plowman, Kimberly Hamilton.

There are many that talked me down when my self-doubt threatened to make me throw in towel, without them it would have been hard to keep going. Gentry Stoumbaugh, Ginx Viegut, Leslie Archer, Karin Southall and Jennifer Keele.

Words could never express my gratitude and love for you all.

Fist of Rage
Do you remember how you felt
when you looked into his eyes?

When he promised that he'd love
you and never make you cry.

Each day he proved his love to
you, showing you romance,

Then you lost your heart when he
pulled you close to dance.

Every night was magic as you
shared your dreams,

Tell me when things changed, this
love's not what it seems.

Now you walk so softly, your love
replaced by fear,

Every night's a battle filled with
pain and tears.

Tell me of that bruise, that's there
above your eye,

Did you try to leave? Did you try
to say good-bye?

What was the reason this time, for
him to raise his hand?

Did you not come running, when
he made demand?

You told me of a gentle man, that
used to softly speak,

Is this the man that left the mark,
that's now upon your cheek?

Tell me why you live this way,
locked up in a cage?

Can't you reach the key, that's in
his fist of rage?

Chapter 1

Olivia

Watching the sun rise behind the Frenchman mountains, the mist settling along the bottom, the darkness of the desert contrasted by the brilliance of the sun lighting the sky in orange, red, and purple, everyday it's a perfect sunrise. My divorce papers rustle in the breeze in my hand, sleep has been elusive, I've read and reread the papers throughout most of the night, the last step in closing this chapter of my life, not just this chapter, I'm closing this whole damn book. In the last five years all that I have ever known has been lost or proven a lie. Greg has twenty days to respond from the time he is served, if he doesn't, the divorce is final, if he does, I don't know, Alex said we would cross that bridge if we come to it. I think he still underestimates Greg, he thinks these papers are a gift to any man getting a divorce, a spouse that is asking for nothing. My only request to the court is to return to my maiden name, not wanting to be tied to him in any way, I haven't been able to impress upon him that Greg views me more as a possession than as a spouse or equal partner. Alex has forgotten the cases that began his career as an attorney, to any of his clients now what I'm offering would be a gift, the opportunity to hold on to their wealth, their possessions, their legacies. Greg, he wants it all, not that we had wealth, but he wants to keep what is his, me being included in that.

Rachel interrupts my thoughts as she comes out the sliding glass door, two steaming cups of coffee in her hands, "Morning doll, you okay?" Yesterday she had given me the space that I needed to process it all after we left Alex's office. He wanted to take her to lunch, but she did what she always does and acted as my support system, I'm surprised her tongue isn't bloody and sore, she went against who she is and offered silent support. She didn't bombard me with questions trying to drag my thoughts and feelings from me, she sat quietly, watching, hovering but never saying a word. She held my hand when tears of relief streamed down my face and she hugged me tight when I cried hysterically. She knew it wasn't the destruction of my marriage that overwhelmed me, it was the fear of what was to come from filing for divorce. Today is a new day, today she will demand that we talk, I see the fear in her eyes, she's afraid that I will slip back into the shell that I was when she first found me, she's scared that I won't come back this time.

"Good morning Rach, how'd you sleep?" I sidestep her question, to be honest, I don't know how I am right now, I've resigned myself to whatever fate may come. In that sense I'm better than yesterday but not as good as the day before that, when I was still hidden in anonymity 2500 miles away from my estranged husband, or am I the estranged one since I left?

"Sorry sister, it isn't playing out like that today, I left you alone all day yesterday, now you have to talk to me." The concern burning in her eyes softens my resolve to ignore her question, she above all deserves a response, I wouldn't be here without her, honestly, I don't know where I would be without her.

"I'm alright, still processing, worrying about what comes next, you know, probably what every person feels when they file for divorce." I try to sound lighter than I feel, Rachel and I have talked about the worst of outcomes, I was going to move out and find my own place just so that she wouldn't suffer any possible consequences. I just don't know what Greg will do and I don't want her to be collateral damage if he reacts the way I think he will. She rejected that idea vehemently, I probably should have put up more of a fight but honestly, selfishly, I'm afraid to face this alone.

"Whatever happens, you aren't alone Ollie, I will be here with you every step of the way, and Alex will too, I think he's almost as protective of you as I am." I can't look at her, I know she means every word, and it splinters my heart to know that I could be putting her in danger.

"Let's just be positive, isn't that what you always tell me, visualize the positive outcome that we hope for." I don't know where I found the conviction in my voice, I can't argue with her anymore about me getting my own place, she knows the hell I came from, and she still refuses to see the reasoning. More than anything, I don't think that I can face it alone.

"I know what you're thinking Ollie, I understand the risks, you're my best friend, if I let you walk out now, I wouldn't be a very good friend." But one that has an inkling of self-preservation, I can't fault her, she is one of two people in the world that know anything about my past.

"What kind of friend does it make me, knowing what can happen?" The last thing in the world that I want to do is put her in danger, but I'm too much of a coward to do anything about it.

"Alex and I talked last night, I know he makes light of things when he talks to you, he isn't oblivious to the possibilities Ollie, he made some arrangements, we will have round the clock security through his foundation. He isn't naïve to the situation, and though it's his story to tell, I will say this, he understands your situation more profoundly than you know." A weight lifts from my shoulders, I could never ask for more than what Alex offered me in taking my divorce pro bono but knowing that there will be someone to keep us both safe sets my mind at ease if only a little. Now she has my curiosity piqued, as much as I want to ask, I would never put her in a position to betray the trust Alex bestowed on her.

"I didn't know he was going to do that. I didn't know he could do that. I don't want to take advantage of the foundation or him, but I am so grateful that he's doing this, Rachel." In addition to free legal services, Alex had offered me more services through Battling Back, the foundation that he and his best friend had started, a non-profit that serves victims of domestic violence, providing services of free legal work, counseling, medical services, resume preparation, clothes for job interviews, and assistance with housing and utilities, giving victims the best possible chance to succeed after leaving volatile situations. When I had asked Alex about it, he had only said that he and his friend were grateful for all the success that they had enjoyed and wanted to give back. They researched resources that were limited in Las Vegas and found that there were few services of this kind, and what was available was lacking severely. What Rachel just said makes me wonder if there was more to the story.

"He worried that you would refuse, be it your pride or that you would feel like you were abusing the system, so he decided for you." While I don't doubt what she's saying, I can't help but feel like his feelings for her also played a role in his decision, and because of that it makes me respect him all the more. Knowing how much he cares for my friend, the doubts about him that plagued me when she first started dating him are all gone. The two of them deserve each other, deserve the rewards of being good people that care about others without asking for anything in return.

"I'll be sure to thank him, now if you're going to be my taxi today, you better go get ready, Alex said my interview is at 11. If I'm going to take back my life, I need a job to start." When we met with Alex yesterday to sign the papers, I wasn't aware he had been on a job hunt for me. Not just a job but a possible career as the bar manager for The Whiskey Wrangler, the new western club opening. The job specifics were minimal, but Alex felt comfortable throwing my name out because of my background as a bar owner. Ian Alessandro, Alex's best friend, client, business owner, and co-founder of Battling Back, agreed to interview me as a favor. I think I'm qualified, I owned my own bar in New York City before it was turned to ash, started by the flames that had already begun to scorch my life.

"I'm not the one that has an interview Ollie, if anyone needs to get ready, it's you." I watch as she makes her way back into our apartment. The presence that she creates with her character is drastically different than her stature, petite at 5'1" and 120 pounds, a perfect hourglass figure, fire red hair hanging just below her shoulders and framing her elfin face, tattooed black eyeliner encasing her green eyes, freckles speckled across her nose. Her red hair is a warning, though she is small, she is a reminder that dynamite comes in small packages. Her big personality sometimes gets her in trouble, but her years in martial arts has bailed her out of every situation she found herself in.

I know that I have at least an hour before Rachel will be out of the bathroom, but it's too hot to stay on the balcony, now that the sun has fully risen it's already sweltering. The desert heat is welcome to the humidity of New York, the temperature is higher here, the dry heat is more comfortable than home, but sitting directly in the sun is too much. I send a quick prayer to my mom that she be with me today, lend me some luck to get my first job in more than three years.

I'm sorting out my explanation of the gap in my work history as I make my way into the kitchen, and my response to the question of the arson that burned down Trinity, no suspect was ever apprehended. I heard the whispers and saw the accusation in people's eyes, hell the tabloids came outright and accused me, the case was never closed. In the court of public opinion, I had set the fire to collect the insurance money and got away with it because my husband was the assistant DA. Those that made those judgments had no idea that I would have done anything to save my bar, it was the business my mom and I had started together. We worked side by side for fourteen years to make it the success that it was. When she died, it was my connection to her, I lost more than my business in that fire, I lost memories and my mom's ashes as well. I just hope that my prospective employer will believe that I had nothing to do with it.

Standing in front of the mirror, I hardly recognize myself anymore, I should have gone for a haircut. My long, black hair is unruly as always and frayed at the ends, I can't remember the last time I had a trim. Brown eyes muddy, dull, and somber, surrounded by dark circles and bags that no amount of makeup will hide. So many tragedies in such a short time have aged me. The death of Greg's parents, the changes in my husband, my mother died in an accident just a year later, then six months after that Trinity caught fire. Since then I had let myself go, I stopped caring about everything, my last bit of hope burned with my bar, my once flat stomach is now full and flabby, my thighs thicker than they've ever been, my breasts always large and full are starting to sag, gravity working against me.

I trace my finger over the puckered red scar the size of a quarter above my left breast. The remnant of the cigar that Greg had extinguished there, a constant reminder from him that I had hurt his heart. I stop myself from falling down that rabbit hole, today is not the day to rehash the past, today I start my future.

I stand under the hot water reminding myself of my qualifications, the experience that I have that will make me the best candidate for this position. As much as I build myself up, in the back of my mind I can hear Greg telling me that I will fail, just as I have at everything, as a wife, a mother, a daughter, a business owner. That I don't have the marketable skills to get this job.

It takes all I have to push all my thoughts aside and focus, silencing his voice, searching for the confidence that I once had. Getting ready for the interview that could be the first chapter of the new book of my life.

Chapter 2

Ian

My morning had started as a shitshow, a 4am phone call that Vivian had overdosed again, this time she was found in the backroom of the Ragtime. I've been on the phone with Alex all morning trying to get my name off that club. When Vivian and I had divorced, I knew she would never be able to support herself, and regardless of how our marriage had fallen apart, I still loved her. Besides, when I started Ragtime Rhythm it was for her, when we split, I wanted no part of it, but she lacked capital. She had no investors to back her, so provided that she left all my other assets off the table, I was more than happy to turn it over to her, retaining 49% interest to help her keep it going. Now that she is strung out, focusing more on getting laid and doing dope, I don't give a damn how she keeps it open. I won't let it tarnish my name or any of the businesses that I have worked so hard for. As much as I loved her, I can't help her anymore, that's what I told her father when he called this morning. Our marriage has been over for three years, I've been supportive of her business and paid for rehab five times, I'm out. I knew we would never get back together, infidelity is not something I can recover from. I had hoped that we could remain friends, I felt that I owed her that. I thought all the years that we had shared was worth that, but this isn't a friendship as much as I'm enabling her.

"Alex, I don't care what you have to do, I want out, I have too much going on right now, I can't bail her out again. The opening of Whiskey Wrangler has most of my resources tied up, until those contracts are complete..." Before I can finish Alex interrupts, "I told you I have it handled, look why don't you go check on her, check on her family, let me handle the mess. Don't forget to tell Michelle about the Daniels file, she is interviewing at 11 and I don't want Michelle being the usual hard ass, this woman has potential, she just needs the opportunity." Michelle and Alex have never seen eye to eye, she is no nonsense, and Alex's mannerisms put her on edge. While Michelle will be part of the interview, I'll be conducting all management positions for The Whiskey, not that I don't trust her, but I need to have good chemistry with my management team. I'm building this club from the ground up, it has to be a success. In the last few months, I've begun to think I may have jumped headfirst without checking where.

"I'll handle it Alex, is Daniels Rachel's friend?" It's the only thing that makes sense, Alex doesn't normally concern himself with my personnel or question the interview process.

"Yeah, that's her, like I said she has potential, so keep an open mind for me." There is more to this story if Alex is asking for a favor, another example of how whipped he is, I've never seen him like this with a woman, Rachel must be something special for him to stick his neck out for her friend.

Rather than check on Vivian, I call my mom, it's been weeks since I've had a chance to speak with her, it's early evening in Italy, increasing the likelihood of catching her.

"Ian!! My dear boy, are you alright?" Hearing her voice, the tension eases off my shoulders. She's been my biggest supporter, without her, nothing I have would be possible. When Poppi got sick it was important for her to get back to Italy to take care of him and Nonie. I bought her a Villa and helped her get moved and her parents moved in with her, that was six months before my divorce.

"Mama! I just had a little time and wanted to hear your voice. Are you well? How are Nonie and Poppi?" My mother has enjoyed this time with her parents, she had lost so much time with them when she ran off with my father.

"Ian, don't lie to your mother, what's wrong?" I could never hide anything from her, even all these miles away, she has a sixth sense, she just knows.

"Vee overdosed this morning, she's in the hospital. I can't keep helping her mama, am I wrong?" Her advice is what I have always relied on. Her honesty, though sometimes hurts, is appreciated, I've always known she would tell me the truth even if I didn't want to hear it. She's never told me anything to save my feelings, she knows that the pain of the truth is bearable, while the pain of a lie can do irreparable damage.

"Ian, honey, you must stop feeling responsible for her, she made her choices. You can't carry the weight of her mistakes with you, you can't bear the responsibility of her actions. How many years did you spend loving her, trying to make her happy? She won't ever find happiness and peace for herself until she learns to love herself." I know my mother doesn't care for Vivian, but that doesn't make anything she says less true. I can't help Vee until she wants to help herself first. "Ian, you have to let her go, you say that there is no going back but you have failed to move on, and you are the first one there to pick her up when she falls. You also need to love yourself more son, you deserve to be loved and be happy, don't spend your life taking care of someone that gave up on you, Ian. You need more in your life than lost love and work." This is why I called her, I needed her reassurance that turning my back on Vivian is the right thing to do.

"I will mama, now tell me of Italy, of Nonie and Poppi." With the deep conversation over, we fall into stories of her home. Poppi has recovered well and the time that they have all been able to share has mended the wounds of the past, mama sounds so happy, so at ease. I'm elated to hear the lightness of her words, she struggled tremendously raising me as a single mother on a card dealers' salary. She took Alex in when he was 10, her hours doubled, but she never complained and never thought twice about her decision to raise Alex.

I spent more time talking to my mother than I had planned, it's easy to lose track of time when speaking to her. I vow to myself that once the Whiskey is up and running, I will go see her in Italy, spend some time getting to know my grandparents. They are the only ones I will ever know. Mother and I stopped speaking of my father years ago, once I came of age, I lost interest in knowing him, any man that can leave a woman pregnant with his child and not look back is not worth the oxygen granted to him. She did fine raising me on her own, he doesn't deserve to be a part of what I have built, I don't even know his name, and I hope I never do.

The offices for all of my operations are all located at The Lost Cities. This is my first casino, where it all started when I was 22, I'm proud of what I've created, I was only able to embark on this journey because of a little luck. I finished my business degree early, after so many years of focus and determination I just wanted a break. I got myself into a poker tournament, and I won. I travelled the circuit each tournament with higher stakes, sitting at a poker table I'm devoid of all emotion. Through college we played nightly, I learned what my tells were and worked hard to learn to hide them. In that year, I earned a spot at the world series, I'd earned enough for my buy in and went on to win the whole thing, the youngest player ever to have won and the biggest jackpot to date. Honestly, it was all luck and just my ability to remain unreadable at a table. My mother told me to invest, she made me promise to not gamble again, she worked the tables for the majority of her life, the cards are always stacked in favor of the house, she always told me, "They don't keep the lights on letting people win Ian, don't waste your money giving it to the casino hoping to get lucky, in the end you will lose." When I won, I heeded her advice, I wanted to invest, ma was thinking stocks and bonds, investing in the market, but I wanted more. I wanted to build something, create a legacy. I bought the most run down, dilapidated casino in Vegas, mama was furious, she called me a fool. She was wrong, 20 years later, I own the largest casino in town, a couple smaller ones, several nightclubs, and am on the verge of opening a club that will host a multitude of events and concerts. I built this. I couldn't have done it without my mother though, and I don't ever forget that. It's because of her sacrifices that I made it to where I am.

I step into reception in the human resources office, "Is Michelle ready for our 10:45am?" I stand before Michelle's secretary, someone new since the last time I was here.

"Your name sir?" I stare at her in disbelief, a look at the calendar would tell her my name, I don't expect everyone to know me by sight, but I am disappointed that she is unaware that I have an appointment with Michelle.

"Ian, Ian Alessandro." Immediately her cheeks redden, she opens her mouth to speak as Michelle steps out of her office, "Ian, we were scheduled for 10:45 why are you wasting my time by standing out here? I have plenty to do on a Tuesday morning, keeping you on schedule is not on that list." Her secretary looks mortified, understanding that she has made a mistake and that mistake has caused me to be late, I give her a slight smile before I turn to Michelle, "Alex is right, you need to relax Michelle, when was your last vacation?" As I round the desk, I see a sigh of relief from the secretary, I set her at ease by not throwing her under the bus. I see no need for further action, she is well aware of her mistake and I'm confident it's not one that will be repeated, if Michelle knew what just happened, at the very least she would be demoted, at worst fired, neither of those outcomes seem justified.

"I've looked over the resume provided by Alex, while this woman may have potential, she's been out of the game for three years, Ian." Michelle jumps straight to business.

"I'm well Michelle, and you?" She doesn't bother to look up from the resume.

"You don't pay me to make small talk, you pay me to do a job, if you weren't interfering, I would be doing that now. As it stands you've requested to be involved in the interview process for management positions at The Whiskey. I'm not sure if it's because you feel I'm not up to the task, or perhaps you feel the need to check up on my work performance, regardless, there is an applicant that will be here directly and I feel it's best that we at least have a game plan for that interview, so if you don't mind." I smirk at the haughtiness she exhibits, apparently, I have stepped on her toes and damaged her ego wanting to be hands on in the hiring of my club.

"Michelle, I've never doubted your ability and have never felt the need to check up on you, what is important to me is that I am able to work well with whomever is hired, your job has always been to weed through the applicants and send the best candidates to department management for a second interview. Until this business is up and running smoothly and making a profit, I fully intend to be in the midst of it all, some people aren't able to work well under those conditions. You have no idea how they will interact with me nor I with them, so rather than hire the wrong people, I feel it necessary for me to be involved. After each interview you and I can discuss what each of us read off the applicants." She stares down her nose over her glasses at me, the sharp angles of her face give her a stern look, her dyed black hair is too harsh for her features and does nothing to soften her characteristics.

"Alright then, Alex submitted her resume, he said she would fill out an application when she comes in if necessary. He stated that she is applying for the beverage manager position, she co-owned a bar called Trinity in New York City, a little hole in the wall place that was frequented by businessmen for about fourteen years. The bar was destroyed in a fire the cause was listed as arson, after that she fell off the map until now." Something about this story is sounding familiar, though I can't place why.

"So, Alex is right, she could have potential?" I know the word arson has her on red alert, it would certainly be cause for concern if Alex hadn't recommended her, I'll still investigate it further, but I don't believe that the issue is with her.

"Well, let's call her in and we shall see." She's still bristled because I'm here, my patience is wearing thin, she doesn't have to like it, it's my business and I will conduct it however I feel is necessary.

Chapter 3

Olivia

I've seen the Lost Cities from a distance, it's hard to miss standing at 56 stories. The outside shines like gold, towering above all the buildings around it. The massive fountain in front of the entrance depicts Atlantis, King Triton in all his glory, trident raised to defend his majestic underworld. The crystal-clear water, providing a cool mist, granting some relief to the heat of Las Vegas. Approaching the doors, I hear the ringing of the slot machines every time they slide open. The grandeur is intimidating but still inviting.

Inside I'm surprised by the brightness, light provided by a sea of enormous crystal chandeliers. The walls a deep navy, adorned with intricate filigree and wall hangings of gold, framed by strategically placed stone pillars. Marble floors at the entrance, giving way to carpet of blue, black, green, and white, patterned to look like ocean waves. I'm reverential in the elegance, the wonder, the peaceful atmosphere. Rachel leads me away from the casino, around the hotel desk, and beyond, we stop in front of a glass door that opens to a long hallway.

"Knock 'em dead doll, follow the hallway down, you'll see a door marked human resources, Ms. Cain is expecting you. Alex says don't let her intimidate you, she's a bitch, but she's good at her job. Just be you." She gives me a quick hug and turns on her heal heading back toward the casino.

My fingers tremble as I reach for the door, I don't know if the heat just hit me or my nerves are getting the best of me, but suddenly I'm sweating. I adjust the collar of my button-down blouse and dab my forehead with the Kleenex from the pocket of my skirt as I head down the hallway. A million thoughts race through my mind, the doubts piling up, what am I doing? Once upon a time I might have been qualified for this position but not now, it's been too long, and my little bar was nothing in comparison to a business of this magnitude. I must do this, I need a job, my funds are nearly depleted, and Alex called in a favor to get me this interview.

Before I speak, I compose myself as best I can and paste on a semblance of a smile, "Olivia Daniels for Ms. Cane." The receptionist greets me with a warm smile before announcing my arrival.

"You can go in and good luck." She comes around her desk to open the door for me, offering me an encouraging look as she passes me.

I falter in the doorway, the stern look from Ms. Cain is intimidating but worse, it seems that I have interrupted a meeting already in progress, "I, I'm sorry, I didn't mean to interrupt." My voice is small and weak, I don't recognize it, my eyes are drawn to the man rising from his chair.

"Please come in Ms. Daniels, I am Ian Alessandro, this is Michelle Cain, I hope you don't mind, but we will be conducting a joint interview." When he reaches his full height, I have to look up to meet his eyes, standing at 5'10" myself, I'm unaccustomed to looking up to most people. He's slim but broad shouldered, muscular build under his gray pinstriped suit, his hand fully envelopes mine in greeting. There is something familiar about Mr. Alessandro, I can't put my finger on it, dirty blonde hair, blue-gray eyes, just the slightest traces of crow's feet, strong jaw, high cheek bones, handsome doesn't even begin to cover it. His eyes are so captivating, and so familiar, his blue tie making them stand out.

"Ms. Daniels, please have a seat." I sit on the edge of the chair provided, forcing myself to sit up straight, knees together, head held high, giving off the air of confidence even if I'm not feeling it.

"Ms. Daniels, have we met before?" Mr. Alessandro addresses me directly, his question startling me because of my own sense of recognition. I'm positive that I've never met this man, the familiarity must be from the papers or the tabloids or maybe a billboard. I would remember if we had met. If that's the case, then why would he have the same feeling?

"Please, call me Olivia, no, I don't believe so. I've only lived here for a year and I really don't get out much." I hate being addressed by my last name, it can't come soon enough that I can be Olivia Mason again. Before he can ask the next question forming on his lips, Ms. Cain interjects.

"Where do you hail from?" She's on a mission, she's ready to conduct this interview and isn't going to get sidetracked. I'm sure she's read my resume, she should know where I come from, I get the impression she is trying to get a read on me.

"New York City ma'am." I answer, careful to be as respectful as I can, it seems that though Mr. Alessandro owns the business, Ms. Cain is in charge right now.

"I knew I recognized you." My body stiffens, I feel the tension radiating throughout my body as Mr. Alessandro speaks. "You're Rae Daniels." I cringe at the name from my past, when I left the city, I left that name with it, preferring to go by my given name in my new life. "I've seen you in the papers." How did he see the papers, I know it isn't recent, I've kept track, curious if Greg would report me missing? How does he remember from so long ago?

"Um... I..." I wasn't prepared to be recognized, though maybe I should have. The media had our faces posted everywhere, I was married to a NYC Assistant District Attorney, but I had no idea that the stories would make it this far west. My first reaction is to leave, I don't want to answer this question, I don't want to be remembered, I want to start fresh, I want a future that isn't tarnished by my past. As I look at the two people in front of me, I know that this is my best shot at having a future and starting over.

"I apologize, I didn't mean to make you uncomfortable, of course I keep track of the markets, I receive papers from all over the country." He looks as though he has more to say, his confidence slightly diminished, embarrassment clouds his features.

"It's fine, you just took me off guard. I was just surprised that the stories published this far west, it makes sense now." The media went crazy over Greg, the devastation of losing his parents, it was a story that sold papers. And as our world was rocked with more death and destruction, the media capitalized as did his boss, pushing us to the forefront, encouraging interviews, giving the circling vultures free rein to use us and our pain to change the opinions of the people.

"Ms. Daniels, please give me insight as to why you feel you are qualified for this position." Ms. Cain interjects, breaking the awkwardness. My confidence grows as I tell her of starting Trinity with my mother, the setbacks that we faced and overcame, the success of our bar. Prior to the fire we were on track to nearly double our profits from the previous year, our profit margin trended up every year, but that last year it skyrocketed.

"While those are all great accomplishments, what makes you think that the skills you acquired in small business will be enough to carry you through as a manager of a business this size?"

"Ms. Cain, I'm sure that I can't answer that question at this time. You have yet to provide me with any information of relevance regarding the position." There it is, a little of the fire that I use to have, it wasn't my intention to be snarky, but the way she presented the question bordered on insulting. Trinity can't compare in size to what the Whiskey Wrangler will be when it's complete, but what Ms. Cain isn't considering is the amount of business that we had. New York City has nearly nine million people, tourism was through the roof, Trinity was so diverse in our clientele, at any given time you would find equal numbers of businessmen, those that worked the stock market, blue collar workers, and of course the tourists. It wasn't a large bar, but the foot traffic was constant from open to close.

"Ms. Daniels, I apologize, Ms. Cain didn't verbalize the question well. As the bar manager it will be your responsibility to hire the staff, keep the inventory, scheduling, and balance the tills. We will also be holding events, because Trinity was a small business comparatively and the amount of staff that you employed, I think that the question she was getting at is, do you think that with the skills that you possess you will be able to adjust to a much larger scale?" It really pisses me off that they keep calling me that. Mr. Alessandro had recovered from his embarrassment and seemed to be trying to ease the tension that's quickly building in the room.

"Please, call me Olivia. I believe that I can, though we didn't have a large staff, it seems to me that doing a schedule would be the same, shifts still need covered." Now I'm unsure of myself but I refuse to let them see it, but really, how much harder can it be?

"Olivia, it wasn't my intention to offend you, so I apologize if you felt I was minimizing your accomplishments, my point is that you will be responsible to schedule for, the kitchen staff, cocktail waitresses, barbacks, bartenders, servers. This club is going to be out of the norm, so to say, it will be open for lunch and dinner. At this point we haven't fully thought out the business hours, but Nevada is much different than New York, alcohol is served on a 24-hour basis, bands will be playing every week, and tourism in Vegas is a different beast. People aren't here for the culture or history, they are here for the party, the experience of Sin City that they can't get anywhere else, because what happens in Vegas stays in Vegas. Are you prepared to manage all of that?" Her tone had changed, she isn't being condescending she is being thorough, and now that she has posed the question that way, I'm well aware that I'm unqualified, I knew that coming in, but I need this job. With some guidance, I know that I'm capable.

"I understand your hesitation, but I am capable of learning, I have the skill set, it just needs to be expanded to adjust for capacity. I understand that this would be on a much larger scale than what I'm accustomed, that would only make it more challenging, but I am confident that I could be the person that you're looking for." Lying has never been my strong suit, and that was a whopper, but I won't be turned away without putting up a fight, I need this job more than I have ever needed anything.

"If we choose to hire you, would you be willing to start in one of the established businesses for training?" This is the break that I need, if I could just get a feel for things, an idea of the pace and what will be expected of me, I have no doubt that I could make this work.

"Of course, I'd be happy to, I am open to starting right away." The sooner the better, the longer that I could work under someone else, the better that I would feel about taking on this position. I won't admit that to them, admitting that would show them how ill prepared I am.

"This position holds a lot of responsibility, when we recruit management, we do so in hope that we can retain our employees long-term. We hope that they can find a fulfilling and rewarding career. There is a lot invested in each employee but especially in management.

So, what are your plans for the future, what are the goals that you are hoping to achieve?" I haven't thought past the end of each day in so long, there are so many unknowns in my near future, I can't hope to look forward too far in advance, and I don't know what I am hoping to accomplish. I don't know what I want beyond the divorce and to be free from Greg. This kind of indecisiveness isn't what they are looking for, they want to know that training and resources won't be wasted on me, that I will stick around.

"I want to find full time employment utilizing the skills that I have spent most of my adult life developing. I'm hardworking and I learn quickly, if given this opportunity, I won't let you down." My response is vague, it doesn't really answer the question, but I don't know what tomorrow will bring. The uncertainty of my immediate future, I haven't thought past the divorce to know what I want or expect, but I don't want to put my drama out for them to see. If they knew the struggles that plagued me right now, they would send me out the door and throw my resume in the trash.

"Excuse me ladies." Mr. Alessandro steps to the window to take a call. The furrow of his brow, the tension in his shoulders, whoever is on the phone doesn't have good news. Looking at him I can't shake the nagging feeling that I know this man.

"Ms. Daniels, do you have any questions?" Ms. Cain pulls me from my thoughts. It's pointless to ask anything, I know I won't get a call back for this job, rightfully so.

"I don't think so, thank you for your time." I rise and shake her hand, Mr. Alessandro is still on his call, but our eyes meet. Unsure if I should wait, his furrowed brow and the tension in his face dissuade me, so I leave the office.

Chapter 4

Ian

I watch as Olivia rises to leave, long, sculpted legs, her dark hair falling in waves down her back, her coffee colored eyes meet mine, I glimpse for just a moment, uncertainty, hopelessness. Lawrence pulls me back into our conversation. "Ian, you need to get down here, I've never seen her this bad, I don't know if she is coming back from this one." As angry as I am with Vee, I don't want anything to happen to her, her father pleading with me for help, I can't stay away any longer. "I'll be there within the hour."

"Is everything alright?" Surprisingly, Michelle hasn't been informed of the situation with Vivian yet, in most cases she is aware of most of what happens within any of my businesses. "I'm sorry Michelle, I have a situation that I need to deal with, can we meet later to discuss Ms. Daniels, and will you also line up more interviews with qualified candidates?" She doesn't question but agrees to my request with a nod.

Five times I have sent Vee to rehab, and five times she has failed to continue the programs once released. I can't help but feel responsible for the downward spiral she fell into after our separation. I didn't have a choice, the lies, the deceit, the infidelity, I was a laughingstock, worse than that, I was miserable. I knew what she was doing even before it was made public. Then the gossip rag, *The Vegas Voice*, had her on the front page with her lovers almost daily. There was no way to repair our marriage, obviously she wanted out, so I don't understand why it affected her so negatively, why she's killing herself.

I'm shocked to see Vee in the condition she is in, the last I saw her she at least looked healthy. Her appearance now is skeletal, how long has it been since I last saw her? The dramatic weight loss is appalling, the skin stretched over the bones of her face, circles around her eyes so dark it looks as if she has gone five rounds in a boxing ring and lost.

My initial reaction is to go to her, to hold her hand and beg her to wake up, to promise her that I will get her the help that she needs, but I stop myself. I need to distance myself from her, from this, I can't get her the help, I can pay for it, but she has to do it for herself. She has to want it for herself. It can't be me, or her dad, or anyone else in her family, it needs be her.

Lawrence enters the room quietly, "You did this Ian." His words are a whisper, but they hit me as if he shouted them. I know that what he said is untrue, but I can't help but to question the validity of his statement.

"No Larry, she did this. You can't hold me responsible for her actions." Though I'm having trouble believing it myself, my mother's voice rings loud and clear in my mind.

"You left her Ian, she has never recovered from that, this is your fault." His voice cracks, the tears running freely down his face. I expected this from him, Vee is his only child, he has never held her accountable for any of her choices in life.

"I did leave her, she didn't give me a choice. I don't know why you thought I needed to be here, I've seen this before, she will recover and, in a few months, she will be right back here or worse, in the morgue." Cold as it sounds, I need to make my position clear, even if it is worse this time, it's still the same scenario. Until she makes the choice to help herself this will be an endless cycle.

"You could have gone to counseling, you could have been a better husband. If you had been, she wouldn't have felt the need to find what your marriage was lacking with others." It's déjà vu, almost verbatim as the last time we were here.

"I'm sorry you see things that way Lawrence, I can't argue with you anymore, you will never see fault in Vivian, could I have been a better husband? Of course, we all learn and grow everyday with ourselves and our partners, but I was never a bad husband. I was good to your daughter and I loved her more than life itself." Since Sophomore year of high school, I had. The first time I saw her I became infatuated with her dazzling smile, she was the most beautiful girl I had ever seen.

"If you weren't a bad husband, then why was she seeing other people, Ian? She loved you, so what did you do to her?" He has asked me this question time and again. It doesn't matter how I answer, he won't accept it. It has to be something that I did because he can't believe that Vee holds any responsibility.

"I have things to do today so I am going to head out, I hope that she comes around soon and that you can get her the help she needs, but I won't be a part of it this time. Additionally, I have started the paperwork to pull out of Ragtime, I won't allow her actions and her reputation to bring down my business." He looks as though I slapped him, maybe now isn't the time to bring it up, but with Vee, I just don't know if there will ever be a right time.

"How can you do this Ian? You gave her that business, it's all she got out of your divorce." She made that choice, she jumped at the offer. At times I have wondered if I shortchanged her but in hindsight, if she had gotten anything more, she would have run that into the ground as well.

"And she still owns it, she will now have to find her own means of keeping it going. I can't let my name or the rest of what I've built be drug through the mud. I'm not going to risk all that I have worked for." A harsh reality that he is going to have to face.

I told him as I left that I would prefer to not hear from him again. I don't want to hear the updates, I don't want to know how Vee is doing, I need to detach myself from all of them. I've enabled Vee to fall into this cycle, and because of that the family has come to rely on me to fix it. As much as it pains me to cut her and them off completely, I can't be a part of this anymore. I can't watch Vee destroy herself any longer and I can't be the one that the family holds responsible for her actions.

I pull into the dirt lot of the Whiskey, I hang back and just watch as the workers climb beams and shout direction to each other, the equipment moving dirt, the crane swinging steel to be placed. This will be my greatest accomplishment, a club for everyday events, dancing, food, pool tournaments, a mechanical bull, and an amphitheater attached at the back. The concerts and shows that I have planned will bring people from all over the state to attend. It's what I've envisioned for twenty years, here it is coming to fruition. Vee should be here with me, she was my best friend, my confidante, my sounding board, she encouraged me for years to make this happen. Is Lawrence right? Did I drive her away, mistreat her? Am I the cause of all of this? I know the answer is no, but watching Vee self-destruct, it's hard not to wonder.

Even all these years later, it's hard not to doubt my decisions. Not that it matters, what's done is done, there is no coming back from where we are, or where we've been.

As I watch the progress being made, I call Alex. "I've never seen her look this bad man, she's so skinny her cheekbones are protruding, she looks like she's been beat up." If I hadn't known it was her, I never would have guessed when I walked into that hospital room.

"Dope will do that to you, how's she doing?" I fill him in on all that transpired at the hospital, the doubts that are creeping in and the guilt that I can't help but feel. "Ian, you didn't do this, she made the choices that brought her to this point, Lawrence only blames you because it's easier than blaming his little girl that is laying in a hospital bed right now. You gave her everything and loved her more than anything in the world. You aren't the first high school sweethearts that end up in divorce. Neither one of you really dated anyone except each other, she didn't stop loving you, she just grew restless and curious. Settling down as young as you two did, to be honest, I'm surprised it took as long as it did, that you both weren't out there experimenting." I never had eyes for anyone else, I never considered an affair even when the women were throwing themselves at me, it was always Vee.

"What now? Have you removed me from Ragtime?" I don't want to be associated with it anymore but it's still hard to let it go. But if it's necessary to give up a business, Ragtime would be the only choice.

"I'm working on it, I'm going to throw an idea out, I think it will help ease your guilt and it will help her to keep it open. I'm suggesting this as your attorney because as your friend it's a stupid idea. I think that you should pay the debts that are currently owed, by doing so you are helping her to keep the place open and giving her a jump start in continuing to keep it open. If you walk away with your name on those debts it can cause you issues later. Overall, your vendors know you and respect you, if you pay them off now, they will appreciate not being left in a lurch if she goes belly up. They will also know that Ragtime business will be conducted only with her going forward." Giving anything to Vee is hard for Alex, he took her betrayal personally, so I know that this suggestion is the best course of action to take. Will it ease the guilt? I don't know, it doesn't matter, this is the stand that I must take.

"Do it, the employees and the vendors shouldn't have to suffer. Make sure all the bills are paid in full including payroll, then sign it all over to her, a clean slate, make sure that they are all aware of the changes and what to expect from here on out." Especially the employees, she's had a high turnover rate for some time now, I expect that number to grow exponentially.

"I'll get started today, now to change the subject on you, how was the interview with Ollie?" As much as I would like to tell him it was great, I can't put her in the position that he wants, she doesn't have the experience, she isn't ready to take this on.

"I recognized her once she introduced herself, she was all over the news in New York for a couple years, that woman has been through a lot." She's more beautiful than her pictures reflected.

"You didn't say anything did you? She likes to live in anonymity." I noticed the way she tensed when I mentioned it, the fear in her eyes, her struggle to calm herself.

"I did, but when I saw her reaction we moved on. Alex, as much as I'd like to help you look like a hero to your girlfriend, I can't hire her for that position, she isn't ready, and I'm not sure that she ever will be. She lacks the qualities I expect in a manager." The strength it takes to be firm with the employees, the vendors, the crowds, she's too meek to take all that on.

"This isn't about being a hero to my girlfriend Ian, you know I wouldn't stick my neck on the line for just anyone, Rachel didn't ask me to do this. You're right that Ollie has been through a lot, but you're wrong about her qualities. I know her resume is short but if you had any idea how far she brought her business you would see things differently." If this isn't about Rachel then how did this come about, there's something he's not telling me.

"Alright, enlighten me Alex." I listen as he explains his position, he offers more numbers than what Olivia had but essentially says the same things.

"She told us all of that, if this isn't about Rachel tell me why you're so invested." Maybe if I understand his point of view it will help me to see in her what he does.

"Well, we need to shift gears again then, we're going to work on some foundation work. Ollie is a client. I was going to speak with you about her anyway, we need security for this case, we're going to need it for Ollie and Rachel, the guy we're dealing with has done some heinous shit and I don't want to take any chances. She needs this job to get back on her feet and start her life over." Her husband, a district attorney, I think, I assumed that they were no longer together, but it's hard to imagine that she would need services through the foundation.

"Her husband, he's the District Attorney?" Surprised by this turn of events, I wasn't expecting to hear that she's a client. I try to recall the information I read, the first article was the day after Thanksgiving, several years ago, his parents were murdered after their guests had departed following Thanksgiving dinner.

"The Assistant District Attorney, that's part of what makes him so dangerous, I'm toeing a line here Ian, I have permission to speak of some of this because we are utilizing foundation resources, but I'm personally handling her divorce." I would never expect him to break confidence as an attorney, but the case has me intrigued as to what the situation is.

"Alright, I'll make some arrangements for security, how long are we looking at?" The best part of the success Alex and I have enjoyed is this, the giving back, being able to provide the assistance that no one could give to his mother. "I'll tell you what I'll do, I'm not offering her the manger position, but I will bring her in as a cocktail waitress, or a bartender, whatever is available and give her the opportunity to move up from there.

"Thanks Ian, plan for a few weeks at least, we filed her divorce papers yesterday, and as far as the job, I think at this point she is willing to take just about anything. So, as a favor to me, I'd appreciate you try to put her somewhere." I'd like nothing more than to find out more about her story. The paper painted a picture of a couple deeply in love, her as a devoted wife standing strong for her husband to lean on. Appearances can be deceiving, no one knows that better than Alex and me.

Chapter 5

Olivia

After wandering through the casino for 20 minutes, I finally found Rachel, I tried calling her, but she didn't answer. We've been sitting here at a machine for over an hour, it's hard to walk away when you're winning, and so far, she's up eight hundred dollars.

While she plays, I tell her about the interview, knowing full well that I won't be offered the position, rightfully so. As much as I tried to convince myself and them that I'm qualified, we all know better than that. If given that job I have no doubt that I'd epically fail and embarrass myself. Mr. Alessandro seems like a nice man and I would hate to be the downfall of something he's obviously worked hard to accomplish.

"Earth to Ollie! Hey doll!" I snap out of the thoughts I got lost in. "Even if they don't offer this one to you, they could have something else, and if not, this town is full of jobs that you would rock! Don't sell yourself short, something's gonna happen."

Her positivity is infectious, it's impossible to wallow if she is close by. Her philosophy is the glass is neither half full nor half empty, it's a damn glass refill it! Her grammar is atrocious, but I love her for those reasons and so many more.

"I know, I guess I just got my hopes up, I wouldn't be opposed to something else." I watch as a cocktail waitress walks by, except that, I can't be a cocktail waitress. The uniform, a deep U cut in the back spanning all the way to her lower back, I can't wear something like that. I try to remember what Rachel's uniform looks like, I guess I haven't paid much attention because I have no idea if hers is similar. I haven't really been out to the casinos, is this how they all dress?

"I know you did doll, I did too, I think with training and working in the environment you could get there though, so maybe they'll train you, don't give up yet. Alex makes miracles happen every day." The way her eyes light up when she says his name, even when Greg and I were dating I don't think I ever looked like that. Now that

I'm nearly forty, I'm not holding out hope that I ever will. Dating is so far away from reality, if it's not off the table completely yet, I really don't know if I will be able to date again or if I really want to. Talk about putting the cart before the horse, I just filed for divorce yesterday and today I'm deciding if I will ever date again. Slow down Olivia, I tell myself, shaking my head in disbelief.

I watch as the reels spin in front of Rachel, her excitement when she triggers a bonus, her laughter when she wins. She is always so easy going, so calm for the most part, but if you get her riled up, she's a firecracker!

It worked well for Rachel, she cashed out at a thousand dollars, built up while she waited for me. As we drive home in silence I get lost in the what if's, what if Greg comes to Vegas? What if he denies the divorce? What if I don't get a job? What if I'm forced to go back? I stop myself with that one, there isn't anyone or anything that could make me go back to that. Vegas is warm, even without a job I can survive as

a homeless person, people survive in the
cold winters of New York being homeless. I
chuckle at my dramatics.

While Rachel gets ready for work, I
disappear into my room. All that is on my
mind is what happens next, there is nothing
to say that hasn't been said. I don't mind
the silence, I revel in it. The solitude is
peaceful, no charades to play, it's healing,
it's strange that I enjoy it so much. I've
spent my whole life never being alone, my
mom was always a prominent figure, I lived
with her until Greg and I moved in together,
so I've never really been alone. I spend a lot
of my time alone now, at first, I was scared,
I jumped at shadows and cringed at noises I
couldn't define. As time has gone on, I've
grown comfortable in the silence and being
by myself, I think it's comforting because I
can hear all that is going on around me. It's
a defense mechanism, if I can hear

something coming, I can be prepared for whatever it is.

The ringing of the phone interrupts my thoughts, Alex's name flashes across my screen. He gets to be the bearer of bad news, I guess he drew the short straw. "Hey Alex!" I wonder if he will be the one to tell me that I didn't get the job. If I remember right from high school, something along the lines of, thank you for your interest in the management position, unfortunately we have opted for another applicant, please apply again in the future. Back then, that response came in letter form, do they call now?

"Ollie! How are you today?" Maybe he hasn't heard how badly the interview went, he's pretty chipper, I can hear the smile in his voice. I've always been told to smile when talking on the phone, that people can hear your smile, I never believed it until I saw Alex talk on the phone. There is a complete difference in his voice when he is smiling as compared to when he isn't.

"I'm good actually, better than I thought I'd be today." It's true, after signing the papers yesterday I was full of dread, I was afraid that was what I would be feeling for the near future.

"Good, I have some good news." My heart leaps, I sit up and listen, Rachel is standing in my bedroom door, she heard Alex's voice on speaker and came running. "The foundation has arranged for your security, I will be by later with the whole team, you and Rachel will be under 24-hour security. I want you both to know who is on the team, if someone new is brought in, you will be made aware through formal introduction." Wow! This is a bit over the top, just knowing someone is watching is enough. "This is important Ollie, I don't want to run the risk of someone telling you they are part of the team if they aren't, this way you will know." Fear builds in my stomach, does he know something I don't?

"Do you have new information Alex? This seems like a bit much." It's not like I don't know what Greg looks like, then it dawns on me, Alex is thinking Greg may send a stranger to pose as security. "Do you think he will go that far?"

"I don't have anything new to tell you. I take my responsibility seriously, this is just a precaution. I would prefer to be well prepared than to not consider all the possibilities and have something happen to you or Rachel. In consideration of his position and the information he can gather because of it, I think this is the best way to handle the situation." This is something that I hadn't thought of, the idea never crossed my mind that Greg could bring a stranger into this, I still don't think that he will.

"If you think it's necessary, we're both home now, but I don't think that Greg would trust anyone else to do anything. He has too much to lose if they get caught or if they talk, his career would be on the line." He's too possessive anyway, the idea of someone being alone with me would drive him insane.

"I'm sure you're right, but I just want to cover all my bases, give me an hour and we'll be there." I look at Rachel, an hour will be cutting it close for her to get to work but she nods her head in agreement.

"What do you think doll?" I see the apprehension in her eyes, she's been my rock through all of this. She has put a smile on her face and let me lean on her, she hasn't shown any fear until now. The idea of twenty-four-hour security has maybe driven home how dangerous this situation may be.

"I think it's a good idea to be cautious. I don't think we have to worry about something like this though, like I told Alex, Greg isn't going to jeopardize his career getting someone else to do his dirty work." Would he? Honestly, I don't know, I haven't seen or talked to him in a year, maybe all of this is for nothing, he could get the papers, sign them and be glad that it's over.

"Okay, I'm gonna finish getting ready, I'll have to hurry out the door once Alex makes introductions." I watch her walk away, the anxiety in her eyes not wavering with my response. She holds herself a little taller, more alert than just minutes ago.

As I wait, questions plague me. I didn't think Alex was taking me seriously, he was so nonchalant about it all, but his approach to security changes those thoughts. If he thinks that we need to know the physical appearance of those working security, it stands to reason that he's afraid someone may try to impersonate them to do one of us harm.

I check the peephole before opening the door, Alex is standing there with several other men in tow. I plaster a smile to my face and try to seem more at ease than what I feel as I open the door. Since I talked with Alex on the phone, several scenarios have occupied my mind, the fear building within, not only for my own safety, but for Rachel, and now these men that stand before me. Will this put them in danger? Do they have families waiting at home that stand to lose more than I do? Who the hell makes a profession of protecting someone else when the cost could be your own life? What a stupid question, anyone who joins the military, law enforcement, firemen, they all join their selected force to protect others, knowing that it could cost them their lives. As they all file into our apartment, the space grows smaller and smaller, it becomes nearly claustrophobic.

As Alex makes introductions, I memorize the features of each man, Mack, I guess to be about six foot about the same as Alex, thinning blonde hair, brown eyes, barrel chested. Ryan, taller, thin, almost wiry, blonde hair, blue eyes, he doesn't strike me as a security guard, to be honest. He doesn't look like he can fight his way out of a wet paper sack. Fletcher, he stands as tall as Ryan but he's thick, muscular, brown hair, brown eyes, and a full beard. Steven, is about my height, built like a linebacker, with a baby face, dirty blonde hair, and blue eyes. Jay is taller than Alex by just a couple inches, his bald head gleams in the light, his brown eyes are hard, like he has seen too much of the ugliness of the world. Nick is about the same size as Jay, unlike Jay, Nick has laughter in his green eyes, his head is also bald, he looks like he keeps in shape, but not like he lives at the gym. And Brett, tall, athletic build, bright smile, something is off about him, I almost pull my hand away as soon as it touches his. Unlike the others his hand is cold, there is a foreboding in his touch and in his eyes. I repeat each name as I shake their hand, grateful that I have learned to not recoil at the touch of a man. How insulting would that be? These men are here to protect Rachel and myself, what would they think if I couldn't shake their hand or recoiled at their touch? It was just a few months ago that was the case. Maybe, in this line of work that's what they expect.

Rachel glances at each man and quickly shakes their hands during introductions, but her eyes are trained on Alex, she can't hide the desire that's burning in them. As soon as Brett releases her hand she throws herself at Alex, the way she falls into his arms, not a thought or a care for anyone else in the room, the warmth between them can be felt, there is no question of the feelings they have for each other. Watching the two of them I feel like I'm intruding on a private moment. The way they fit together, it's intimate even though they are sharing just a warm greeting.

Knowing that Rachel needs to leave soon to make her shift, I wait before saying anything, my questions will keep until they are done. Their opposing schedules make it hard for them to spend time together, her late nights running cocktails and his early mornings in the office, like the sun and moon, only seeing each other in passing. They make time for each other, but stolen moments like these are a rarity that they both deserve to enjoy without interruption.

As Rachel walks out the door with Ryan following close behind, I can feel the warmth go with her, as does Alex's easy-going smile. As soon as the door closes, he gets down to business. "Let me start Ollie, I think this might be a bit overwhelming for you and I'm sure you have a lot of questions. Until we know how Greg is going to react to the divorce papers, you and Rachel will be under security at all times. In most cases you won't even be aware that they're around, they'll watch the apartment at a distance but will stop anyone trying to approach your front door. If you leave, they will follow, remind Rachel of that, she drives like a nut, she might unintentionally lose them." Just the mention of her name brings a smile to his face. "If you need to go anywhere and Rachel isn't here, one of these men will take you, it's part of their job so don't hesitate to reach out to them. I have here a schedule, they work six to six, throughout the month they will rotate through. Pay attention each day to who is working that day. On the schedule is each of their phone numbers, put them in your phone, if anything seems out of the ordinary don't hesitate to call whoever is on shift. I mean it Ollie, anything, that's why they're here. When you and Rachel are together there will be two of them watching you. The point of introducing you all is so there is no mistake of who you can trust, if there is a change in schedule you will be aware of it and it will only be one of these guys filling in." I take it all in, I don't pay as close attention to the schedules, I can read that later, I learn the security protocols, what to do if someone comes to the door. Then Alex hands me what looks like a key fob for a car, there is a single button. "This is your panic button, if anything arises and you can't make a call, press this button, this will alert whoever is on shift that there is an emergency, they will be here within seconds."

My stomach drops, will I need this? Is there something he knows that he isn't telling me? When Rachel said security, I don't know what I expected but this isn't it. How the hell does a non-profit organization have access to this kind of security? More so, how do they pay for it? This can't be cheap, and now guilt is setting in, I feel like I'm taking advantage of this resource, I'm sure there are other women out there that need this more than I do.

"You said that any man would consider what I was offering a gift, that you think that he will sign the papers and move on, if you really believe that Alex, why all of

this? This doesn't seem excessive to you?"
Before he responds he dismisses the
security team. Now I'm beginning to feel
silly, this all seems so extreme.

"It's not excessive, I know what
you've told me Ollie, and in my experience,
women like you, that have gone through
what you have tend to downplay some of
the specifics. I would rather err on the side
of caution, than not take enough measures
and be wrong, I've seen what happens
when a case like this is underestimated. Has
Rachel told you about my mother?" I shake
my head, Rachel said that he understood
more than what I realized, but she didn't
tell me why. She is loyal and would never
break the trust of someone that she cares
about, she never broke mine with Alex. She
begged and pleaded for me to allow her to
speak to him about my situation, until I was
ready the answer was a hard no. She
honored that until I made the decision
otherwise.

"When we were kids, Ian and I lived
down the hall from each other in our
apartment building, our mothers would

trade babysitting. One day, we were at my apartment when my father showed up. He was in and out for as long as I could remember. On this particular day he came looking for money, he killed my mother for the money she had stashed away for rent. He knew she had money and when she refused to give it to him, a fight ensued." His voice is quiet, his eyes trained on the wall. "The neighbors called the cops, it wasn't the first time their presence was required but it was the last. By the time they arrived, he had beaten my mother to death and had turned his attention on Ian and me. When the police broke down the door, he attacked them instead of us. They opened fire, I became an orphan that day, Ian and I were ten years old and together watched both of my parents die. Over less than three hundred dollars." He shakes his head at the horror. "I spent my childhood watching my father beat my mother. I witnessed my mom take beatings that were meant for me, but she intervened on my behalf. I have seen abuse Ollie, I've lived it. I knew you came from abuse long before you ever told me." Tears shone in his eyes, my heart hurt for the things he must have witnessed, no child should ever have to see what he did.

He went on to describe the signs that led him to believe that I was abused. I always choose a table at the back of a restaurant with my back to the wall so that I can see all my surroundings, that I flinch when someone makes a sudden movement, the panic in my eyes and the way I search for the cause when I hear a loud noise, and his first clue was the way I shrank away from him and refused to shake his hand or meet his eyes when we first met. I had no idea he was evaluating me or paying that close attention to my mannerisms, he was so infatuated with Rachel, I didn't think he noticed me at all.

He didn't stay long after he revealed the tragedy of his childhood, I had been so wrong in my assumptions of him when Rachel first met him. I had seen his picture in the gossip rag, he was always attending different charity functions and grand openings, and for all of them, he had a new woman on his arm. I told her he was a playboy that would break her heart. Rachel was right though, she said he had a warm heart and swore that he was a good man, that has just been searching for the one to be his equal. I'm glad that she was right, she deserves a man like him.

I know I'm in for a long night, imagining the horror that two young boys witnessed, with flashbacks of my own living nightmare invading my mind.

Chapter 6

Ian

The great advantage of converting the top floor of the hotel into an apartment for myself, is coming down to the office when I can't sleep. After tossing and turning for hours last night, I gave up, and spent the night working. Catching up on reports, responding to emails, and sending management notice that the security schedule will need to be updated to reflect those that will be working off premises for the time being.

It's the largest security detail Battling Back has needed, I'm confident with all but one of the men I sent Alex. Brett Jones has only been with my team for a year, the rest of the guys Alex and I have both known since college or high school. Those six work for the foundation whenever the need arises, their employment within the casinos and clubs is just to keep their paychecks coming in. Under normal circumstances, Brett wouldn't have been an option because of his limited history with the company, he was chosen due to lack of options and his previous service record. I'm hopeful this decision doesn't prove to be a mistake.

My curiosity got the best of me, I found myself searching through the archives of the New York papers I subscribe to. Searching by her name Olivia Daniels turned up little, but when I typed the name Rae Daniels, I hit the jackpot.

The brutal detail of the first article I opened nauseated me, a 911 call requesting assistance for a possible intruder. The officer that arrived at the residence thirty minutes later, found the door frame broken, upon entering the house, he found a grizzly scene. The house in disarray, broken furniture, lying at the bottom of the stairs with a gunshot wound to the head was George Daniels. Anne Daniels was found in the master bedroom, beaten and raped but still breathing, she succumbed to her injuries at the hospital. This case was highly publicized because of the brutality and because the victims were the parents of Assistant District Attorney Gregory Daniels. The investigation went on for months, Daniels suspected retaliation possibly stemming from one of his cases, in the end the case was labeled as a home invasion, the suspect or suspects were never apprehended.

I study the pictures included with articles, her long dark hair is the same, her eyes haunted, in the first couple articles I can see her strength, standing tall beside her husband as he pleads with the public to call the hotline that had been set up with any information they may have. In the beginning Olivia crowds close to her husband, supporting him. As time goes on, I notice subtle differences, in the way she looks at him, where she stands, how she stands, not as straight, lacking the confidence that can be seen in the first photos. I had read this story as it unfolded, sympathetic to Mr. Daniels, reading it now, from a different perspective, I deduce that this is when the abuse began. Pictures speak a thousand words, these ones tell a story.

Several more articles are attributed to her, the death of her mother and the subsequent search for the car that hit her and fled the scene. When he was eventually caught was the biggest news of all because of who he was, the most recent article available is regarding him. Angus Kelley, notorious enforcer for the Russian mob was driving the car involved in the hit and run, he's up for a parole hearing at the end of next month. The press speculating whether Rae Daniels will attend to contest his early release. And a few articles relating to Trinity and the fire that destroyed it.

How does so much happen to one person in such a short amount of time? I empathize the sudden loss of her mother, I can't imagine that devastation. The distance between my mother and I is painful, but I have the luxury of still speaking with her.

Losing her to death will be a crushing moment in my life.

Will she go back to be present at the parole hearing? Probably not, between what she said and what I've learned from Alex, she essentially dropped off the earth for the last year. It's curious that her husband hasn't filed a missing person's report. Not a single word about the missing spouse of an Assistant District Attorney. Is he biding his time, waiting for her to return? Is he planning a reunion of sorts? Is he worried what the press will dig up if he reports her missing? It seems to me that the fact that she has been gone so long, one would think that if anything happened to her it would put him on the spot, I can't be the only one that would find it suspicious if a man's wife had been gone for a year and he made no mention of it.

The more that I consider these things, the more that I'm convinced that Alex is making the right call with the security team. If he hasn't filed a missing person's report, he's waiting. Waiting to find her himself, that's the only reasonable explanation. He didn't want the publicity. When the police didn't come knocking on his door after she left, he knew she didn't report him. He's afraid if he draws attention to the fact that she's missing, that she will spill her story if she is picked up. Is it possible that someone can disappear for a year and no one know? Does she not have any other family that would question a long absence?

Remembering my promise to Alex to offer Olivia a position within the company, I draft an email to Michelle, requesting that she find a position suitable and send an offer. Ignoring a call from Lawrence, I close out the tabs that detail the destruction that has rocked the life of Olivia Daniels. When I searched her name, I had hoped that I would find answers. As it stands, I found only more questions.

Alex meets me for lunch in my office, all the documents are ready to be signed. I appreciate that he's worked so quickly on this, he knows what's at stake and he knows how restless I'll be until this is done.

Our history has made us more than friends, more than business associates, Alex is my brother. My mom fought tooth and nail to gain custody of him after the death of his parents. He slipped into foster care for months while social workers looked for blood relatives. Mama pled with the state to allow her to foster him, she was beating her head against a brick wall, no one would listen to an immigrant, single mother living off the wages of a card dealer. They told her time and again that it would never happen, that a child needed structure, stability, security, and family with a mother and father. Alex ran away to our apartment twenty-three times in two and a half months. Every time a social worker would show up with a cop and take him back kicking and screaming. Then one day out of the blue, her presence was requested at social services, she came home with Alex that day and promised he would never have to leave again. I don't know how she accomplished it. I don't know what strings she pulled, but Alex officially became a part of our family that day. There was an adoption hearing later, but the day she brought him home is the day that sticks out for me. It was the best day of my young life.

Alex doesn't say much as I read through the paperwork, he eats his sandwich as he waits, answering questions as they arise. It isn't until after I sign the last page that he tells me what is on his mind. "Something about this case has my hackles up, Ian." I look across my desk at him, he's waited for three years to get my name off Ragtime, what the hell has his hackles up?

"You said this was the best course of action, so what's the problem?" Aside from the fact that Ragtime will be shut down in a year, the employees are going to suffer, unfortunately there isn't anything I can do about those things.

"Not that Ian, the Daniels case. This one's different." Realizing we are on foundation business, I relax a little. It's different because his girlfriend could end up in the crossfire if this goes badly. "I've been looking into this guy, his stellar record ends about four years ago, he's been in some trouble, he's been on administrative leave a few times. In the last year he's had two cases dropped, both because the complainants are missing. Both cases were mob related." How is that not suspicious? Is anyone looking into that?

"What's the story coming out of the DA's office?" If the witness fails to appear in court, charges are usually dropped, but there must be some sort of protocol if the witnesses disappear, especially if they are involving the mob.

"So far, they've been quiet, the families of the victims haven't pushed the issue. Both are kids in their twenties, long lists of petty crimes and histories of disappearing only to reappear in a few months. Something about all of it and him, I just don't like it." It is odd, two cases where both victims fail to show up and the family just lets it go?

"What's your plan then?" I'll do whatever I need to help, I let Alex take the lead on Battling Back, I hang back and just make sure he has the resources to keep it going and to help the victims, I step in when he asks, or if I see he's got more going than what he can handle in addition to his practice.

"I don't know yet, I'm waiting to see what happens when he gets served, but it has me on edge and I can't explain it. You're probably right though, I've never been involved with anyone that's so close to a case, but Rachel's a badass, she will kick someone's ass. I don't really think its fear for her safety, she really is meaner than a rattlesnake when she gets pissed off, she's been training since she was four. She's been to a lot of exhibitions and she even had a few cage fights, she's undefeated and she now has armed security. I'm confident that she's safe." He speaks of her with such reverence, the pride in his voice while he lists her accomplishments. I wonder if she's it for him. They've been seeing each other for almost a year now, it's the longest relationship he's ever had.

"What else can you tell me about the case?" I might have other ideas that could help, but mostly I'm simply curious about this woman. I haven't been able to get her off my mind since I met her yesterday.

"Can we get access to a safehouse if it becomes necessary? I know it's not something we've done before, and maybe I'm being paranoid because of Rachel, but I just want to be sure that all our bases are covered, and we have a plan." He hasn't given me any more information so I'm unsure if this is based on concern for the client or concern for his girlfriend. After his speech highlighting her ability to take care of herself, was he trying to convince me or himself?

"Of course, it's possible, I'll get someone working on it." Is Greg Daniels this dangerous? I make the mental note to look him up later, this is the problem with being involved with someone that is close to a client, I don't know if Alex is overreacting or if there is genuine need for more resources.

The information I find online isn't much more than what Alex had given me. I make the decision to call on Markus Baxter. Markus works as head of security, he oversees the department on a whole. I've known Marcus since high school, when he hacked into the school system and changed my D in history to a B. He never got caught and he saved my ass, if mama had seen a D, I would have been toast.

He went on to the military, worked in intelligence, and retired honorably a few years ago. He has connections and the know how to get information on anyone. With his experience and knowledge, I knew he would be an asset to not only my security team but to the foundation.

I shake his hand when he enters my office, "Markus, I've got a name. I need all the information you can find on a Gregory Daniels, he works for the District Attorney's office in New York City." I've known Markus long enough to not bother with small talk, he considers it a waste of his time and finds it pointless. I get straight to the point.

"Are you looking for something specific or general information?" He's a nice enough guy, just zero personality. I assume it has to do with the years in the military, because he was a completely different person in high school.

"I want his employment record, his personal life, whatever you can dig up. This will be for the foundation, so document the time spent on this accordingly." He doesn't give any acknowledgement, he just leaves my office.

Chapter 7

Olivia

The week drug on endlessly and has continued into a new one, every day is filled with filling out online applications and searching for more places to apply. I didn't expect to be offered the job at the Lost Cities, but I thought at the very least I would get a polite not interested letter. No letter is delivered, no email scheduling an interview somewhere else, and worst of all, the only news I've received from Alex is that the divorce papers have been served. Since then, my anxiety has grown each day, Alex says that it's normal, we won't hear anything until he retains his own attorney. It makes sense, probably not the best idea for him to respond himself.

I find myself looking out the window often, I take more notice of the vagrants in the street, more skeptical of the passersby. I seek out the men that I know are down there somewhere, watching, waiting, and I feel guilty, it seems a waste of their time.

Rachel's been gone a lot, one of the other waitresses had to have an emergency appendectomy. I really miss her company right now. She has a way of easing my worries. As time has gone on without hearing a response from Greg, she's grown complacent, she sees it as a good sign that it will all be ok. I wish that I could feel the same but as the days go by, I only feel more apprehensive. Apprehensive that Greg will show up, that I haven't found a job, that I won't get another interview to get another job, that I am going to run out of money soon and wont' be able to pay Rachel for rent and utilities.

I spot Mack across the street, leaned against an old beat up car smoking a cigarette. His demeanor is relaxed but the more that I watch him, I see that he is vigilant in his duty. His nonchalance is to blend in, to not be noticed by anyone. Funny, until now, I've been comfortable and secure in this apartment, I've had no desire to venture out. Now, I feel like a caged animal, growing more restless as time goes on, frustrated at my situation. I'm ready to go somewhere, anywhere, just to escape the monotony that last week I was grateful for.

Rachel appears in the kitchen, her red hair a tangled mess, makeup smeared down her face. I know better than to speak to her yet, not until she's had at least one cup of coffee, even then it's better to wait for her to address me. I smile inwardly, as friendly, kind, and sweet as she is, in the morning she's a bear that has just come out of hibernation, hungry, groggy, and in no mood to deal with anyone.

Squinting at me through tired eyes, she raises her mug to me in a silent greeting. Every day it's the same, just as the audible sigh she makes after her first sip of coffee is. I feel better already, there is normalcy in this, the routine is comfortable. Even in silence, I don't feel so alone, I don't feel so nervous.

I continue looking out the window, Mack has disappeared from across the street. Everyday this has been my entertainment, find the men charged with my security, when they disappear, start again, a perpetual cycle.

"Morning Doll." Rachel has finished her first cup, pouring her second, she smiles warmly, eyes are fully open. "How was your night?" It's hard not to be snappy, she knows last night was the same as every other night this week. I looked out the window, I read a book, wrote some nonsensical words trying to make sense of my thoughts, and watched TV. That's the story of my last year, not just this week, every week.

"It was fine, monotonous." Same response I always give, just better word usage. I say it with a smile to try to take the sharpness out of my tone. It's not her fault, hell, until I filed for divorce, I was perfectly happy with monotonous.

"I've got the day off, get ready, I'm taking you out." Now that the opportunity to leave presents itself, dread fills me. I'd rather stay here. Suddenly venturing out seems like the worst idea ever!

"You don't have to entertain me, you should probably use your free time to see Alex. Between his workload and your work schedule, I know you two don't have a lot of time for each other." Until she suggested it, going out has been all I could think about this morning, now that the opportunity presents itself, I'd rather not.

"Nope, you let me worry about the time I get to spend with Alex. I don't want my life to be consumed by him, I have to make time for girl time as well." I know by the look on her face that I'm not getting out of whatever she has planned.

"Will you at least tell me what our plans are?" Preferably something that doesn't require wearing anything more than something comfortable.

"We have a spa date, I need to unwind, I need a massage, I need to be pampered." This is my out. I can't afford a spa, I need to be mindful of every penny, I can't blow any amount on something so frivolous.

"I think I'll sit this one out, I promise, once I have a job, I would love to do something like that with you, but I just can't do it right now, Rach." I know what she is going to say before she says it.

"Sorry doll, this is my treat, you need it as much as I do. You need a haircut, a facial, a pedicure, maybe even a manicure. You can get a facial while I get my massage, I know you won't join me for that even though you should." She's obviously thought this through. "Besides, I'm a grand richer because of you." It wasn't because of me, I just sat there and watched. "No more excuses, get ready, we have an appointment at 12."

Maybe this is what I need, at least I can stop complaining about being stuck in the house. Regardless, I know she isn't going to let me off the hook, once she gets something in her head there is not dissuading her.

I'm surprised when Rachel pulls into the valet of the Lost Cities, I don't know where I expected her to take me, but this isn't it. I'm still feeling bitter that I haven't gotten anything at all from them. Rachel pulls me from my thoughts of self-pity. "They really have the best spa in town, I wouldn't have had any idea how awesome this place is if my stylist hadn't taken a position here. You're in for a treat, doll." Again, I'm blown away by the grandeur, I've seen beautiful buildings, I've been in five-star upscale New York establishments and somehow, they pale in comparison to this.

As we make our way to the elevators, I feel a prickle on the back of my neck, I can feel eyes on me, bile builds in my throat, and I ball my hands into fists to stop them from shaking, I quicken my pace to catch up to Rachel, I am wishing for the comfort of our apartment, the monotony of each day, at least I know what to expect. Before I reach Rachel, a hand touches my shoulder, I recoil in fear and turn sharply, my hands up, I come face to face with Ian Alessandro. Humiliation consumes me, I breathe in deeply trying to slow my heart that is beating out of my chest. "Ollie, calm down." Rachel is at my side, speaking softly, Ian backs up, his hands out in front of him.

Five things I can see, I see Mr. Alessandro's eyes, filled with concern and still strangely familiar, behind him the smoke from a cigarette rises, I see a woman's hand as she pulls down on the arm of the slot machine, making the reels spin. I see a roulette dealer watching the people pass by his table, I see a chandelier sparkling in the brilliance of its own light. Four things can feel, I feel the lightness of Rachel's touch on my arm, I feel the air blowing down on me from the vent above, I feel the floor beneath my feet, and the whisper of Rachels breath. Three things I can hear, I hear the whisper of Rachels words soothing me, the shouts of the players at a winning table, the ringing of the slot machines. Two things I can smell, I smell the smoke in the air, and a touch of the familiar scent of Rachels shampoo. Lastly, one thing I can taste, I taste the bile that rose up in my throat. I quickly make it through the grounding technique.

"I'm sorry Mr. Alessandro." I'm feeling much better, grounded, centered, more at ease. My breathing is under control, my heart rate down to normal levels. I thought Rachel was full of shit when she handed me instructions on how to ground myself. I've used it before, but I've never had an attack like this since she gave it to me. I'm grateful that she made me try it.

"Please don't, I should have done things differently, I apologize for startling you." That's a polite way of describing my almost meltdown, a normal human being wouldn't react that way, I'm embarrassed and angry with myself for letting my fear control me like this.

"Let's just start over, nice to see you again, Mr. Alessandro." Rachel smiles warmly and offers her own greeting.

"Please call me Ian, have you been in touch with Michelle?" I haven't been in touch with anyone, the puzzlement on my face must clue him in. "She will be contacting you directly." Hope again starts to stir, I don't allow myself to get too excited, I know it won't be for the management position but that's actually a relief.

"I look forward to it, thank you." Not knowing what else to say, I stand quietly while Rachel and Ian talk. I allow myself this time to continue to recover and be proud of myself for using the tools that Rachel has been working on teaching me. When confronted I didn't cower, I reacted in defense instead of defeat. I reacted, prepared to defend myself. Internally I smile, this is another step in the right direction.

While they speak, I continue to notice Ian, I'm drawn to his eyes, trying to place them. I've seen him in the news, in the papers, in the gossip rag, but none of these ring true. I feel as if I should know him, but I can't explain my reasoning.

"Ollie, we have to go, we're going to be late if we don't hurry." I blush as Ian catches me staring at him, he offers a boyish half grin, it makes him look twenty years younger. I've been caught, all I can do now is smile in return.

"It's nice to see you Mr..." I stop myself when he raises his eyebrows at me. "Ian, it's nice to see you." Why does his name roll off my tongue like that? What the hell is wrong with me?

"You ladies enjoy your spa day." I watch as he walks away, while being pulled into the elevator by Rachel.

I feel rather than see Rachel's gaze on me, I turn my head to meet her eyes. "You were totally checking him out." I'm not dead, he is an attractive guy, but really, more than anything I'm intrigued by his eyes and why they are so recognizable to me.

"Maybe, wouldn't it be more noteworthy if I wasn't?" I know why she's surprised, I'm just as shocked, I haven't been sure if I would ever be attracted to another man again. Now so much is happening at once, my divorce, looking for a job, seeing someone as attractive, learning who I am again, taking back control of my life.

In the spa, Rachel and I go separate ways, her to her massage and me to my facial, it's been years since I've done anything like this, there came a point when I couldn't hide what was happening at home and frankly, I just didn't care to try anymore. So today, I'm going to let it all go, I'm going to relax, soak it all in, for today, I'm just going to be.

Rachel and I meet back up to sit in the hot tub, I know she has something on her mind. I quietly wait for her to work it out in her head, she will say whatever it is when she's ready, from the looks of her she doesn't need the added pressure.

"Ollie, can I talk to you about something?" Trepidation written across her face as I look at her through the mirror. I wait for her to meet my eyes then nod. I don't like the way she asked, I'm afraid of what she's about to say and I don't trust myself to speak.

"So, I know you have a lot going on, and I know you need my support." Dread is consuming me, she's changed her mind, she wants me to move out, she's realized how dangerous it could be to be my friend. I try to hold back the tears forming in my eyes. "Doll, don't cry, never mind, this is stupid." She can't tell me to never mind, I don't blame her one bit, if this is the choice she's made, she needs to know that I understand.

"Don't Rachel, please just say what's on your mind." She has done so much for me, I can't let her feel guilty for wanting to save herself.

"It's really not a big deal doll, it was just an idea Alex had. But the time isn't right, it can wait." Now I'm confused, maybe it's Alex that wants me to move out, he's afraid of what could happen to her.

"If it was important enough to bring up then it is a big deal Rach, what is it." I brace myself to hear the words that will rock my world. I won't fault either of them for it. In the back of my mind I always knew that this could happen, I've always known this is what should happen.

"I've got some comp time because of the hours I've been working, and Alex needs to be in Tahoe at the end of the week for a conference. We were kind of thinking that maybe we could go together and have a weekend." My breath comes out in a rush, I've been holding it waiting for her reply, seriously, all the build up for a weekend getaway with her boyfriend.

"You really just asked for permission to hang out with your boyfriend? Rachel, you scared the shit out of me, I thought you wanted me to move out." The tears that had been building spill over as I laugh, this is not a conversation I thought we would have. "Of course, you should go with him, that sounds like a lot of fun." All the tension melts away, but a small nagging voice in my head telling me that if I was any kind of friend, I would move out while she's gone.

It explains her answer when I suggested she spend the time with Alex.

"Oh doll, I don't want you to leave, I'm sorry, I really should have thought this out better. It's not that I'm asking permission, just that you just filed for divorce, you're scared, and I don't really want to leave you alone with all of that, but this weekend really sounds amazing." The way her eyes twinkle, even if I didn't want her to go, I would be an asshole to make her stay with me.

With that settled we kicked back and let the warm water and jets work their magic on the sore muscles and tension.

Chapter 8

Ian

On the way back to my office I had stopped in to see Michelle, irritated that Olivia hadn't heard from her yet. After speaking with her, she said she left a message early this afternoon but hadn't gotten a reply, we have a couple open spots in cocktails, it's a starting point for Olivia, we can build her up from there.

Lawrence's name flashes across my phone again, I've been ignoring him since last week, I meant what I said, I've washed my hands of the whole lot of them. But the genuine concern for my ex-wife finally prevails and I answer.

"She's clean, she's doing much better now, not that you give a damn." No greeting, just more of the same anger and resentment as before.

"Thank you for the update, is there anything else?" This is the reason he's been trying call all week, because he needs someone to lash out at, a whipping boy.

"She wants to see you, only God knows why, it's not like you haven't already done enough. She said she tried to call but it went straight to voicemail." As it should have, I blocked her number, there's nothing more to say.

"For once Larry, I agree with you, you can let her know I feel that way and that I won't be in contact with her again. She has Ragtime, I've paid all the vendors, payroll, and deposited enough to cover payroll through the end of the month, that should be enough for her to get back on her feet. She needs to know though, this is it, I won't do anything else, the success or failure of Ragtime is on her now." As much as I hate to walk away from this, it's the only option I have.

"Then I guess that's it, I'd appreciate it if you stick to that. Seeing you again could be all it takes to set her back again, Ian." The audible click on the line, I know he's hung up. I rake my hand through my hair, this crap has been going on for five years. I stuck with her for two, trying to make our marriage work, trying to get her the help that she needed, trying to be a better husband. Two years of accepting everything she laid at my feet, two years of bending over backwards trying to be the man that she expected. When the pictures published, it was the last straw, it wasn't just any pictures, these were explicit. My wife engaging in sex with a stranger, in front of a club full of people, at the time, it was my club.

I couldn't even speak to her, I went to the house, packed a bag, and moved into the hotel. I left my key, I left it all, I didn't want any of it. It was a life built on love that faded into lies and deceit. Everything I left behind could be replaced, I didn't want to fight with her about any of it, none of it mattered.

There's no reason left to speak to Vee, the tattered remains of the life that we shared can't be sewn together. There are no words left to say to each other, I can't and won't continue to take all the blame for our failed marriage.

As I take a swig of my coffee, the color the same as Olivia's dark caramel colored eyes. I knew better than to reach for her the way that I did, her reaction was better than a lot of others that have been through what she has. She turned on me as if she were ready to fight, she didn't try to retreat, she didn't back down, I misjudged her thinking she is meek or passive.

I search my email looking for an update from Markus, I've yet to hear anything back since we spoke. I'm tempted to send him a request for an update, but I know that if he had anything for me I would have it. Instead I open an email from Alex, an update on the security detail. The weekend trip he planned is a go, he's leaving the security schedule as it stands, no reason to change it, just to rearrange it again on Monday. I respond with my agreement and wish him good luck and a safe trip, he's going to need it.

As much as I try to get work done, I'm distracted, not having any information from Markus is starting to irritate me. It can't be that hard to get information on this guy, with his contacts, I feel like he should have something by now. My thoughts continuing to go back to Olivia. She's beautiful, olive skin, almond shaped eyes, high cheek bones, full lips... I shouldn't be thinking of her like this, soon enough she will be an employee. I have a hard stance against engaging personally with employees, she's a client with the foundation, she's still married, and I'm quite certain that dating isn't on her priority list. Get it together Ian.

A commotion in reception gets my attention, the door to my office swings open. "I'm sorry Mr. Alessandro, she wouldn't take no for answer." Vivian stands in my doorway, my secretary Stephanie right behind her. "Should I call for security sir?" As much as that would make my life easier right now, I'm sure it will only make things worse later.

"Thank you, Stephanie, I'll handle this." Vee sneers at her as she closes the door, then sits in the chair opposite of me. I lean back in my chair and wait. She's called this meeting, rudely, by barging into my office, it's up to her to speak. She looks better than before, her hair is clean, looks like she's put on a little weight, but she's still too thin to be healthy, her cheekbones still protruding. I look for signs that she's under the influence, it doesn't appear so but it's hard to tell.

"Why'd you give up your share of Ragtime?" No greeting, no thank you, just her demand for answers that she already has.

"It's your business Vee, you need to step up and run it, and I need to step away from it and you." That's really all the reason I need. She just continues to look at me, not saying anything. I can almost see the wheels turning while she prepares her argument.

"Ian, I'm sorry, I've let things unravel out of control, I know that the choices I made have brought me here and I know that you've tried so hard to help me, I just want you to know that I'm going to put in the work." That's not what I expected at all, for added effect she turns on some tears. "I still love you Ian, I want to fix all of this, I want to fix us." There was a time I would have done anything to hear these words, that's why I tried so long to stay with her, I wanted the opportunity to do all of that.

"It's too late for that now Vee, there's nothing left to fix, all that we had isn't broken, it's destroyed beyond repair." Oddly enough, as true as the words are, there is no pain saying them. Walking away from her tore my heart out, until now I haven't looked at another woman. Though Vee is sitting before me telling me all the things I once wanted her to say, now I'm just hopeful that she will leave soon, so that I can get back to what I was doing prior to being interrupted.

"You can't mean that we have too many years behind us, we can make it work. Do you still love me?" Not enough Vee, but I can't say that to her, if I give her that, she still has hope and there is none.

"No. And I can't forgive you for any of this Vivian, those years are behind us, I don't have room for you in the years I have left. If there's nothing else Vee, I have work to get done." It's hard to be so dismissive to her. Yes, I still care about her, I hate to see her in the condition she's in now and worse last week, but there is no going back. We have nothing to build off, and I can't ever forgive her.

"I know your lying Ian, you didn't just stop loving me, just like I didn't stop loving you. I'll prove to you that I'm better, I'll prove that I still love you, and I will show you that we can still have a future with our broken past." Tears spill from her eyes, but that is the only emotion she shows with the passion in her speech. I sit quietly, I'm not going to argue, I don't have it in me to fight her, so I just wait. As the silence continues, I worry that I may have to ask her to leave, and just as I'm about to speak the words, she rises from her chair and blows me a kiss. When she reaches the doorway, she stops. "This isn't over, I'm going to show you, Ian, and then you'll come crawling back to me.

If she had said those words a year ago, she probably would have been right. I was willing to look past all her indiscretions,

I was ready to forgive it all, I wanted the life we had when we were happy back. I know now that even if I was willing, it doesn't mean I would have been able. I can't and don't feel the same when I look at her. More than anything, all I feel for her is pity. I can't learn to respect her again, I can't forget all she has done, and without respect any relationship will fail.

As much as I don't want to, I worry that the exchange with Vee may be upsetting to her, rather than call, I send an email to Lawrence, just a heads up that he may need to check on her. My refusal to engage or accommodate her could be the excuse she's looking for to contact her dealer, to fall off the wagon, to harm herself. Maybe I should call, but I don't have the patience for what I'm sure he'd have to say.

Chapter 9

Olivia

Watching Rachel parade around the apartment in every outfit in her closet while she giggles like a schoolgirl, lifts the weight from my shoulders. I think she's picked enough clothes to last a month in Tahoe, yet she continues to bring out more.

Three days ago, when we got home from our spa day, there was a message from Michelle Cain on our answering machine, and I had an email from the Desert Sands casino for an interview. Tomorrow after Rachel and Alex leave, I interview there as a bartender, immediately followed by a meeting with Michelle Cain at the Lost Cities.

Everything seems to be falling into place, still no word from Greg or an attorney on his behalf. Alex doesn't seem to be concerned, he says it's possible Greg hasn't been able to see an attorney yet. My confidence is building, the fear isn't overwhelming, there's a good possibility I can be employed by next week, and soon be divorced and back to my maiden name. It's all that I want and it's all possible in the next couple weeks.

I laugh as Rachel comes out in yet another outfit, this one a sequined little black dress, Alex has been pretty tightlipped about what they are doing, she doesn't have any idea what to pack for. She asked him and he told her to bring a little bit for every occasion. Everyday should be this easy and carefree, I hope that this is just the beginning of the trend. As much as I don't want to see her go, I'm excited for her, right now my apprehension of being alone for the weekend is minimal. Alex planned with security to take me to my interview and my appointment with Ms. Cain. Rachel and I went shopping yesterday, there's enough food in the house to sustain me for a month. With each passing hour, my excitement for her grows, while at the same time nervousness for myself.

Sleep is impossible for me, I can't shut off my brain long enough to fall asleep, mentally I'm trying to prepare for my interview tomorrow, wondering if I should even go. I know Ms. Cain is going to offer me a position, am I wasting someone's time interviewing at the Desert Sands. On the other hand, do I really want to take a job at the Lost Cities? Ian is privy to more intimate details of my life than a normal boss would be, not that I think he will use it against me, I just feel like it's improper. And what about my attraction to him, dating my boss would be out of the question. Whoa! Slow down Olivia, what the hell? Where did that come from? 1. You're married, dumbass. 2. You aren't ready to date. 3. You don't want to date, do you? 4. What makes you think that he would even be interested in you? Greg's voice chimes in, he isn't interested in you, you're old, you're fat, you're fucking ugly, you're worthless, you've accomplished nothing in your life, he's successful and good looking. No Rae, you don't have to worry about that.

I push that voice aside, I try to ignore it, I'll go to the interview, it'd be better to take a job there anyway. Ian has access to too much information about me, no matter what happens at the Desert Sands tomorrow, I'm going to decline whatever Ms. Cain offers me. With that decision made I drift off to sleep.

A crash in the living room sends me flying from my bed, backed into the corner of my room watching the door. "It's me Ollie, sorry!" Rachel's voice not at my bedroom door as I expected. Curious what's going on, I open my door slowly. "Can you speed it up a little Ollie? I'm stuck!" I round the corner to the living room, I'm met by the sight of Rachel lying face down on the floor, a suitcase as big as she is on her back and the coffee table flipped over leaned against her and her suitcase, and an explosion of clothing. The laughter that erupts from me is deep, try as I might, I can't stop. It only takes seconds before my sides hurt and tears are running down my face. When I regain control of myself as much as possible, I set the coffee table upright and roll her suitcase off her.

"How the hell did you accomplish that?" Mid-sentence the laughter starts again, the frustration, embarrassment, and anger on her face fades and she starts with a giggle that quickly turns into laughter. It's a full five minutes before she can gather herself to tell me what happened.

"My suitcase wouldn't close, I put it on the table and was trying to squish it down, then the table flipped over, and the next thing I know I'm on the floor being suffocated by my suitcase." We fall into another fit of laughter, the more I survey the scene the harder that I laugh. "I'm sorry Ollie, I didn't mean to wake you, and I probably scared the shit out of you." I'm so glad I didn't miss this.

"My day couldn't have started any better than this, I only wish I had gotten a picture." I help her fold and repack her clothes, as much as she has packed, I'm certain she's prepared for anything. "When's he going to be here?" The suitcase is securely on the floor, I squeeze the zippers together while Rachel zips.

"A couple hours, I couldn't sleep, so I went through my checklist again and was gonna start getting ready. Do you want to shower first?" I'm no fool, I jump at the opportunity to shower first, I can be done in 10 minutes. If I wait for her to go first, I'll be late for my interview. I leave her at the breakfast bar with a fresh cup of coffee.

Both of us are ready and sitting at the dining room table, still giggling over Rachel's mishap, when Alex arrives. I notice immediately there's something off, no sign of his carefree attitude, he seems stressed, I start to think maybe he has something to tell me, but he hardly notices me. I chalk it up to the conference he's going to. Maybe he's speaking and he's nervous, or maybe I'm reading too much into things, Rachel doesn't seem to notice, her excitement bubbling over.

"You sure you'll be okay this weekend?" Alex looks as if he dreads my response. It doesn't matter if I am or not, I wouldn't interfere with their getaway if it was my last act on earth.

"I'll be fine. I have a team of security, a full fridge, cable tv, and if all else fails, I have Rachel's password to Netflix. Stop worrying about me. You guys need this weekend, and no one deserves it more." Relief washes over him, but still there's something else, I'll be interested to hear what has him so worked up.

"Fletcher will bring the car around when you're ready to go, text him, then wait for him to come to the door." Maybe this is what's bothering him so much, Alex likes to be in charge, he likes to have control of the situations he's involved in, it's probably just the loss of that control and being so far away that's bothering him. Rachel gives me a hug, makes me promise to call if I need anything at all. Alex surprises me with a hug of his own and makes me promise to call only if there's an emergency. He grabs Rachels suitcase. "Jesus woman! What the hell did you pack?" There's the Alex I've come to know. It's his fault she packed everything but the kitchen sink, if he would have just given her an idea what the weekend entailed, she could have narrowed down her choices. I laugh as I shut and lock the door behind them.

The silence and emptiness settle quickly, they've only just left, and already the loneliness is encroaching on me. What happened to my appreciation for silence, for being alone? Stop it Olivia, you're being ridiculous. I have an hour before I need to leave, I busy myself cleaning the kitchen, placing our coffee cups in the dishwasher, and wiping the counters.

I feel silly waiting by the door for Fletcher to knock, maybe I'm getting complacent, but all of this seems unnecessary now. There's been no word from Greg at all, I can't say that I expected him to sign the papers as soon as he got them, my thoughts were more sinister than that. I was positive that he would show up, track me down, or reach out to me. Not hearing from him at all, sets me at ease. He's looking for a lawyer, whether he contests the divorce or not, he hasn't found me, he hasn't come to my door. It's possible that we can get this done civilly.

All these thoughts lift my spirits as Fletcher drives me through the city. My nerves are settled, I'm interviewing for a bartending job, this I can do, this is what I've done for nearly all my adult life. I'm prepared for this interview and I'm confident that I can do this job. Parked in valet, Fletcher opens my door for me, Alex hadn't told me anything else except what to do at home. "So, how do things work now?"

Will he be waiting here for me, do I have to call him before I leave, send a text?

"I'll follow you in miss, I'll wait nearby, and then I'll follow you out." I hadn't prepared for this, where the hell is he going to wait nearby? I don't even know where the hell I'm going. I don't want him to be conspicuous, the last thing in the world I need is to draw attention to myself having personal security. Who in their right mind will give me a job if it's necessary to have security following me? My irritation builds, but I try not to let it show, it's not his fault, he's doing exactly as he's been instructed. Knowing I have no argument and even if I did, it would only make me late, I make my way into the casino. I hurry to the help desk, it's quicker to ask than to try to find HR on my own. True to his word, Fletcher remains a good distance behind me, a casual observer would have no idea he is watching me, following the directions given to me, I hold the elevator for Fletcher, as frustrating as this situation is, there is something comforting having him near, a familiar face in a sea of strangers.

I lose sight of Fletcher while waiting to be called, I didn't need to worry about anyone knowing I have a security detail. Even though I can't see him, I know that he's here, somewhere close by.

I'm led back to another office. Roger Burroughs introduces himself as he stands and shakes my hand. He waits for me to sit before following suit. Jumping right to business, he fires off typical interview questions, I've prepared for every one of them, this is how an interview should go. "Well Olivia, do you mind if I call you that?" I'm pleasantly surprised he used my first name and shake my head in response. "I think you are a great candidate for this position, I'd like to set up another interview with Brian Jones, he's the food and beverage manager, are you available early next week?"

I thank him as I leave, excited that I'll be coming back next week, as I make my way back through HR, I look around for Fletcher and still don't see him, I look at the clock on my phone, I don't have a lot of time before my meeting with Ms. Cain. I start typing a message to Fletcher, but before I can finish, "Are you ready miss?" He's standing before me.

Traffic in Vegas is nothing like home, I worried over being late for nothing, Fletcher got me to the Lost Cities in no time, early even. I fidget in my seat waiting to see Ms. Cain, unsure what she's going to offer and unsure how I will respond.

"Olivia, please come in." She's friendlier this time, not so curt. "Mr. Alessandro and I discussed your interview, unfortunately, we aren't prepared to offer you the position you interviewed for, it's my understanding that you are willing to take another position?" I appreciate her trying to break the news to me gently, but it isn't necessary.

"Depending on the position, that's correct Ms. Cain." I don't want her to think that I will take anything that's offered. After so much thought last night, it really doesn't matter, I can't work here.

"We would like to offer you a position in cocktails, would you be interested?" Internally I cringe, grateful I have another interview at the Desert Sands, the job itself wouldn't be bad, but there isn't a chance in hell I'm putting on that uniform.

"Thank you, Ms. Cain, but I don't think that will work for me. I really appreciate the offer, but I'm going to pass." That made it easy, if I was completely desperate, maybe. If I could wear something else, definitely. But I have the opportunity to tend bar instead, I would rather do that anyway.

"Oh, I can't say that's the response I expected." Now she's back to who she was the first time I met her, the niceties expired the minute I said no. "Well, I'm sorry you feel that way, good luck to you." Her dismissal is clear, she acts as if it's a personal affront to her that I turned down what she offered.

Now that all my appointments are over, as I get into the car, I start looking forward to a quiet weekend, next week it starts all over again, with another interview Monday morning.

Chapter 10

Ian

Overall, my morning started productively, meetings with each of the construction superintendents. The Whiskey's coming along but production is going to slow due to delays in materials. They don't expect it to set us behind but prepared me for the possibility.

As I drive to the Lost Cities, I return a missed call from Michelle. "This is Cain." I may need to invest in some phone etiquette classes for her. If I was anyone else, I would probably hang up.

"Good morning Michelle, how are you this fine morning?" I enjoy irritating her by being pleasant when she is obviously in a bad mood.

"She declined." Who declined, what? I wait in silence for her to elaborate. "Olivia Daniels. She opted to not take the position offered." Alex made it clear that she needs a job, why would she refuse?

"Did she say why?" Truthfully, I was hoping she would be in the casino when I got back, I was looking forward to seeing her.

"Maybe Alex can tell you, I've wasted enough time on this, have a nice day Ian." Silence fills my car momentarily until the music cuts back in. Michelle and I will have to have a sit down, in the near future, she seems to have forgotten who works for who.

I start to dial Alex before I remember he left this morning for Tahoe. As much as I would like to understand what happened, unfortunately it will have to wait until Monday. I'm not going to interrupt the weekend he worked so hard to plan. When he told me his idea for a romantic weekend, he really threw me off when he said he was going to propose. I'd been curious if he was getting serious about Rachel, but I wasn't expecting that. I come up with multiple explanations just trying to understand until my thoughts are interrupted by the phone, Markus's name flashes across the screen. I may not have answers for this puzzle, but he holds the answers to another.

"Markus." I keep the greeting brief, he's not one for small talk and I really just want to hear his report.

"Sir, I have the information you asked for, are you available to meet?" I hate being addressed as sir, it's too stuffy, too formal. I've asked repeatedly for him to use my first name, or even my last, but for some, old habits die hard, the years he spent in the military groomed him to be this way.

"I'll be in my office in ten, I'll clear my schedule." I know him well enough to know that if he was willing to speak on the phone about whatever he found, he would say it, I resist the urge to ask any questions. The music fills my car again, indicating that our conversation has concluded for the time being. I put my foot a little further in the gas, so many questions surrounding Olivia, I'm eager to start getting some answers.

Markus is already waiting when I arrive, "Stephanie, please clear my schedule and hold any calls." I don't think I have anything pressing, it doesn't matter, whatever there is can be rescheduled. Markus carries a thick manila envelope. He seats himself across from my chair at my desk.

"Sir, I would have gotten back to you sooner, but once I started digging, the more skeletons fell out of the closet. Is he a threat to you or your corporation?" What the hell did he find on this guy?

"As I said before, this information is for the foundation." The details of it all are none of his concern, his job is to find the information. If he found what I think he did then he already knows.

"Gregory Andrew Daniels born, July 30, 1979 to George and Anne Daniels in Jersey City. Graduated high school in 1997, joined the army right out of high school, served four years, continuing his education while enlisted. After the army he went to law school and went to work for the firm he interned at after passing the bar. In 2004 he met his current wife, Olivia Rae Mason at Trinity, a bar in Lower Manhattan. They dated two years and married on May 20, 2006." I take notes of dates and names, I know he will provide the full report, but I don't want to have to search through the whole thing for the bits of information that I may need.

"They led a pretty simple life, bought a brownstone in Brooklyn, his wife and her mother ran a successful business, he worked his way into the District Attorney's office. In 2009, he was put on administrative leave and ordered into drug counseling after a random test returned positive for cocaine..." I listen closely as Markus continues with his report.

"He had a few run ins with superiors that cost him promotions and raises. Then in 2012 he was placed on leave for evidence tampering, but nothing was ever proven.

Circumstantial evidence led to Daniels but not enough to pursue a case." Drugs, disciplinary action, evidence tampering, how much of this does Olivia know? How much of a part did she play?

"Also, in 2012, Daniels was placed under surveillance by District Attorney Derek Long, Daniels had a few meetings with leader of the Russian Mob, Fedor Morozov, as it turned out, Daniels got himself involved in some gambling. Long turned the other cheek, surveillance was dropped." This guy dug himself out of one hole just to fall into a deeper one.

"By 2013 his gambling had become a problem, he was in debt to the Russian mob over $100,000. He worked out a deal with Fedor, Fedor's son Viktor was up on assault with a deadly weapon, battery, breaking and entering, and a few minor offenses. Fedor offered to forgive the debt if Daniels could make the charges disappear, the evidence in the case disappeared and the victim refused to testify. The DA couldn't make any of the charges stick so Viktor walked, Daniels got out of his debt." He's been in a downward spiral for years, I thought I had it figured out when the abuse had started, but hearing all of this, I wouldn't be surprised to find that it started much earlier than I originally thought.

"He was released from that debt, he stayed away for a while, toward the end of 2013, he was back at it. By June of 2014 he was in neck deep again, the brownstone was going into foreclosure. He borrowed enough money to save the brownstone and got caught up on payments. About the time that it was starting to all fall apart again, his parents were murdered. The details of that case are appalling, what made the papers doesn't even scratch the surface." Were his parents murdered due to his debts? A mob hit to send a message to him?

"The case is still open, it's listed as a home invasion, no suspects, but Daniels collected a hefty life insurance policy, paid his debts, and got his mortgage back on track. He went out on leave for a couple months, worked the investigation on his own and did some counseling. His wife started paperwork to give up her share of

Trinity, but never did anything with it." In just the short time I spoke with Olivia, I know that bar meant the world to her, what would make her want to give it up?

"In December 2014, Olivia Daniels fell down a flight of stairs, she fractured four ribs, broke her wrist and had to have corrective surgery to fix her nose. January of 2015, Daniels went back to work, he was put on leave again for insubordination, then in May he went back on leave to care for his wife. She'd fallen off a ladder and pulled a shelf of booze down with her, multiple facial lacerations, more broken ribs, and her left tibia was broken. While on leave he was nearly arrested for destruction of property, harassment, battery, and vandalism. Him and his mother in law, Natalia Mason, had an argument, he'd busted a few stools and a mirror, when the police arrived, Ms. Mason was telling him to leave and he struck her, one of the patrol guys that showed up was a friend of Daniels, he was able to smooth things over and Daniels went home without any charges." It seems Olivia became quite clumsy after his parents were killed, coincidence? Anger builds inside of me, as I consider the possibilities of the ways that he could have caused all those injuries, it heats my blood envisioning his hands upon her and her mother.

"His wife consulted a divorce attorney after he attacked her mom, shortly thereafter, she was checked into the hospital again, the medical report said she was mugged, no suspect was apprehended, she was beaten pretty badly." What the hell is the matter with the doctors? The cops? Is protecting the District Attorney's office more important than the life of a victim? How does this happen?

"Things stayed quiet, Greg Daniels got back on track at work, Olivia Daniels continued working with her mom, their relationship was showing signs of deterioration, police were called on a couple of occasions, one or the other was required to leave. Fall of 2015, Greg Daniels had burned through his parents life insurance, and his debt with the mob was rising, their home was again on the verge of foreclosure., Almost a year after his parents deaths, Natalia Mason was walking across the street, she was hit by a car and the driver took off, she died in surgery. Interestingly enough, Angus Kelley, the enforcer for Fedor Morozov was the driver of the vehicle. A witness was able to positively identify him, he stood trial and went to prison on a six-year sentence for vehicular manslaughter, he has a parole hearing coming up. The witness disappeared after the trial." Did the mob kill Olivia's mother to send a message to Daniels? Was she a casualty of his recklessness? I'm seething at the possibility.

"Once again, through life insurance, Greg Daniels saved his home and paid his debts to the mob. Six months later his wife lost her bar in a fire, the fire investigator ruled it arson, his wife went under scrutiny, but it was short lived. Greg Daniels called in a few favors and the investigation went in a different direction, still unsolved. After the fire, either the police or the ambulance was called to their home eight times in two years, she had five hospital stays in that time, the last was over a week, a day after she checked out she cleaned out the money in her business account, that included the insurance money she collected from her business." Five times in the hospital? Was it because he worked in the DA's office that they all looked the other way? Flashbacks of when I was a kid cycle through my mind as I listen to Markus, mama called the cops to Alex's apartment a few times a week. I'm livid that this woman had to endure so much, that anyone would believe that she fell down a flight of stairs, fell off a ladder, I wonder what other excuses were made and accepted. She started planning her escape back then, she put money in the one place he couldn't get to it, but why did she wait so long?

"On the work front, Daniels has been in some trouble, he's currently on administrative leave again, showing up to work late, showing up under the influence, not showing up at all. You told me that I would be billing my time to Battling Back for this, so I assume that his wife is here. This guy is dangerous, I haven't been able to get a twenty on him. I know that he's been served divorce papers, he was served at work, the same day he was put on leave. There were a lot of questions that were asked, but it worked in his favor, his superiors are blaming his behavior on a pending divorce now." He knows Olivia is in Las Vegas, is he here? If he's here or on his way, we need to protect her, it won't end well if he finds her.

"I checked flight information, unless he has an alias that I haven't uncovered, he didn't fly. I caution, if he doesn't want to leave a paper trail, he's driving, using cash, and my best guess is that he is coming here. He's due back to work on Wednesday." The look of terror on her face when I said I recognized her, she had fled from a nightmare, now I understand. I need to contact Alex, I think things are about to heat up, he may need to put his plans on hold for the time being. I would talk to Olivia directly but I'm not sure she would be comfortable with that.

"I'll keep working on this, I'm watching his bank and credit card activity, if

I get any hits, you will be the first to know. I would recommend, if it's possible, to have her under surveillance and security, I can't prove it yet, but he is coming for her." I watch as Markus leaves my office. Before I call Alex, I contact Mack.

Chapter 11

Olivia

I felt liberated when I left the Lost Cities, I felt so good that I stepped out of my comfort zone and asked if Fletcher would take me to the Hoover Dam. Standing here, awed by the architecture, impressed by the feats it must have taken to build something like this. I look out over the water, the wind blows through my hair, for the first time in as long as I can remember, I'm not afraid, strangers pass me by, some with a smile, others with a nod, rather than hide from them or avert my eyes, I return a smile and a wave.

Everything that's happened that has brought me to this point has weighed me down to the point of feeling like I was suffocating. The fear has been paralyzing. To stand here and feel free, to feel at ease, to know that I'm going to be okay, just a little more time and I will be able to start completely over. I walk the path across the dam and take in the beauty of all that is around me. I notice the children and the happy couples, I envy them, maybe someday. I surprise myself with a thought of Ian, his blue-gray eyes that are so familiar to me, they draw me in, the gentleness in his voice, and his demeanor, so calm and understanding. I shake my head, that's not a road you're willing to travel girl, stop it.

I couldn't take the job as a cocktail waitress, the uniform would be too revealing of my secrets, people would speculate, the whispers, the questions, the shame. No, taking that job isn't an option, I only hope that Alex understands. I'll have to tell him, he deserves an explanation, for all that he's done for me, but especially for trying so hard to get me a job. I don't want him to think I'm ungrateful.

I lose track of how long I've been here, I have crossed the dam and back several times, soaking in the sun and the energy of those surrounding me, enjoying the peace that has been missing from my life for so long. I want to absorb it all before I hide myself away again, I remind myself that it's only for a short time longer, soon all of this will be behind me. Noticing the change in the light, seeing the sun dip further down in the sky, I look for Fletcher.

"Did you enjoy your walk miss?" I appreciate Fletcher's quiet demeanor, I didn't really know what to expect being driven around by security, but it really hasn't been terrible, I don't think it's obvious to anyone, and that sets my mind at ease.

"I did, thank you, and thank you for bringing me here and giving me the space to enjoy the scenery." I haven't ventured out much since arriving, Rachel has drug me out to a few places but overall, I prefer to stay home.

As we pull onto the freeway, I lose myself in how I got here.

After being released from the hospital, I knew I had to do something. I knew that if I stayed, I probably wouldn't survive my next trip to the ER. The insurance money from the bar was still in my business account, the only place Greg couldn't get to it. The bank didn't care that he worked with the DA, his name wasn't on the account. Without a warrant there was nothing he could do, except try to strong arm me into closing the account or adding his name, I suffered for refusing both options. Looking back now, it was worth it. The dilemma of where to go was my next obstacle, I was racing an unseen clock, when would he lose his temper again, my father was out, the only conversation we had had in twenty years was when I called to tell him that mom had died. It was an unnecessary conversation, he didn't care, and couldn't be bothered to come to the services either. I had no other family, I had alienated all my friends, I was truly alone in this world. Greg had successfully managed to remove everything and everyone except him.

With limited access to the outside world, I decided that when the opportunity presented itself, I would just go as far away as possible. I'd never had passport, leaving the country was out, and a plane ticket left a trail. I couldn't take my car for fear he would call it in stolen, my only option was a bus ticket. A day after being released from the hospital Greg was called into work, I waited for half an hour, then left. The bank was my first stop, then straight to the greyhound station. A small suitcase was all I carried with me. I was able to catch a bus heading for Los Angeles, only having to wait for a half hour before it departed. Sixty-seven hours later, we stopped in Vegas, I couldn't sit on the bus any longer, my whole body hurt, and I was exhausted, I took a taxi to the first casino I saw.

Rachel saw me struggle into the casino, my body hurt, not just the broken and bruised parts, all of me, being on a bus for that long would make anyone sore. I was having trouble catching my breath, the doctor had said that my lung would heal naturally, when he released me, he said I should be fine without the oxygen, but I was questioning that now. She made her way over to me with a full tray of drinks in her hand and picked up my suitcase, leading me to the nearest empty seat.

"I'll be back as soon as I deliver these drinks, wait here for me." She wove her way through people and slot machines and was gone before I could respond to her. I knew that I looked terrible, thankfully no one knew why, but they still stared and whispered to one another, so I hid my face as much as I could, and I waited.

"Can you walk now doll?" Rachel startled me when she returned, I had been so preoccupied with hiding that I didn't see her.

"I think so, but probably not far." She picked up my suitcase and held out her arm to me, I didn't need the support, but I took it anyway. She led me through the casino to a little coffee shop and ordered us both burgers and fries. Her kindness to me, a stranger to her, overwhelmed me and I cried. She slid into the booth next to me and just held me while I cried the tears that I had been holding back for longer than I

*could remember. By the time my tears
started to dry up, our food arrived.*

*"Thank..." I wanted her to know that
I appreciated her kindness, but she stopped
me.*

*"Shhh... eat now, talk later." She
dove into her food like she hadn't eaten in a
month, the burger looked delicious, but I
knew that I wouldn't be able to take a bite
without reopening the split in my lip, for the
first time in my life, I used a knife and fork
to eat a burger.*

*"My name's Rachel." She had
cleaned her plate and set it aside. I was still
slowly getting mine down.*

*"I'm Ra... Olivia." I'm starting a new
life, I don't ever want to be called what Greg
called me again. I had always preferred my
middle name, Olivia seemed so old
fashioned, Rae had stuck since I had asked
to use it in third grade. But it isn't who I
want to be any longer, Rae cowered at the
hands of a man that tried to destroy her, I
won't ever be her again.*

"Look, I want to help you, I don't know what your story is, and you don't have to tell me, but you can at least tell me your name." She assumes I'm lying, I guess that should be expected when I started with one name and ended with one completely different.

"Olivia really is my name, just not the one I'm accustomed to using, but Olivia is who I am, and who I want to be." Olivia is strong enough to take back her life.

"It's nice to meet you Olivia, you scared me when you came through the doors, I thought you were going to fall over, are you alright?"

What would have happened to me if I hadn't met Rachel that night? Would I have made it all the way to Los Angeles? What would I have done if I had? The only reason I've made it this long is because of Rachel. She left her shift early and took me home that night. She tried to take me to the hospital to get looked at. When I refused, she called her uncle, Dr. Tony Matthews, a surgeon, and he made a house call. He said I was lucky that my broken clavicle was still in place, and brought oxygen to make it easier to breathe, the punctured lung would heal, but after the trip I took, I set myself back.

"We're here miss." I was so lost in my thoughts, I missed the whole drive. I hope that Rachel is having the time of her life, no one deserves it more than her. I hope that one day I can do something to repay her for all she's done for me, for being a great friend, my only friend.

Fletcher escorts me up the stairs, I stop at the landing, Brett stands in front of the door, but it's not my unease of him that takes my breath away or stops me cold on the top step. Beside him on the ground, a vase of red and white roses, the preferred non-apology of my soon to be ex-husband. "When did those arrive and who brought them?" I knew he wouldn't just let me go, now the fear and disappointment are crushing me, I had gotten my hopes up, but the reality of my life is sitting beside my door in the guise of flowers.

"About an hour ago ma'am, the courier said it's a gift to you from Rachel." Rachel would never send me roses, she knows that I despise them, she knows what they mean to me. Greg has been doing his research, he knows a lot more than what I'd like. I pull the card:

It's been a long time, Angel

I can hear his voice saying those words as if he is speaking them in my ear, the scent of the roses is nauseating. I put my key in the lock and run to the bathroom, unable to stop the vomit that is threatening. As I heave, I hear his explanation in my mind, "Red signifies the passion of our love that drives me to react the way I do, and the white represents the purity of that love no matter what. I love you Rae, I'm sorry that you angered me." I never got the I'm sorry I smashed your face, I'm sorry I broke your leg, I'm sorry that I killed our unborn child, no, the only apologies I received put the blame at my feet. Like he wouldn't have hit me if I hadn't angered him, but it was never about me angering him, that was just the excuse he needed to justify it.

"Miss, are you alright?" Fletcher knocks gently on the door. At least he is here for now, I wish I paid closer attention to the schedule so I knew who would be here next, I know it isn't Brett, for that I'm thankful. Something about him troubles me, but I don't know why.

When I open the door, Fletcher hands me a cool rag, "Thank you. Did you read the card? Those aren't from Rachel." I press the cool rag to my forehead, focus on just breathing in and out, keeping calm. I can't freak out right now, I need to keep it together, and stay focused. I won't let this derail me.

"Yes ma'am, this is why we're here. I just wanted to check on you before I call Mr. Sutton." There has to be something else we can do. I don't want Rachel to worry and I don't want to disrupt their weekend. The sound of the doorbell stops my heart. "Wait here miss." Before I can respond Fletcher is gone. Is Greg so brazen that he is outside my door now?

Hearing a friendly exchange in the living room, I sneak a glance, peering around the corner. I recognize Mack standing in the doorway, Brett looming behind him, a chill runs down my spine, what is it about that guy? "Ms. Daniels, I'm here at the request of Mr. Alessandro, but it seems you are already aware of the situation I've been sent to brief you on." Ian had sent Mack to tell me that Greg was going to send me flowers, that doesn't make any sense. "We have reason to believe your husband is here in Vegas or on his way." The room starts to spin, before I can stop it, my knees buckle beneath me, and I crumple to the floor. Fletcher and Mack both dive forward in an effort to catch me, neither of them make it. "Are you alright?!"

Five things I can see, the roses on the table, the card lying beside them, my keys where I dropped them, my purse with its contents scattered, the boots on the feet of Fletcher. Four things I can feel, the scar on my hand, the material of my shirt against my skin, my hair brushing my arm, and the carpet beneath me. Three things I can hear, the hum of the refrigerator, the fan spinning above me, the tick of the clock on the wall. Two things I can smell, the roses that brought on this attack, the vanilla candle on the coffee table. One thing I can taste, the mint of the toothpaste.

"I'm fine." As fine as I am going to be for now, on shaky legs I rise and take a deep breath. "What does Mr. Alessandro suggest?" If Ian sent Mack over, maybe we can get through the weekend without bothering Alex, there really isn't anything more that he can do. As much as I'd like Rachel to come home, I'd rather have her as far away from this mess as possible.

"Security will be increased for the time being. Now that your husband has made contact, we will assume that he is in the area." Will it matter? I don't know but I look at these men tasked with my safety

and I'm both grateful and scared for them.
Greg didn't waste any time.

Chapter 12

Ian

"Did you ask her yet?" I never thought I would see the day that Alex settled down, I think part of the reason he never got deeply involved with anyone was his fear that he would be like his dad. Something about Rachel changed that for him. I've never seen him happier.

"Not yet, we have a hike scheduled tomorrow morning, we'll be on top of a mountain overlooking the lake, I have a photographer that's going to pose as a hiker, women like pictures, right?" I hear the nerves in his voice, I only hope he doesn't look as uncertain as he sounds.

I can't tell him about the brief from Markus, nor the news from Fletcher that Greg made contact. As soon as he proposes, I'll fill him in on all of it, until then, I'll handle things on this end. "Yeah, they do. I hadn't heard from you, so I was curious if she turned you down." I can't help the grin that forms.

"Is it too soon? Do you think she's going to say no? Should I wait?" Alex has never been this nervous or unsure of himself, I'd like to keep messing with him but it's pitiful to hear him this way.

"Relax man, she won't turn you down." I hang up, Alex, for the most part handles the clients with Battling Back, I'm out of my realm diving headfirst into this one, the reasoning behind it, is her, I can't stop thinking about her. I read through the file Markus left with me, I justified it as needing to fully understand the situation. Truthfully though, it was to know her better, now the guilt is eating away at me, no one deserves to have their privacy invaded. I hope that when I confess that she will understand.

I adjust the schedule, if her husband is here, I want only the most trusted in the team to be watching. "Mack, I put you and Ryan on for the next three nights, tomorrow and Sunday it will be Nick and Fletcher during the day, keep the area secure, no one makes it to her door." There was time when Ryan wouldn't have even

been in the running, then Mack took me to
see one of his fights. That tall skinny kid is
brutal in the cage, no mercy for his
opponent, he is smart and agile and has a
keen eye. "Will you let Ms. Daniels know
that I would like to speak with her as well?"
I'd like us to be on the same page with Alex
and Rachel, I don't know if Alex told her
what he had planned this weekend, I want
her to know that she is still safe even
without them and as much as I'd prefer not
to, I need to tell her what I found out.

"You got it boss, are you looking for
a face to face or a phone call?" A phone call
would be the coward's way, I'm not a
coward. I'm willing to admit my mistakes
and take any consequences for my actions,
face to face is the way it has to be. I tell
Mack to send me a text with whatever she
decides, she may not want to see me.

I pull into the parking space and wait for Mack. I let him know I was on my way, I'd like a briefing before I go up to Olivia's apartment.

"Sir, it's been quiet, nothing out of the ordinary, do you want me to go up with you?" Should I take him up with me? I hadn't considered the possibility it may be uncomfortable for her, but then again, would she have agreed to meet with me? I decide against it, I don't know how far into the conversation we will get but her privacy should be respected, I already invaded it.

"No, just keep an eye out." I make my way up the stairs, at the landing I stop. The door is open just a crack, a thin line of light shining through, I hear the distinct sound of Phantom of the Opera, a smile plays on my lips. My mother took me to see this in San Francisco as a boy, it's still the best vacation I've ever been on. Did Mack alert her of my arrival? Even still, the door should remain locked until she knows who's behind it.

I rap on the door, it moves only slightly, no response, the crescendo of the music blaring, I give the door a nudge as I knock again, "Olivia!" Still nothing, I push against the door meeting some resistance, able to get my head in, it's her blocking the door, face-down on the carpet, unresponsive. As gently as I can, I push it open far enough to enter. "Olivia! Jesus!" I check her pulse, her shirt is torn down the back, there is a roadmap of scars, all shapes, sizes, and colors. She groans slightly and shifts her body, blood covers the carpet beneath her. "Olivia, it's Ian, can you hear me?" I'm unsure what to do, my instinct is to call an ambulance, I'm not sure how she will react, or how she'll take me being here. She moves again, "Olivia?" She pushes her body off the floor, scrambling to the corner of the room, her eyes wild in terror, but she doesn't scream. Her breathing is rapid, her face smeared with blood and tears. She looks at me in confusion.

I stay kneeled down, fearing that I might send her over the edge if I move. I need to turn off the music, the sound is coming from the TV. "Olivia, it's me, Ian, I'd like to help you if I can, I'm going to turn off the TV." After clicking the power button, the silence is deafening, I call Mack, "Someone's been here, check around, don't come up here until I call you." Seething, it takes all I can to keep my voice even. I watch her, waiting, she takes a deep breath, holds it, then forces herself to let it out slowly, all the while her eyes scan the room.

Her blouse ruined, slides down her shoulder, the scars from her back wrap around over her shoulder, an angry red mark the size of a quarter over her heart. "Olivia, I'm not going to hurt you, I need to get you a new shirt." She looks down at herself, it's all too much for her, she slides down the wall, hugging her knees to her chest and buries her head. She doesn't make a sound, I see the movement of her shoulders, her body wracked with silent sobs.

Moving through the apartment, I look for anything for her to put on. I know that I've found her room, the walls are bare, sparsely furnished and only a few things hanging in the closet. I grab the first thing I get my hands on. Returning to the front room, I slow my stride, "Olivia." I speak softly, not wanting to frighten her any more than she is. "I brought you a new shirt." Flashbacks of Patricia, kneeled on the floor, blood spilling from her nose. Olivia takes the shirt from me, I find paper towels in the kitchen and get some wet, I approach her slowly. "Will you let me help you please?"

"I'm not going to freak out if that's what you're thinking. I know who you are, I know where I am, I'm fine." She puts herself together again, not at all what I expected, I'm still waiting for the meltdown.

Kneeling again, I wipe the towel gently down her face, wiping the blood, "Looks like it's all coming from your nose, how does it feel." It's not the breakdown I'm expecting, but she falls into me and releases all the emotion that has overflowed tonight, her face in my chest, what else can I do? I wrap my arms around her, I stroke her hair and speak gently, and hold her, trying to reassure her. Waiting until she is ready to ask what happened.

The longer she cries the more my anger builds. Anger at her husband, anger at my men, anger at myself for not preventing this. I knew he was coming, I knew he knew where to find her, why didn't I take the steps necessary? The safe house is ready, Mack could have taken her there once the flowers were delivered. This is why Alex is in charge of the foundation, Alex would have made sure this didn't happen, he doesn't let shit fall through the cracks. There's no getting around it, we need call him, he needs to know this. When Olivia is ready, we'll call him together.

A calmness settles over me, sitting here like this with her. Her vulnerability on display, leaning on me, knowing that right now, nothing can hurt her, there is nowhere else I would rather be.

"I've ruined your shirt and jacket, I'm sorry." Her words startle me, I don't know how long we've sat like this, her tears subsided some time ago, but she didn't let go so neither did I.

"I have a great dry cleaner." It's a shirt, it doesn't matter, all that matters now is that she is ok, and that this doesn't happen again. "Can you tell me what happened?" I don't want her to have to relive it, but I need to know, there are holes in the security plan, they need to be closed.

"I was watching tv, I went to the kitchen, when I started back to the couch, I was pushed from behind. It wasn't Greg, I didn't see who attacked me, but the man spoke to me, it wasn't Greg's voice, he sent someone." He came from the hallway, he gained entry from one of the bedrooms. "I fell into the coffee table, I hit my face on the edge, he grabbed my shirt and jerked me back up, but it ripped, and I fell again." I wait, not wanting to pressure her, letting her tell me as she is ready. I don't want to upset her again. "He said, it isn't over." Her lip trembles, I pull her in closer. I assume the message implies her husband doesn't want a divorce.

"You didn't see the person that attacked you?" Having a description would be helpful to the guys. She doesn't speak, only shakes her head. "Are you sure it wasn't Greg?" If she didn't see him, it's possible it was her husband, though not likely. I don't think he would have left her alive if he left her at all after all that I've been told.

"It wasn't his voice, it wasn't him. I can't explain it, I spent four years of my life being knocked around by him, this wasn't his style, he likes to get face to face." That's a great explanation.

Olivia goes to the kitchen and uses the sink to wash her face and rinse her mouth. I call Mack, within seconds, him and Ryan appear in the doorway. Mack surveys the room, he watches Olivia at the sink, "I need to check the apartment boss, we haven't found how the perpetrator gained entry." I glare at him but say nothing, I don't trust myself right now. Mack doesn't wait for permission, he and Ryan start down the hallway, Ryan going right, Mack going left. Ryan returns first, there isn't much to see in Olivia's room, he checks the sliding glass door that leads out to the balcony, then checks the window, both are locked.

Mack emerges from the hall, "One window unlocked but unless he brought a tall ladder, he didn't gain entry there, possibly used it as an egress. If we are going to file a report, we need to do so and we should probably have her checked out, we can build a paper trail." A glass shatters in the sink, our heads all turn to Olivia. Her eyes wide in terror.

"Are you alright?" It dawns on me, she's afraid to have the police come here, who could blame her for that, they haven't done anything to help her yet. She's been failed by the system. "No, we'll handle this internally and I don't think she needs to be checked out, if we aren't involving the police, a paper trail means nothing." Olivia doesn't speak but she's visibly relieved by my statement. "How the hell did he get in then? Did either of you see him come to the door?" Olivia busies herself cleaning up the glass. Eyes should've always been on the door. If this bastard walked in because someone was sleeping on the job, there will be hell to pay.

"I can assure you, one or both of us have been watching all evening." Mack looks as perplexed and angry as I feel. Something isn't adding up and I intend to figure out what it is.

Chapter 13

Olivia

Physically, I've had worse, the bleeding has stopped, my nose isn't broken, the split in my lip is superficial. Mentally, I don't know how much more of this I can take. On one hand, now I know, my divorce won't be easy. On the other hand, what now? He knows where I am, he's proven that I'm not safe anywhere, even my own home. I wish Rachel was here, I could use some of her positivity.

Or maybe not, positivity sucks, when everything falls apart, you feel worse because of it. If I had stayed in my negative state, at least I wouldn't be surprised by tonight's events. Maybe I would have been more alert and could have done something.

I feel like I'm going to cry again, not because I'm upset, or hurt, because I'm really fucking pissed, and I don't know what to do with it. I want to scream, I need to yell, I need an hour in the ring with the bastard that invaded my home! Yeah, that's just what I need, time in a ring to get my ass kicked again. Who the hell was that guy? And how did Greg recruit him?

"Olivia?" I jump, I was deep enough in my own thoughts, I didn't hear Mack and Ryan leave. I don't know what they talked about, I faded into myself after Ian shut down the suggestion of making a report. In a perfect world, it wouldn't be a question, something bad happens you call the authorities, they do their duty to protect and serve, the bad guy goes to jail, and everyone lives happily ever after. In my world you don't know who the good guys are, you don't know who will protect who. In my world the bad guy doesn't go to jail because his image and the image of his office is what's important. "Olivia?"

"I'm sorry, I'm a little distracted." I guess that's one way of putting it, I'm scared, tired, sore, frustrated, irritated, there's more, but those are the only feelings I can pinpoint right now.

"I know you are, can we talk for a minute, come up with a game plan?" If he's the one that's going to come up with it. My brain is fried, I'm not able to even suggest any ideas right now. "I'm going to share a secret with you, do you know why Alex took Rachel to Tahoe this weekend?" I'm confused by the question, what's a secret have to do with Alex and Rachel? I don't trust myself to speak, so I shake my head instead. "Alex has put in a lot of work to plan the most romantic setting so he can propose to Rachel." That explains his behavior this morning, he was nervous.

"That's fantastic!" It really is, Rachel will be so happy, she is so in love with him. She's told me before that he's it for her, he's her happily ever after. A little good news after a very crappy evening.

"Agreed, so now I need to ask a favor of you, normally, I wouldn't work this way, but, Alex's plan takes place tomorrow morning, if it's alright with you I'd like to wait until after to fill him in on what's happened today." This isn't a favor, this is what friends would do for other friends. I don't want to ruin whatever he has planned, and I don't want him thinking about what's going on here while he's proposing to my best friend. "We can call him tomorrow afternoon, I wouldn't ask this of you, but it's taken a lot of courage for Alex to do this, I don't want him to put it off." I bet it did, and Rachel will be dumbfounded, she's still positive that he isn't ready.

"We need to wait until they get back, the memory of his proposal isn't going to end with them flying home because of me." There's nothing that can be done that isn't already being taken care of, and I prefer Rachel out of harm's way. Home isn't that place.

"I think we both may get an earful if we wait that long." He's right, we will, Alex will be pissed, Rachel will be furious, and they will both get over it. If they don't, they can blame me.

"Look, I don't have control of much of anything in my life, and I haven't for a long time, so can we just let me have the reins to decide something that affects me, I need that." A decision that I can make for myself, because it's the choice I want to make, I'm not doing it out of fear, I'm not doing it out of compulsion, just because it's the choice that I think is right.

"You hold the power to control your life, you just need to believe that yourself. Don't yield to anyone that tries to override what you want." Is that what I do? Do I yield to anyone else that has a different thought than me?

"You can put the blame on me, I'll tell Alex myself, we aren't going to tell them anything until they get back." If I want to make changes in my life, it's time that I start. I can't be led around and told what I should do and how I should do it, it took a near stranger to make me see that.

"Alright, we wait." I lean against the counter watching him sit at the breakfast bar, how is it that I can feel so at ease with this man I hardly know? It seemed so natural when I buried myself in his arms, it was so comforting to be held by him, I felt safe and I didn't want that feeling to end.

"So, what now?" So much has happened since this morning, it feels like a lifetime ago that Rachel had a fight with her suitcase and lost. They aren't due back until Sunday night, so what do I do for two full night and days. This is part of why I don't have control of my life because I can't do anything without the help of someone else. I'm dependent on so many people just to get through a day.

"Do you mind my asking, why did you turn down the job at the Lost Cities?" Ah, damn. I'd forgotten, I'm sure Ms. Cain didn't have anything nice to say about my meeting with her.

"Isn't it obvious? You saw my scars, I can't parade around a casino wearing next to nothing." I hear the bitterness in my voice, it's not his fault, and I shouldn't treat him as if it is.

"Is that the only reason? We could have arranged for a different uniform." I guess I hadn't considered that. It doesn't matter though, I couldn't ask for special treatment and even if I could, then I would be expected to explain why. More hassle than I want to deal with.

"That's it, I saw a cocktail waitress after my interview while I waited for Rachel, I knew I wasn't going to get the management position, but I decided that if you offered me any job I would take it, except that one, that uniform exposes too many of my secrets." I don't feel embarrassed that he's seen my scars, the first time Rachel saw them I was so humiliated and ashamed. I do blush at what I don't tell him, my thoughts of dating him, how improper it would be. Not that I will ever tell him that may have also been part of what affected my decision. After all that has happened tonight, how can I feel giddy right now? Because I think that is the perfect description of how I feel at this moment

His gaze drops from mine, "I have something that I should tell you, but I'm not sure how to say it." And just like that the giddiness is gone, my insecurities raise all their ugly heads.

"Then just say it." I hold my breath while I wait.

"I recognized you in the interview, later I went back through the old articles that I knew you from, then Alex called and asked if I would secure a safehouse, just in case." I let my breath out, I know there's more coming, but I don't know what to expect. "I had someone get me information on your husband, I would tell you that I wanted to know who I was dealing with but that's only partially true. I wanted to know more about you, I wanted to know what you had been through." Who can access that kind of information? How much more could someone get than what was in the papers. I felt like my whole life was in print back then. Until the story of his parent's murders published, Greg had kept the details of the scene from me. When the article ran, I was mortified knowing what had happened to them.

I know that I should be angry, but I'm not. Why aren't I? He invaded my privacy.

"Would you have told me this if tonight hadn't happened?" I guess part of the reason I'm not upset is the raw honesty.

He could have kept this to himself, I would have never known. Another part, I believed he already knew, at least what Alex knows, I just assumed that Ian would be told because he's part of the foundation, he helped with the security team. I guess I don't really understand the attorney-client privilege.

"This was part of the reason I asked to meet with you tonight, I wanted to tell you and I wanted to ask that we not tell Alex about the flower delivery until after his proposal. The man that gathered all the information for me is who clued me in that your husband was here or on his way." I don't know what to say, it didn't matter that he found out Greg was coming, more than anything, I want to know what he was able to find. "I'll understand if you want me to leave now, I'm sorry that I threw this at you now, after everything that's happened tonight." He rises from the stool, his eyes are apologetic and remorseful.

"Please don't leave, I don't want to be alone. Will you tell me what you found out, without expecting me to elaborate?

Can you tell me what you know without expecting explanations?" I can ask that much right? To know what he knows without telling him more. I don't want him to go, I want to continue to feel this sense of security. I know that it'll evaporate as soon as he steps out the door.

I sit on the opposite side of the sofa as Ian, my legs curled beneath me, facing him, hot cup of tea in my hands. I watch him struggle with how to start, I don't encourage him, I just wait. As he speaks my disbelief grows. The only parts of what he says that are familiar are the trips to the hospital.

From the beginning of my marriage to Greg, he had always controlled the finances. He made all the payments, I was just so busy with the bar that I never really thought anything of it. My card was never declined, the lights always stayed on, but according to Ian, my house was nearly foreclosed on, multiple times. My husband was in debt to the mob, gambling? It makes sense now why he shut down the investigation of the arson, it wasn't to protect me, he was covering his own ass. Ten years of my marriage, so much was happening that I didn't know. Greg's suspensions, he never missed a day of work, where did he go when he was on leave? What was he doing? I never knew, I lived with a stranger, our whole life was a lie, even before his parents died. Drug abuse? How did I not see that?

"Olivia?" My body is trembling all over, I can't describe what I feel, maybe this is shock? Chills run up my spine, hatred, and resentment course through me. I want to cry but no tears form. I start the anxiety technique again, but before I make it through the five things I can see, Ian slides closer to me on the couch, I want to feel the warmth of his arms. I want to feel safe, I lean into him and breath him in. I inhale his scent, not a hint of cologne, just fresh and clean. The trembling slowly subsides, his warmth drives off the chills. "I will never take your power from you, you will always have the freedom to make your own choices, so I'm asking Olivia, do you want to hear more or is it enough for now?"

I get to decide? Am I ready to hear more? How much more is there? It doesn't matter, whatever is left, I can't take more tonight, "It's enough, I can't." I don't feel like I need to explain my answer, I don't need to elaborate, and I don't. I just sit here wrapped in his arms, absorbing the secrets of my life that have just been revealed to me.

Chapter 14

Ian

I had barely begun, I could see by the look on her face she doesn't know a lot of what I'm telling her. Her olive skin grows pale, her forehead wrinkles in confusion, I lose track of the emotions that flash in her eyes, I keep my distance and keep talking, but when she starts to tremble, I can't hold myself back any longer. Once my arms are wrapped around her it feels right. There's still so much more that I haven't told her yet, but I meant what I said, I will respect her wishes. I'm glad she made the choice she did.

It's not long before her breathing deepens, I can't see her face, but I know that she's sleeping. Her mind needs the break, a little sleep will do her good. As she sleeps curled against me, I try to solve the mystery of the stranger in the apartment. Mack said that one window was unlocked but it wouldn't be possible for anyone to get in that way without being noticed. Mack and Ryan are both top notch in their field, I don't believe it would be possible for anyone to go through the front door with them watching. So, what does that leave? Fletcher took Olivia to an interview and to the Lost Cities, then over to the Hoover Dam, they spent several hours there. When they got back the flowers were beside the door, and so was Brett. My body stiffens, tension rolls through me. Olivia stirs, I stroke her hair until she stills, she needs the rest. Why was Brett at the door? He wasn't yet aware that Greg could be in town, he said the courier told him the flowers were from Rachel and he said he didn't read the card. Until late this afternoon, protocol has been to keep Olivia and Rachel safe, from a distance, we didn't want anyone aware that security was in place.

I look down at the top of Olivia's head, it's my fault that she suffered tonight. Brett had to have let that man into the apartment, I know it, I can feel it. I sent him here to protect her, not fully trusting him, I should have gone with my gut. The guys could have worked extra shifts, there were other options besides sending him. She paid the price of that decision.

I need to get a handle on this, but I need a plan. I don't have proof that Brett did this, but the circumstantial evidence is mounting. I text Mack, *When is Brett scheduled again?* I silence the ringer, I don't want to wake Olivia, I watch my phone for his response.

Monday morning. That gives me the weekend to come up with a course of action, for us to come up with a plan, Fletcher, Ryan, Mack, Nick, and Olivia, I intend to include her. Show her the power that she has at her fingertips, she gets to make the decisions that affect her life, this isn't about me, this isn't about the rest of the guys, it's about her, she should have a say. When I reveal my suspicions to all of them in the morning, I want her to be there, I want her to have a voice in the discussion, I want her to be a part of deciding how to proceed.

Say nothing to anyone about the events of this evening, until we talk in person, make sure Ryan gets the message as well. Plan for a meeting in the morning when Fletcher and Nick arrive. I put my phone back in my pocket without waiting for a response. I lean my head back against the couch, it's not the most comfortable position, but I won't risk waking her to move, I settle in for a long night.

Quiet murmurs and the smell of bacon frying rouse me. It takes a moment to orient myself, my back is sore, and my neck is on fire. I awaken in the same position I eventually fell asleep in. It was a long night of restless sleep. At the dining room table sits my security team, I catch a glimpse of Olivia in the kitchen. It seems I've slept in.

"Morning boss." Fletcher is the first to greet me, followed by the rest of them. Olivia rounds the corner with a shy smile and a hot cup of coffee. I see the creamer and sugar on the table and pull up a seat with them.

"I've got breakfast going, Mack sent me a text when you didn't answer. I invited them all to breakfast, it's nearly ready." I'd forgotten to turn my ringer back on. The only sign of last night's events is her swollen split lip. It's a reminder to me of my failure, I had one job and I failed within 12 hours. She's been busy this morning, the apartment set back to order and it appears like a full breakfast spread cooking on the stove.

"Morning, sorry I kept you waiting." I don't elaborate on why I requested to meet with them, I'll explain my suspicions when Olivia can be involved with the conversation. While the men talk sports, I watch her in the kitchen. I'm taken in with the way she moves, gracefully, as she turns retrieving plates off the counter, spinning back to the stove to fill each with potatoes, eggs, and bacon. Her hair loose, fluttering behind her while she moves back and forth. She shows no sign of worry or fear of the events of last night, shows no stress that it may happen again.

I join her to help serve, once both of us are seated at the table, I begin, "I don't want to keep Mack and Ryan late, it's been a long night and they need to get some sleep for another. Last night I had a thought, if it's impossible that anyone was able to enter the apartment, I suspect that someone was allowed access." As soon as I've spoken the words, I can almost see a lightbulb light up above Fletcher's head, Olivia waits for me to go on.

Fletcher takes over where I left off, "Brett was at the door with the flowers when we got back." He doesn't say anything more, but it's enough for the other three to understand where this is going.

"I don't understand, what's the significance of him standing at front of the door?" Olivia asks between bites.

"He shouldn't have been there, the door can be seen from the parking lot, there's only one entrance into the complex and only one set of stairs to your apartment. Our instructions were to stop anyone prior to them taking the stairs." Mack explains quietly, he understands the implication I'm making.

"I want all of you to think of a plan to expose him. We will play this quietly, this conversation doesn't leave this room. The story is we think the intruder gained entry through the bedroom window that was unlocked. If he did do this, I want to give him the opportunity to do it again." Olivia shifts in her seat, uncomfortable with the thought of something happening again. "If you have any ideas Olivia, I'd like you to share them, we aren't going to let anything happen to you again, I promise." I don't make promises I can't keep, I will keep her safe, one way or another. "Brett comes back on shift Monday morning, so I want to have a plan in place tomorrow afternoon."

"Boss, I've been thinking the same thing all night, once Mack filled me in, it was the only thing that made sense, but I didn't want to just start throwing out accusations. I've got an idea that can put this to rest on Monday." Ryan doesn't speak a lot, so when he does, people tend to listen. "Today or tomorrow, let's set up a few cameras inside, put one in each room, when Miss Olivia is gone, we can turn them on, then we know what's happening all the time." It sounds like a great solution until I see the horrified look on Olivia's face.

"No! I'm sorry but I don't like the idea of having cameras in my house that will be capable of watching my every move. Don't take this personally, but I am not going to feel like a prisoner of my home, and I refuse to give anyone the capability of watching me all the time." She speaks with vehemence, she drew the line in the sand and set her boundary.

"It's a good idea Ryan, but you heard her, lets come up with something a little less invasive to those that have to live here." She's lived for years in a relationship with an abuse of power, she would never trust that the cameras are off.

"I'm sorry Miss, it was just a thought, but I have a plan B. My sister, her and I own our gym, what if we hire her to come hang out, she's always asking if I can get her into the security team, if we can set something up that she will be gone during one of his shifts, Grace can be in here waiting." This may be more acceptable to Olivia, but I'm still not sure she will agree.

"Why would you subject your sister to the possibility of getting hurt or worse, if Brett did do this, and tries again, how do you think he will react to find someone in here that has caught him red-handed." It's not a no, she doesn't know anything about Ryan or his sister, Grace. Ryan isn't the only one that does cage fights, his sister holds the current women's title, undefeated in 48 fights. I wouldn't challenge her.

"She can handle herself, don't worry about that, she'd get a kick out of it." I don't interject my thoughts, I want Olivia to decide, if it was a bad idea I'd say so, but this could work, and I think Olivia would like Grace. I think Grace could help give Olivia some confidence and teach her a few things. I don't hate the notion, I think it would be the best option given the alternative. It will most likely be a fruitless endeavor anyway, I can't imagine he would risk it so soon after the attack.

"Why can't one of you do it? I think it's a good idea, but I don't think your sister is the best option, no offense, I just would hate for her to be hurt." She looks at me questioningly, as much as I want her to make the choice, I want her to gain her confidence and to feel like she has control of her life, I feel like I should help her with this. If something were to go wrong, she would live with the regret of a choice she'd made, regardless of what anyone would say to the contrary.

"Olivia? Do you want me to make the call on this one?" This way she still has a say, I'm not taking the decision from her, if she willingly gives it to me, she still retains her power.

"I don't know what the right choice is here, I don't want to put anyone at risk trying to help me, I can't make this call." Her eyes forlorn, the weight of last night showing through the mask she carefully created to hide behind.

"Get a hold of Grace, I want a sit down with her, if she's willing to do this and if she proves her merit, I will put her in the pool for any future details we have. Her and I need to talk to first." I like Grace, I've met her on several occasions, every one of those she's asked to join my team, not for regular duty, she specifically wants to be used for foundation detail only. She told me it would give her the opportunity to show an abuser what it's like to have the tables turned, I would pity any man that had to go toe to toe with her. "Set it up for tomorrow morning, I want time to come up with more details and a complete plan."

As the men file out, Ryan and Mack on their way home and Fletcher and Nick downstairs to start their shift, each of them thanks Olivia for her hospitality. She really is a great cook, breakfast was delicious.

Olivia doesn't speak, she goes to the kitchen and starts cleaning up. I see the rise and fall of her shoulders and I know that she is crying. I hesitate, do I go to her? Do I stay back? I don't know what she needs from me. I opt to help with the cleanup and follow her lead, I want to pull her into my arms again, I'd like to wipe the tears from her face, but I know that I can't push her, she's been through so much.

I lean against the counter beside her, her hands are bracing herself against the sink, she makes no sound, her head is bowed, face hidden behind a curtain of ebony waves. When she raises her head and meets my eyes, I can't stop myself from reaching for her. I move slowly, when I touch the skin of her arm, I gently pull her toward me. Just as last night, she sinks into the cradle of my arms and buries her face in my shoulder. I don't speak, nothing needs to be said, this is enough.

Chapter 15

Olivia

Why is it so easy for me to trust this man? How can I let down my defenses and want nothing more than to be wrapped in his arms? I don't even know him, but right now, beside him is the only place I feel safe, at ease. I don't know how he feels about me invading his space, but he's willing enough, I don't know what I must look like to him. It's been so long since I've felt this way, that I will take full advantage while I have the opportunity, being in his arms gives me a chance to relax, to push all my thoughts, my fears, and all my feelings away. The weight that I carry with these burdens is exhausting, it feels good to let it all go.

I was embarrassed when I woke, my head in his lap, he slept sitting up and I curled in a ball. If I hadn't been afraid of his rejection, I would have asked him to lay with me on the couch, to cocoon me in the safety of his embrace. Already I've expected too much, he has obliged, but soon, when

Alex is back and Ian no longer feels the responsibility for me, we will go back to being the strangers that we were. For now, I will take this, I will use this to have the reprieve that my mind needs. I am not disillusioned that this will continue, but I'm intrigued that I want it to. Only a short time ago I was planning my life in spinsterhood, knowing that I would never be able to trust another man, knowing that the fear that has plagued me for so long would continue. Yet Ian changed all that, I don't know why, but I do trust him. I'm not afraid of him nor do I feel fear when he is near, and the biggest surprise is how much I am attracted to him.

When I pull away, I don't speak. I look into his eyes, we still say nothing, his eyes search mine, but I don't know what he's looking for. Once released from my safety net, my mind goes into overdrive, what happens next? I can't ask him to stay, but I don't want him to leave. I don't want to be in the apartment, but I don't want to be pushed from my home by fear either. I won't let Greg do that again, even if I did, where would I go? There is nowhere else.

In silence we work together to clean the kitchen. We move together in sync with each other, our bodies speak but we are quiet, peaceful, we don't need words. This is a connection that I have never shared with another person.

Ian breaks the silence when we sit down at the breakfast bar. "What would you like to do today?" Is this an invitation or just a general question of what my plans are? Stop driving yourself crazy Olivia, ask him.

"I don't have any, I've been wondering that myself." Okay, I'm a coward, but it leaves it open to get an idea of what he might be thinking, doesn't it?

He thinks about what he is going to say before he speaks, "I wasn't really prepared for last night." I wait for him to continue. "I need a shower and some clean clothes, but I was hoping you might take a ride with me, there's something I'd like to show you." I wasn't really prepared for that.

What do I say, where does he want to take me? But the thought of going with him doesn't frighten me.

"I'd like that. If you want to go to your place, I'll get ready, when you're done you can pick me up?" I hate the thought of being here alone, but I need to face this fear. I don't want to be terrified of being in my house.

"I hope you don't take this the wrong way, but I'm not ready to leave you here alone. I know the guys are out there, but they were out there last night and look what happened." His sense of obligation protesting.

"Ian, you aren't to blame for what happened last night, I don't want you to think that I'm your responsibility. You can't change your whole life around to accommodate me, even if it's just for the weekend. I don't want to go through a night like last night again, the fact of the matter is that the chance is there, but it isn't your burden to bear." That lets him off the hook.

His eyes darken, a frown forms on his lips, he takes his time before responding, "I'm not ready to leave you alone because I feel drawn to you, being with you just feels right. I didn't say that because Alex asked me to look after you, I don't want to leave you alone anywhere because I want to be with you, wherever you are." His cheeks flush but only a little, if I hadn't been looking him in the eyes while he spoke, I might have missed it. Through the stubble of his chin I notice a slight cleft, it adds a little more ruggedness to his features. I'm at a loss as to what to say, he just described how I felt, like he read my mind. I feel a pull to him, truth be told, I want to be near him. "I'm sorry if that was too forward, but since I've already stepped in it, I don't know how to tell you or show you what I'm feeling without coming off as completely insensitive to your situation or what you've been through. I haven't felt an attraction to or a desire to be near a woman since my ex-wife and I divorced." I'm shocked by his admission, butterflies flutter in my stomach, did I hear him say that? "I wasn't sure I should say anything, I don't know how to navigate this situation. I've never been in this position before, and I really don't have a lot of experience with women in general, but I can't sit by and listen to you speak of yourself as if you're a burden. I'm here to be, your friend, your defender, an ear to listen, if you need to be held, I can do that too. I don't expect or want anything from you Olivia, I would just like to enjoy your company and I hope that you would enjoy mine as well." He holds my eyes for a just a moment longer before looking down at his hands. I try to articulate what is going on in my head.

"Thank you." I can't just leave it at that, he just bared his soul, he deserves more than that. I dig deep to find the courage to match his honesty. "Thank you for answering every question I've been afraid to ask. Thank you for being so truthful. Thank you for doing it gently and trying to be considerate of my past. I want to live a normal life, I don't want to be handled with kid gloves, I know that I will face hurdles in learning how to deal with people and I know that I will face setbacks, especially in times like last night, but I'm so glad you were here. When I first came to, I was scared, I was confused, but you set me at ease. I felt safe and I didn't think that I would feel that way with a man again, and yet I did with a stranger. I don't know why I trust you, but I do. I wasn't embarrassed that you had seen some of my darkest secrets and I've been puzzled by that as well. Hearing you say all of that to me, I realize that it doesn't matter why, I do, and I just want to enjoy feeling safe, and I want to enjoy time with you. Now that I know that you feel the same, and that you don't view me as your charge." So much is happening so quickly, some things I was mostly prepared for. If not prepared, at least aware that they could happen, but this? I wasn't expecting this. It doesn't matter, it is happening, and I want it to happen. I lean closer to him and lay my head on his shoulder, this proximity to him is soothing.

His shoulders relax like he had been bracing himself for what I would say. "I don't want you to ever be ashamed of what you call your darkest secrets. I know what they represent to you, but to me those scars represent your strength, your endurance, and your will. Those scars represent you as a warrior, you went into battle and you fought your way through hell to survive. The scars that mar your body could never diminish the beauty that is you. Both physically, because you are Bellissima, but also inside. Your beauty radiates from within you, nothing could ever overshadow that. Now that we've cleared that up, if you would like to get ready, I'll wait, then we can leave together. I meant what I said, I'm not ready to leave you alone. This isn't just for you Olivia, this is for me too." I don't know how to respond, I feel the heat rise in my cheeks, I accept the compliment without a reply. Hearing the Italian word roll off his tongue, somehow made what he said more meaningful, I wonder if he speaks the language or if he just picked up on a few words.

With the door securely locked, Ian and I descend the stairs. I can't find Fletcher or Nick, but I know they are watching, I know they can see us. I wonder what they will do now? Will they follow us? How does security work if I'm leaving with Ian? As if reading my thoughts, Ian answers the questions I don't verbalize, "Fletcher will follow us, Nick will stay behind and keep an eye on things." I nod my head in response, surprised that again he knew what I was thinking.

I'm able to pick out his car without him telling me, it's so far out of place in my parking lot, nobody but him would ever bring a car like this here. It's beyond the price range of most people. I stand in awe, it's the most beautiful car I've ever laid eyes on. The color seemed to change from silver to white, the light color enhanced with black accents. I've never seen anything so nice, let alone ridden in it.

"Olivia, meet Bella, she's a bit pretentious, but she's fun to drive." I realize he is talking about the car. I blush because I had looked for a person. "She's a Bentley

Continental Supersports." The pride in his voice, having this car is an accomplishment that he values.

"You named your car?" Who the hell names a car? And why use a female pronoun?

"Of course, be careful, you'll hurt her feelings." I laugh at the thought, and the half smile that plays on his lips, his lightheartedness is welcome. The tension I felt this morning is gone, it's what a normal morning with a friend should look like.

Ian opens the door, takes a deep bow, "Mia signora" and waits for me to step in. More of the Italian, I sink into the soft, gray leather of the bucket seat, the smell of the leather permeating the interior.

As we leave the complex, I see a black SUV pull out behind us, my heart sinks, this is my reality. As free and easy as I felt just a moment ago, the SUV is a reminder that I'm not free nor is my life easy. I need to stop getting caught up in these moments, but I don't know how to stop, it just happens. It's Ian, somehow, he makes me forget my situation.

For a time, we sit in a comfortable silence, I don't know what to say, I don't want to talk about last night, or the plan to see if Brett is the culprit, what else is there? I'm afraid to ask him questions because they may lead back to me. He doesn't seem to mind, he turns the music up just enough to enjoy but still low enough that if we speak it wouldn't drown out our conversation. Another surprise, the tuner is set to a country station, Miranda Lambert singing about something bad about to happen, fun and upbeat, the weight of all that's happened easing off the further we get from my apartment.

The car doesn't roll down the freeway, more accurately it sails. The ride is smooth, like we're floating above the road rather than on it. I take in the place that has been my home for the last year, it's sharp contrast to what had been my home my whole life. It was an adjustment not seeing trees, the ocean, the lack of humidity. Nevada, the driest state in all the country.

"Where are we going?" I break the silence as we get closer to the Lost Cities, he said he needed to go home first.

"I renovated the top floor of the hotel to an apartment after my divorce, it made sense, and it was easier than trying to find a new house." I forget that he was married before, I guess she got the house, I would say lucky her but is it lucky? To live in a place that you once shared with someone you loved alone, or even someone you hated. You either have all the memories you wish you could bring to life, or all the nightmares that you never get to escape from. Maybe he's the lucky one, to be able to start over from scratch.

"How many floors are in the hotel?" I follow my question with another question before he answers, "Wouldn't it have been easier to find an apartment?" Seems like a lot of work and loss of revenue to occupy a space with that kind of view, I'm sure a lot of people would pay a lot of money to be able to look out over all of Vegas.

"The Lost Cities has 56 floors, and maybe, but renting is a waste of money. If you're able to buy you should, if I lived off property, I wouldn't be able to work at night when I can't sleep." Isn't that the point of having a home to go to, to get away from the pressures and stresses of work?

"If you're going to your office to work at night, it probably isn't good for your health, sounds like you need a vacation." I bet his doctor would agree with me.

"You're probably right, I haven't had a vacation in years. I'll take that under advisement." There it is again, that half smile that makes him look younger than he is, joined with a soft chuckle.

In the parking garage, he presses a button on a remote, a garage door that separates a section of the first floor opens, only a few cars are present in here, an electric blue Ford truck, a silver Mercedes, and a couple of SUV's, the door slides down behind us, on one wall is an elevator. He backs the Bentley into the spot closest to the elevator, when I pull the handle of the door nothing happens, Ian is already at the passenger side, the door open, his hand outstretched. Child locks or is he really this chivalrous? "Thank you." I say softly.

Inside the elevator, it looks like any other, rather than push a button, Ian slides a card through a reader, I assume it ensures that only he can reach the 56th floor, I note that the panel only reaches to 55. The slight jar when the elevator starts rolls my stomach, I'm not sure if it would be better if I hadn't eaten breakfast. The ride to the top is quick and aside from the initial lurch, smooth. I'm speechless when the doors slide open, the view is breathtaking, every window giving a panoramic picture of Vegas, I bet at night it's even better. The inside of the condo doesn't look lived in, it looks like a model set up for showings. Clean, stark, it looks almost sterile, few personal touches. Dark gray carpets, light gray and white walls and doors, a fireplace in the middle with a few pictures on the mantle, that is all the décor there is, no paintings on the walls, nothing to make this a home, it looks like a place to exist not really to live.

Chapter 16

Ian

Though it was comfortable to sit back and listen to the music on the way over, I struggled to find something to say. I wanted to ask her questions, to learn more about her, but no matter the question, each would lead to her past and the hell that she went through. I don't want today to be tainted with the life that she escaped from, I want today to be an easy, carefree, and fun day. After the events of last night, she deserves that, I can wait for her to lead our conversation.

She hesitates in the elevator, I assume she is taking in the view, aside from walls separating rooms, there is nothing that obstructs the view of Las Vegas, all outer walls are glass. When I left Vee, I didn't have a plan, I moved into the hotel on the temporary basis until I could decide a course of action. I looked at a few houses, toured a few condos but nothing felt right, you buy a house to build a family. I was in the middle of leaving that dream behind. As time went on, I liked the convenience of being able to go to the office anytime, as little sleep as I was getting back then, it was a good way to escape. It was Alex's idea to convert, the more that I thought on it, the more I liked the idea. Being able to look out and see the city made me feel a part of it from a distance, and the brightness helped to guide me out of my misery, The view made me appreciate all that I had, even if I no longer had the person I wanted to share it all with.

I reach for her hand, "Let me show you around." She takes my hand and allows me to lead her into my home. The main living space is open, a large kitchen, a space for dining, and living room all open to one another, an electric fireplace in the center wall of the living room, separating it from the bedrooms and the library.

"This view!" Her eyes are wide in reverence, the excitement in her voice. I swell with pride and happiness that she seems to like it.

"It's something else, isn't it?" The best view in the city, to be able to look out not only on the city but the vast desert that surrounds it, an oasis in the desolation of Nevada. "Make yourself at home." The words sound foreign to me, few have been to my home, inviting someone to make themselves at home is a new concept in this place.

"How long have you lived here?" Her eyes no longer taking in the scenery of the windows, she is focused on the mantel.

"Nearly three years." I realize the deeper meaning in her question, to see this place through her eyes, nothing adorning the walls, no personal touches aside from the pictures above the fireplace. "I left everything behind when Vee and I split, I guess I just haven't gotten around to making it homier." Truth be told, I had never really thought about it, this place was meant to serve a purpose, a place to lay my head at night and a place to retreat from the outside world.

"I didn't mean to sound critical, you have a beautiful home." Honesty resonates in her words but still, I feel slightly embarrassed, in three years I should have made this my home, not just a dwelling.

"Thank you, I'm going to go get ready, can I get you anything?" I think I have some tea, maybe coffee, not much else. But one of the perks of living here, it isn't necessary, if need be, I could call room service. It's not something I take advantage of often but for this occasion, I would make an exception.

"I'm fine, thank you." It won't take me long to get ready, just a quick shower, a change of clothes and we can be on our way, I can show her who I am, and in the process learn more about her without prying into her past.

Before the water gets hot my phone rings, I consider ignoring the call but when I see it's a call from Carl, one of the casino managers, I answer.

"Ian, Ms. Michaels is in the lobby creating quite a stir, she is demanding to see you. I wouldn't have called but the only other option is to have security take her out." As much as I'd like to send security, I know it will only make things worse.

"Put her on the phone." Today is not the day that I want to deal with her, now that all ties have been severed, both business and personal, I shouldn't have to.

"Ian?" She purrs my name as she always has when she wants something from me. "I really need to talk to you, and it needs to be in person, can I come up?" Not once have I allowed her to come here, I never wanted her to have the impression that she was welcome here.

"No Vee, what do you want?" I'd rather her just say what's on her mind and be done with it.

"It needs to be face to face Ian, if I can't come up there, you'll need to come down here." That won't be happening today, or ever if I can avoid it.

"I'm not on the property Vee, so you can say what you have to say or don't." I don't owe her honesty and I know that she won't give up until I cave.

"Then I'll wait, when will you be back." I'm not interested in having a discussion with her at all but if I must, it will be on my terms.

"Call Stephanie on Monday and schedule an appointment and stop causing trouble or security will remove you, good-bye Vivian." I disconnect the call before she can respond, afraid that she may continue her rampage, I send a text to Carl, telling him to call me if he encounters anymore problems with her.

I expect to find Olivia at the windows after my shower, instead she is at the mantel, looking at the few pictures I have. My mother and I at my college graduation, my mother with Alex when he graduated law school, a few photos of the three of us on vacation in southern California when Alex and I were in junior high, and one of Alex and Patricia taken at a barbeque a few months before she died.

"Your mother is very beautiful." She touches the frame of my mother and me. There is a sadness in her voice.

"Thank you. Would you tell me about your mother?" I don't know if it's right for me to ask, I don't want to bring her sadness or melancholy today, but I want her to know that I am interested in her life and that she can talk to me. I don't want her to feel like she has to avoid subjects.

Her eyes look across the room to the window, a sad smile plays on her lips, just when I think she isn't going to say anything she begins. "She was an old soul, nothing ever came to her easy in life, but she worked hard and did all she could to give me the best life she could. She was my best friend, my biggest supporter, and never failed to be there for me." She pauses but I feel like she has more to say. "My father had an affair when I was in eighth grade, looking back now, it wasn't an accident that my mother caught him. He didn't have the balls to leave her, but he knew she wouldn't hesitate to leave him for being unfaithful, he was right, and she did. Their divorce was quick, and he married his mistress Sandra, the next day. After that, it was just her and I, I tried to maintain a relationship with my dad, but his wife gave him a lot of grief over it, it didn't take long for me to understand that I wasn't a part of his new life." There is sadness in her tone, but I don't sense anger or bitterness.

"Were you ever able to reconcile with him?" I can't say if I were in her situation I would want to. I don't know who my father is. I have the resources, I could track him down if I wanted to, but I have no desire to know a man that ran out on my mother.

"No, I never really wanted to, my mother was enough, she put all of her energy into helping me through the hard parts. Once I got past the initial hurt of the rejection, I realized that she was all I needed, I didn't want him. I couldn't trust that even if we did rebuild our relationship, he wouldn't walk out again." Her words struck me deeply, it's just how I feel about my mother and father, the only difference, I didn't have to watch him walk away. "My mom worked her 9-5 as an accountant and got a part-time job bartending on Friday and Saturday nights. She refused to work at all on Sundays, those were our days, we would go to the museum, take in shows, or just walk through a park. Sundays were the days that we reconnected each week."

"She sounds a lot like my mom, I really wish I could have met her." Her mother's sacrifices are similar to those of my mother. I can see her mother's will shining through Olivia, her spirit is a driving force.

"You have no idea how much I wish she were still alive, how much regret I have for the way that I treated her. We started fighting a lot, she knew something was going on with me. I hid things well, but I started having too many accidents. She suspected what was happening and tried to talk to me several times, I would get defensive and pretty soon we were fighting. I wish that I could tell her how sorry that I am, and I wish that I could go back, she would have gotten me through all of this, or she would have killed Greg." She giggles for just a moment, then continues. "Sometimes I think that things would be much different if I had let her help me. That she would still be here, it should have been me that day." I can't listen to her blame herself for an accident.

"Do you think your mother would feel that way, do you think she would rather it be you that had your life taken too soon?" I hear the anger in my voice, but I do nothing to rein it in, this isn't a thought process she should have.

"You misunderstand, I should have taken the deposit to the bank that day, it was supposed to be her day off. I know that if given the choice my mom would have died a thousand deaths to save me from one, my regret is that I failed her. If I hadn't called in that day, things may have been different all together." I wasn't expecting that, the what if will always nag at her mind.

"I'm sorry, I can't imagine the weight that you carry, but it isn't your fault. My mother taught me that everything happens for a reason, that there is purpose behind all things in life. It doesn't take your pain and it won't ease your suffering, but I hope that you know that, even if you don't understand why." I can't let her feel like her mother's accident is her fault, I wish that I could offer her more.

"That's what got me through for a long time, my mother always said the same thing. I don't carry the guilt all the time, I know better, she taught me better than that, but sometimes I just can't help but wonder." We stand in silence for a moment, the weight of the words pressing on us. "Enough of the serious, sad talk, you said you had something you wanted to show me. This view is impressive, but it's not what I expected." Her resilience surprises me again, I know that her heart aches, and that she has a lot that is worrying her right now, but she lets it all go, moving forward as if it's a normal day. That takes a strength that most people don't possess or understand.

"I wasn't thinking about the view when I asked you to join me, I'm ready if you are." I will do my best to keep the mood light, to show her a good time. Whatever I need to do to keep seeing the smile that she has right now.

In the elevator we shoot meaningless questions to each other, what's your favorite color, music, sunrise or sunset, we fire them at rapid pace. By the time we reach the garage we are both laughing, before either of us could finish our one word answers the other was asking another question.

As the doors open, we are breathless but still asking questions, every answer that she gives is burned in my memory. While they seem like simple questions, every answer is insight of who she is. Unfortunately, the light and easy mood is broken when I see Vee leaned against my car.

"So much for honesty in our relationship Ian." Vivian spits the words at me.

"You mean so much for me being honest Vee, you haven't been honest with me in years. If you will excuse us, we have plans. As I said earlier, call Stephanie and make an appointment." I don't know how she got in here and right now I don't really care, that's a problem that can be solved later. Right now, it's more important to get Olivia away from Vee.

"You aren't going to introduce me to your girlfriend?" Her words are like venom. Olivia stands quietly, confusion etched on her face. "I knew after I left your office you were seeing someone else, it's the only explanation to your response. I don't know who you are, but you better start looking elsewhere. Ian and I have history, you won't be anything but a memory soon." Vee looks Olivia up and down, with what can only be described as disgust.

"Vivian, you need to leave, my relationship status, or lack thereof, is none of your business. Olivia is a friend and I won't tolerate your lack of respect toward her." I keep myself between Olivia and Vee and open the door, irritation boiling through me. Just as Olivia starts to step into the car, Vivian stops her.

"Honey, I'm warning you, you better steer clear. I won't allow you to come between me and what's mine." Before I can say anything, Olivia steps around me.

"Are you threatening me? I can only assume that you're the ex-wife. Now that I've met you, I can understand why you're the ex, but let me tell you something, you don't get to tell me what I can and can't do, instead of making threats, make your move." Olivia's eyes have narrowed, grown darker, her whole body tensed, this isn't a reaction I would expect from her.

I touch Olivia on the shoulder, whisper in her ear, "Let's go, we have places to be, let's not let her ruin it for us." She steps back, with a final glare at Vivian she slides into my car.

"Vivian, this is the last encounter that I hope to have with you." It takes all my restraint to not lash out at her.

"This isn't the end Ian, I meant what I said, and you know that I'm the only woman for you." It will do no good to argue with her, I don't intend to allow this conversation to go any further.

Chapter 17

Olivia

"I'm going to go out on a limb and guess that is your ex-wife? She's uh... pleasant." As hard as I try to keep a straight face, I can't, maybe it isn't the time, but the laughter erupts from me. Maybe it's the stress of the situation, or maybe I have to laugh as an outlet, this is the first confrontation that I've had with a stranger since I lost Trinity. Even back then there weren't a lot of instances, our crowd was pretty laid back, they were just in to unwind a little after a long day. They stuck within their crowds or to themselves.

Ian chuckles for a moment but he doesn't share in the hilarity I find of the situation, "I apologize, Vee was out of line." The moment is no longer funny, his somber reaction changes the atmosphere.

"I'm sorry, I shouldn't have said that." Concerned that I have upset him, I realize that this could be painful for him. I'm not sure of the circumstances of his divorce, regardless, I shouldn't make light of what just happened or how he may feel about it all.

"You have nothing to apologize for, I didn't expect her to be in the garage. Maybe I should have, when I refused to talk to her earlier, I should have expected she would find a way. If nothing else, she is determined." He isn't upset with me, I don't even think that he's angry, I think he's embarrassed. "Are you ready? I'd like to pick up where we left off in the elevator, not let the dark mark of my ex-wife put a damper on things." I'd like to know more about her, their divorce and her assumption that we're dating and because I'm nosy, their conversation in his office, I'm feeling better that I'm not the only one that has a crazy ex, she's a different kind of crazy, but crazy, nonetheless.

As we pull out of the garage, Ian starts in again. The questions come in quick succession, what's my favorite flower? Iris. Favorite place? I stumble on this one, after a brief pause, he moves on to the next one. Favorite movie? PS I love you. Favorite TV show? Guilty pleasure, court TV. That answer stops him, he looks at me questioningly, "I know, it's dumb and it's all scripted but there is some truth in there somewhere, the absurdity of some of the things that people take to court, it's kind of entertaining, but I think what appeals to me the most, it's mindless. I don't have to think about it, I don't have to pay close attention to know what's going on. My mind wanders so much that I miss a lot of plot lines and then things don't make sense. The plot in court TV is reiterated so much that I don't miss it." He nods, my explanation satisfying his curiosity. Favorite activity? Writing.

"What do you write?" I'm just as surprised by my answer as he is. If I had time to think of a response, I'm not sure I would have been able to answer. I do enjoy writing, but I never thought of it as my favorite thing to do.

"I journal and write some poetry, sometimes the thoughts in my head get so jumbled that I can't make sense of any of it. If I sit down and write it all, I can organize my thoughts in journaling, and my feelings in my poetry." I haven't even told Rachel about my writing. Did I answer because he caught me off guard or because he just sets me so at ease? I'm on the fence of how I feel about him knowing, my writing is my secret. I stopped keeping journals when I was with Greg, about the third time he found it and read it, but it was easy to start again once I felt secure that they would remain private. Poetry was harder, Greg ridiculed all the things I wrote. I struggled with whether or not what I was writing was even poetry, but I decided it didn't matter, it wasn't for anyone else except me. If it helped me to understand what I was feeling, that was what was important.

"It matters not how straight the gate, how charged with punishments the scroll, I am the master of my fate, I am the captain of my soul." He recites the last lines of Invictus, that poem had become my mantra over the last several years, it was my glimmer of hope that I would escape, that I would not always live in fear.

"You know William Ernest Henley?" I shouldn't be surprised, Ian is well educated, I'm stunned that out of all the poetry in the world, this one in specific is what he recites, because this one is my favorite of them all.

"I do, my mother found a plaque with that poem on it and gave it to Patricia as a gift, she hung it in Alex's room so his dad wouldn't see it. When the fights would begin, Alex and I would read it aloud but quietly." Yet another parallel.

The depth of his revelation leaves me silent and reflective, internally trying to make sense of the parallels in our stories, though from two different perspectives. "We're almost there." Ian interrupts my thoughts. We've pulled away from town, more on the outskirts. Before me I see the cranes in the air, he's brought me out to see the Whiskey Wrangler. I've seen the progress in the papers, but the pictures don't do it justice, when it's complete it will be spectacular!

"Welcome to the Whiskey Wrangler, or what it will soon be." I hear the pride in his accomplishment, and see the satisfaction shining in his eyes.

"How did you come up with the name?" Every article I've read, the name has stuck out to me, I've been curious since I first saw it.

The boyish smile that has come to be my favorite of his expressions so far, flashes. "My mother was a card dealer, every year for as long as I can remember, the cowboys, their crew, their families, would come to Vegas for the National Finals Rodeo. They all spent some time in the casinos, usually before or after the event, my mom started calling them Whiskey Wranglers because of how much they would drink. As the event neared, my mom would talk about how the whole town had to prepare for them Whiskey Wranglers." A tribute to his mom, his explanation makes it perfect, and gives me understanding of the importance of this project.

"It's beautiful." I see beyond the girders and trusses, what is standing gives my imagination enough to see what it all will be when it's complete. More than before, I also understand that my skills aren't enough to manage the enterprise this will be.

"Would you like to see more?" I hesitate, not because I don't want to see, but because I don't want to be in the way of the work that's being done. Men and women moving with purpose to accomplish the task set in front of them, deadlines to be met, I don't want to impede the progress being made. "It's ok, I talked to the Superintendent, besides, I have special privileges." The half grin playing on his lips, his outstretched hand patiently waiting for me. Just as I start to reach for him, my phone rings. Rachels face lights up my screen, I give Ian an apologetic look but see that he has also pulled out his phone. His smile widens, I assume it's Alex on the other end of his call.

"Rachel! How is…" Before I can finish my sentence, Rachel interrupts with an excited squeal, followed by, "I'm getting married!! Will you be my maid of honor? Please?!?" I laugh at her exuberance, I can feel her happiness radiating through the phone. In this moment, all is right in the world. I feel genuine joy for my friend and gratitude that it's me that she's chosen to share her most special day with. "Oh Rachel, no one deserves this more than you, of course I will."

It's all I get to say, the next ten minutes I'm regaled with the details of Alex's proposal, the plans he set in motion last night, a candlelight dinner on a boat on Lake Tahoe, gazing at stars not obscured by the lights of the city, a moonlight stroll along the beach when they got back to shore. Her fear that something was distressing Alex because of his quiet demeanor. This morning a hike with a waterfall along the path, leading to the peak dotted with snow that looks down on the vivid blue Lake Tahoe. While she was preoccupied with the view, Alex set in motion what I can only imagine he's been planning for some time. The photographer prepared for the moment, other hikers patiently waited for what the photographer had quietly let them in on as they all ascended the trail. "I turned from the lake to thank Alex for such a special gift and he was down on one knee, I will never forget what he said... Rachel, I never believed I would find someone like you, today, here with you my world is brighter. The light that you bring to my life makes the sun pale in comparison. I don't ever want to find a day that you aren't by side. I want to create memories with you, I want my present to be filled with you, and I want to build my future with you, because now that I know a life with you, a life without you would be a life without light. Will you marry me?" Tears pool in my eyes at the beauty of his words to her.

"I think that is the most romantic thing that I've ever heard Rachel." I watch Ian a little off in the distance, his smile is wide, and I pick up on sounds of his laughter. My thoughts are curious if he is as romantic as Alex. I cut the thought short and bring myself back to what Rachel is saying, I don't think I missed much, at least I hope that I haven't. I wasn't required to say anything, Rachel kept the conversation going all on her own, I just reveled in her happiness. As she finished telling me all about the proposal, some of it twice, her excitement abated, "How's things at home?" So much had happened in such a short time, none of it I want to share with her. I want her to bask in the happiness she has right now, I can't even tell her about the interesting events of being with Ian, as that would only pique her curiosity as to how our time together came about.

"You know, same shit, different day Rach, not much changes with me." I try to make my tone light, I don't want her to suspect that anything is amiss, I hate lying to her, but I would rather mislead her than let her worry about me and the things that have happened while she's been gone.

Fortunately, she is so immersed in the moment that she doesn't question me any further. "Oh! And the ring Ollie, I can't forget to tell you about the ring, it's perfect. The band is silver, I think, but there are little diamonds on each side of the band that leads up to this beautiful solitaire, it looks enormous on my finger but it's so beautiful. I can't stop looking at it, I can't wait to show you!" I would imagine her ring is either white gold or platinum. I can't see Alex giving her anything less, but her description tells anyone all they need to know about her. She doesn't care what the ring is made of, she would probably choke if she knew what the ring cost. Knowing Alex, that ring probably cost more than Rachel's car, it never even crosses her mind and that says a lot about her and what she values most. "Ollie, I gotta go, I guess we have reservations somewhere, I love you! I can't wait to see you!

She didn't wait for me to respond, I turn around to face the Whiskey Wrangler again, Ian is only steps away. "Did she ask you to be her maid of honor? Alex said he thought she was more excited that you would be her maid of honor than she was about being the bride?" I smile, not at the words but at the humor in his voice. "She did, but I think Alex is being sensitive, I definitely get the vibe that he just made all her dreams come true." He did, and without even trying, all she's ever wanted is just to be loved unconditionally. To be respected and treated well, even without the proposal he accomplished all of that and more.

Chapter 18

Ian

I knew Rachel would accept Alex's proposal, it was good to hear the relief in his voice when he told me though. While talking to him I watched as Olivia spoke with Rachel, I saw a true smile emerge from her while she listened to her friend, it was a genuine smile, one that lit up her whole face and made her eyes sparkle. I'm making it my mission to see that same smile all day.

"Are you ready to see? I'd like to see what's new since I last walked through myself." I know there isn't anything new for me to see since yesterday, but I want her to feel comfortable and I want to show her all that I envision this place to be. I want to see what this will be through her eyes, and I hope that she will be able to see it through mine as well.

Entering the construction office, I greet the Super, I pull my hard hat off the hook and retrieve a new one for Olivia. I may be able to walk through the site of my own accord, but safety precautions can't be ignored while I do. As we leave the office, my phone vibrates in my pocket once again. Unknown Caller flashes on my screen.

"This is Ian." There are too many things going on right now for me to ignore a call. Alex being unavailable for Battling Back being my main concern, but there is also Vivian to consider. Whatever mischief she may be causing, not to mention Olivia's uninvited guest last night. While under other circumstances I would have sent the call to voicemail, right now that isn't a luxury I have.

"Mr. Alessandro, you and I have some business to conduct, we need to talk alone, so step away from the woman." I don't recognize the voice on the line, and I'm puzzled by his knowledge that I am with Olivia. Tension rolls through me, Olivia looks around, sensing my apprehension.

"I'm afraid that you have me at a disadvantage, with whom am I speaking?" With my best impression of sign language, I ask Olivia for her phone, I want Fletcher to be on the alert, without making it known to the mystery man on the phone.

"It doesn't matter who I am, what matters is what I'm about to say. Get back in your car, take the woman back to her place, and leave, take your security with you. If you do all of that, we will never speak again. If you don't, then you're about to have a problem on your hands." I suspected as much. I scan the area, further down the road are some warehouse buildings but there is nothing close by. I send a quick message to Fletcher.

"Mr. Daniels, I presume?" The color drains from Olivia's face hearing his name. I try to reassure her with a look. The terror overcomes her, she becomes hyperalert, looking all around, scrutinizing every face that she sees.

"Nope, sorry, I don't know that name, just do what I said, and everything will be everything." He may not be Greg Daniels, even so, he does know who Greg is.

"I'm afraid I find your terms unacceptable sir. I don't conduct negotiations with strangers, nor do I conduct them over the phone, so might I suggest a meeting? You can present your terms, I can decline them, and then we can really get to the bottom of the situation." The eyes that were so happy only moments ago are consumed with panic and confusion, hearing only one side of the conversation. I pull Olivia into me, wanting only to chase the demons that have resurfaced.

"This was the only chance you were getting, good-bye." The line goes dead, I guide Olivia back into the office, the Super looks up from the plans he is studying, "Problem sir?" I shake my head at him, "No we're fine, we'll do a walk through on another day, something has come up. Can you give us a moment please?" He nods, placing his hard hat on his head and leaves through the same door we entered.

"What did he say?" Her voice trembles.

"Before I get into that, I need you to understand that his request is denied, and I don't want an argument from you. Can you accept that?" She looks at me silently, slowly shaking her head. "Olivia, I will tell you what was said, but I need a compromise from you, you have to let me handle this. Can you do that?" I hate giving her an ultimatum, but I know what she will say otherwise. She doesn't respond, she only looks at me waiting for me to continue. I know it's the best that she can offer right now, I tell her all that was said in the short communication.

She takes a moment to take it all in, she breaths deeply, gaining more control of herself with each one. "So, he's watching us right now? He knows where we are?" It's the only assumption that there is, I nod. "You need to take me home before this gets out of hand. I want you to do exactly what he asked."

"You can't ask that of me, I told you, you have to let me handle this." I know she isn't listening, she's made up her mind and now it's up to me to change it.

"No, Ian, I don't, I..." I cut her off before she can say anymore.

"Yes, Olivia, you do. I don't want to tell you what to do, so don't make me. What do you think will happen if I leave you there alone, unprotected? Are you considering that? After last night, I can put together a scenario and it's not one that I care to see come to fruition." I hate using her fear against her, but she's leaving me no other choice.

"You don't understand, I don't know if that was Greg or someone working on his behalf, regardless, he doesn't make empty threats, it may already be too late." He may be able to threaten and intimidate her, but there is nothing he can do to me. His threats are empty, and intimidation has never been a way of motivating me.

"No, you don't understand Olivia, I won't give in to demands that will result in you being hurt or worse. There is nothing that he can do to me." Her resolve is wavering, so I keep pushing. "Tell me, what would happen if I left you alone at your place?" I want her to say it, because I need her to feel the full magnitude of what she is asking. "Tell me, what would happen?"

"I don't know, it doesn't matter. I can't let him wreak havoc on you, I can't let him come after you." My goading seems to be having an opposite effect.

"What kind of man would that make me? Do you think that I could live with the repercussions of that?" I know that I'm needling her, I know that I'm driving her fear further, I'm trying to keep my promise to her, that she always has the final decision, that vow may   come back to bite me in the ass. "Here's what I think, let's continue our day, let's go on like this never transpired. I will get someone on this, if Greg is here, we will find him.

"And then what, Ian? What happens when he's found here in Vegas? There is no stopping him, there is no reasoning with him. You conducted the investigation, you learned a lot more than what I knew, knowing now that he also has ties to the mob only solidifies what I've always known.

Not only does he have his office to protect him, but he apparently also has friends at the top of the Russian mob. I can't fight against that, and no matter your wealth, your power, or influence, neither can you." I let her get it all out, her anger rising then morphing into hopelessness.

"For the time being, keeping you safe is the priority. Learning his location is secondary, we will talk to Alex tomorrow. We can put our heads together and decide a course of action then." It's a large desert, that may be the only option that we need.

Another unknown caller flashes on my vibrating phone. "This is Ian." The voice on the other end is different than the last. "Ian, I'm a friend of your mother's." My heart speeds up its beat, dreading what this stranger may say next. "I owe it to her to give you a warning, the woman you're with is going to bring down a rain of hellfire on your life. It will burn you and those around you if you don't step away from her." Before I can respond the line goes dead. What the fuck is going on? Was that Greg? I don't know his voice, but who else could it be? He's been doing research on me, I need to check in with mama, make sure she's okay. Olivia waits quietly while I try to make sense of it all. I know she wants to know if it was the same person, or if the call even involves her.

"Another warning, different voice, let's get out of here." Do we go back to her place? I'm ready for that, if nothing else to just end this shit and be done with it, but I can't take her back there.

"Let's go, but I want to go home. I think the day has already been ruined, I can't forget this, there is no salvaging." Her agreement surprises me, but I still need to convince her that her apartment is not the place to go. So much for keeping that genuine smile on her face all day.

"Why don't we go back to my place?" I can have the security team meet me there, them in conjunction with casino security will set my mind at ease until I can think of a solution.

"Sorry Ian, I gave in, I'm letting you keep your security, I'm not even going to oppose your presence, but I will not be driven out of my home." Her resolve strengthening with each word, determination etched in her eyes. I'm getting the distinct impression that there's something she's not telling me.

As we walk to the car, I ask her, "Are you going to ask about the last phone call?" Her disinterest is what's tips me off, what's raised my suspicions that she is keeping something from me.

"Another warning, that's what you said? What more is there to tell?" Her demeanor is cold, I feel the distance growing between us, not physically but she's withdrawing from me. Her answers are curt, to the point, there is no warmth between us.

After opening the door for her, I stop at the Escalade and give Fletcher the reader's digest version. He is also opposed to taking her back to her apartment, but unless we are ready to force our will upon her, it's the only option there is. Fletcher will get in contact with some of the other guys, he'll bring in a few, the extra security will give us time to put a plan into action. She's compromised on not sending me or the team away, if I renege it will make me untrustworthy. This is why Alex is in charge, I've backed myself into a corner, in doing so I either have to put her in harm's way or lose the fragile trust that she's given to me. I don't have another choice but to take her back to her place, perhaps during the drive I can work out an acceptable alternative to this dilemma.

As I get in the car, she doesn't even look at me, her senses on high alert, eyes searching for what may be lurking. Wanting to give Olivia time to sort through all that's transpired, I make a call to Markus, keeping the call through my phone rather than the car, I know that she will hear my side, if she's interested, she will ask. "Markus, I need a twenty on that subject, do you have anything yet?" He hasn't been able to pinpoint him. "Utilize whatever resources that you need, I want to know where he is now!" The obscene amount of money that I pay him for these special projects, I expect to see better results in a timelier manner.

Chapter 19

Olivia

"It isn't his fault, you shouldn't take it out on him." Ian remains silent, not responding to my admonishment. The nagging voice in my head is trying to convince me that Ian's anger is at me. My common sense is warring with that voice, saying it's the situation. Though, possibly, there is some for me as well, I have used his good intentions against him. While he may believe that what he's doing is right and that Greg can't do anything to him, he doesn't know who he is dealing with. He can read reports until he goes cross-eyed, but he won't ever understand what Greg can do. He isn't one that can be understood unless you've dealt with him personally.

I appreciate what Ian's trying to do and I understood the point that he was trying to make in asking what kind of man it would make him, what he isn't understanding is what kind of person will it make me to allow whatever evil Greg has in store for him? When he failed to see my side, I shut down, I shut him out, I compromised. It seems like my whole life has been about bending to the will of someone else, so here and now I took my power, I'm using it to make concessions so that I can have control of the result. Whether Ian knows it or not, he will need protecting as much as I do. I have the inside information, I know the enemy before me, it's my job to use my knowledge to shield Ian from Greg.

I pay close attention to the direction we are heading, unsure if Ian will try to take me somewhere other than my apartment, so far, we are going in the right direction. The silence between us is deafening, the tension thick and unnerving, but still I feel safe. I feel the same comfort in his presence as last night and I will soak in as much of that as I can. I hope that it will stay with me when I have to send him away. Greg isn't just going to give up, he isn't going to walk away, for me to end this, whatever that end may be, Ian has to go, security has to go, those were the demands. Greg won't stop until those demands are met. I must decide my course of action, whatever it is, Ian won't be part of it.

I see Nick in the car on the corner, if I didn't know better, I'd think he's taking a nap. Their job is to blend in, to be part of the scenery, to draw as little attention to themselves as possible. None of that matters, Greg knows they're here, him or whoever he has working with him made the demand for them to leave. Frustration builds, anger at myself, irritation with Ian, rage against Greg. As soon as Ian stops in the parking space I get out of the car, I want the sanctity of my home, I need to take some time for myself to think. Having all these players makes this all so much more complex. Hell, when it was just me it was complex. Ian follows close behind me, Fletcher takes long, hurried strides to catch up. I should have known that I'd have to wait to enter my apartment, after the threat today, security is on high alert. I climb the stairs as close to the railing as I can, giving Fletcher room to pass me, handing him my keys as he goes by.

Ian and I avoid eye contact, he stands on the landing with me while we wait for Fletcher to check the apartment. My resolve is starting to weaken, my courage starting to abate, the safety and comfort that I felt in the car dissipating. Just two steps and I could close the gap, if I could take two steps, I know that Ian wouldn't deny me the warmth that he can offer, the security that I feel with his arms around me. But taking those two steps would be selfish and misleading and only temporary.

Fletcher returns with the all clear, I see a look pass between him and Ian, I know that they are waiting for me to go inside. They want to speak alone, what a difference a few hours make. Was it only this morning that we all sat around my table having breakfast? When I was included in the conversation? How can it seem like a lifetime has passed in just a few hours?

With only a nod I brush past Fletcher, I close the door behind me but lean against it hoping that I might hear what they will say. Disappointment fills me when I can only hear murmurs, will Ian tell me if I ask?

What's my play? How am I going to handle this? The only solution I can see, is to make the call I've been avoiding for the last year but then what? I know what will be demanded of me, will I concede? Do I sacrifice myself to keep the rest of them safe? Curled up on my bed, I stare at the phone, Greg's preprogrammed number, just seeing his name on the screen is daunting, my thumb hovering.

"Olivia! We need to go! Now!" My door crashes open, the panic in his voice, pain in his eyes. "Grab some things, we won't be back for a while." I want to ask what's happened, but his demeanor deters any questions I have. I scramble to gather things that I will need, things that I may want, in minutes I have nearly all of my possessions packed back in the small suitcase I came to Vegas with.

With his arm wrapped around me, pulling me close, I allow him to guide me to the living room, Fletcher has tears in his eyes, I hear the wail of an ambulance growing closer, fear clenches in my stomach. I don't know what's happened but whatever it is, it's awful. I don't waste time asking questions, just allow myself to be guided back outside. Ian looking in all directions, Fletcher close behind, at the bottom of the stairs Steven and Jay stand solemnly, stepping out into the parking lot I catch sight of Ryan and Mack. Ryan watching the surroundings, Mack leaning in the driver's side of the car Nick was in. Realization sets in, something's happened to Nick.

"Oh God! What happened? Is he okay?" Choking on my words, tears blinding my vision, I stumble away from Ian, I try to go to the car, Ian grabs my arm, pulling me back to him. Memories surface, flashes of Greg fill my mind, my anxiety threatening to consume me.

His fist smashed into my nose, blood started pouring. He struck me twice more and I fell to the ground, the world around me slowed, my vision hazy, the coolness of the hardwood floor on my face, and then pain. So much pain. He landed a kick to my stomach, before pulling me up by my hair. He is screaming, but I can't make out what he is saying. I try to get my feet under me but stumble and fall to my knees. He is pulling me to the staircase, I stagger to my feet, pulling away, trying to twist out of his grip. My hair being ripped out strand by strand at the root, I can't let him get me upstairs, if he gets me up the stairs I'll be handcuffed and confined in the closet again, the thought helps me to find my strength, I kick out at his legs, trying to connect with his knees, if I can just break free of his grasp, escape just to the street, my efforts...

Flailing my arms, I make contact, again and again, "LET ME GO! LET ME GO!" He only pulls me tighter, cocooning me in his arms, whispering, "Olivia, it's me, it's ok." It's his use of my given name that pulls me back to the moment, I can't see through my tears, but his voice is soothing, it's Ian, it's Ian holding me, it's Ian comforting me.

My knees buckle and he catches me, lifting me into his arms, carrying me to the car and I submit.

Ian guides the car onto the roadway, the ambulance is just arriving as we pass by, what happened to Nick? Is he ok? The sobs still wrack my body, I can't get the words out. Ian still talking quietly, reassuring me, holding my hand, keeping contact with me, maintaining a connection. His friend is hurt or worse and he's here with me, calming me.

I don't look where we are going, it doesn't matter, so long as it isn't here. The guilt of all that's transpired pressing down on me. I did this, I brought all of this upon these people. Whatever happened to Nick is my fault, whatever Greg does to Ian will be on my conscience as well. I'm going to lose it again. Five things I can see, Ian's hand holding mine, the emblem on the dash, the car that is beside us, the man in the car on the phone, the song description on the screen of the radio "Under Your Scars, Godsmack." Four things I can feel, Ian's thumb rubbing on mine, the air blowing on my face, the soft leather of the seat, the seatbelt across my neck. Three things I can hear, Ian whispering words of comfort, the music faintly in the background, the sound of my own cries. Two things I can smell, the leather in the car, the scent that is Ian, clean, masculine. One thing I can taste, the salt of my tears.

Back in control, as much as I can be in this moment, the fog starting to lift, Lost Cities looms ahead of us. He's taking me back to his place, putting me up in his golden tower to keep me safe, I don't doubt that I'll be safe, but to what end? Who else is going to pay a price for the sake of keeping me safe? And what's the price going to be?

In the garage, Ian pulls into his spot, the Escalade next to us. Fletcher steps out of the driver's side and I hear the passenger door close as well. Ian comes around to open my door, Steven comes into sight, my suitcase in his hand. Both men checking the surroundings, guarding me and Ian. What have I done? Which one will be next? How long will I allow for this to happen?

"Let's get upstairs." Ian offers his hand to me, I don't want to take it, I don't want to learn to depend on it, I don't want to get used to it, so I ignore his gesture. Because this isn't going to last, I can't let this happen to any of them. I'll contact Greg and I'll do whatever he says, it's me that he wants, if I give him what he wants, then all of them will be safe. I need to do it soon, before Rachel gets back, visions fill my head of what could happen to her, only I can stop it all. I allow myself to be led to the elevator, Ian at my side, though I refused his hand, he guides me with his hand at the small of my back, Fletcher and Steven close behind.

When the elevator stops and the doors open, the beauty that I saw earlier today is gone. Now this is my cage, a prison, not to keep me in but to keep the monsters out. All the hope that I once found in this city, I had allowed myself to believe that this place would set me free. I chased that dream to my detriment and to the detriment of others as well. "What happened to Nick?" All three men face me,

Fletcher's face masks whatever he may be feeling, Steven's face darkens with anger, and Ian, Ian's reveals the guilt that he feels. "Is he..." I want to know if he's still alive, but I can't say the words, my voice fails me.

"He'll make it, we only know he was beaten pretty badly, whoever did it got the drop on him, I couldn't find any signs of defensive wounds. When he comes to, we'll piece it all together." The monotone of Fletcher's voice is chilling. Exhaustion washes over me, learning that Nick is going to be ok, triggered a fatigue I'm unprepared for.

"Ian, I'd like to lie down, is that okay?" I don't want to hear anymore, I don't want to see the worry on their faces for their friend. I just want to be alone. I want to rest and clear my head, I need that.

Chapter 20

Ian

I don't want her out of my sight, but she doesn't need to hear the details, right now she doesn't need to know. Initially, I started to take her to the spare room but as I drew closer to the door, it felt wrong, it felt foreign, my room is safe, it's comfortable, I know she won't know the difference, but I will. She can stay in my room, I'll take the spare.

The same coldness between us has returned, she lays on my bed without looking at me. I'm at a loss, I want to comfort her, to reassure her that things will be ok. I want to just take the time to sit with her so that she knows that she isn't alone, right now, I can't. I have a lot of arrangements to make and phone calls that must be placed. I retreat, leaving her in solitude.

Mack bought us some time with the police report, the hospital has my number, Fletcher is on his way to the hospital and will keep my apprised of any changes. Right now, Nick is unresponsive, but his heartbeat is strong, the bleeding is controlled, staff will continue tests and ensure that he gets the best care. That was the most important task before me.

Markus is working on my phone records and tracking down Greg, it's all I can do on that front. I need to let him do his job and give him the room he needs so he can, breathing down his neck isn't going to produce results any faster.

I can't believe that the person on the phone would have real knowledge of my mother, but it's necessary to reach out to her just to be sure. I know it was a scare tactic. This guy wants me to believe that he knows her, he wants me to focus on mom rather than what is happening here. It's the only explanation. "Mama, I know it's getting late there, I'm sorry to disturb you." The worry in her voice when she answers the phone, she knows it's important. She remains quiet waiting for me to continue. "I can't go into a lot of detail, but I got a call today from someone that says they are a friend of yours, they warned me to stay away from a client that I'm working with. You haven't encountered anything strange today have you?"

"No Ian, I haven't, are you alright?" I hear the other questions she refrains from asking. I can see in my mind the worry creasing her face.

"It's okay mama, I think someone is just trying to use our relationship to force the outcome they are trying to achieve. Please don't worry, I just wanted to call to be sure you are alright." She knows that I won't say anymore on the matter, she has always respected the privacy of my work. When the time is right, she'll have the answers to the questions that she has. "I love you ma, be well, I'll call you soon."

"I love you son, be safe." I loathe causing her this stress, until she has the answers to what she won't ask, her concern will keep her up at night. If I could've avoided this call, I would've, there's nothing she can do. Unfortunately, now she will just worry.

I stand before my bedroom door, resisting the temptation to open it, my hand hovers in preparation to knock. Does she need anything? Can I help her? Would my presence help? Not knowing what I can say or do, is new ground. I'm a problem solver, methodical in my approach, taking one step after another to resolve whatever is before me. Here and now, I don't know how to proceed, this situation is beyond my knowledge, not only in that I don't work with the foundation this way, but that I've made this personal, she is more than a client. I'm unaccustomed with being unsure of my next move. I rest my forehead on the door, rather than disturb her, instead I send Alex a message and wait for him to call. He has the experience, this is his domain, I now regret not informing him of the events of last night.

"Alex!" Shit, where do I start?

"Hey man, I sent Rachel to get a massage, what's up?" I hear the apprehension in his voice. I start with the information that Markus had gotten and proceeded with all the events that have happened since. He takes it all in, not interrupting, only muttering under his breath as I detail the events since yesterday.

"God damn! Why didn't you call me last night?" I should have. We're partners, but he has more at stake in Battling Back than I do. His is the face that represents, he is the one that handles it all, I am just the silent, silent partner, my role is helping behind the scenes. A breach of this degree should have been disclosed immediately.

"Alex, you went away for the weekend to propose to your lady, there wasn't anything you could've done to prevent it, all that could be done was. I wanted you to have the weekend that you planned. Rachel deserved to have it as well." I'll take the heat for this one, Olivia has enough going on she doesn't need the ire of Alex to add to it.

"The detectives aren't going to be patient long, they're going to need a response. Are you going to take her to the safehouse?" The thought had never entered my mind. Right here, she is safer than anywhere else in the city, security in the library, security downstairs, no one is getting in here.

"No, we're going to stay here, I'll keep her with me. I need you to get a hold of the detectives and handle that when you get back tomorrow, so far, I haven't heard from them. Don't let Rachel go back to her place alone. You don't have to tell her any of this right now, let her have her moment. I can put off PD until you get back. My biggest concern was you walking into this shitstorm not knowing what was happening, as well as you going to Rachel's apartment when you get back." As much as I'd like for Rachel to talk to Olivia, it can wait.

"How's she doing? We won't be able to avoid making a report, Nick's been injured, she's going to have to talk to them. No matter what, do not let her talk to them until I get there." That's the next obstacle that I need to address. I think in part that's the reason for her silence. She knows, she's married to an Assistant District Attorney, she knows how things work. I need to help her feel safe, make her understand that things aren't like they were before, Alex and I know some good cops here.

"She's really withdrawn into herself, we were making a connection, she leaned on me a lot after I found her last night, but I'll take care of her." With nothing else to say, we exchange our goodbyes, Alex and Rachel will come here when their flight gets in. The weight that I felt has lessened. Knowing that Alex will take the reins on the investigation, frees me up to work on things with Markus. Knowing that she's safe for now, allows me to help her work through all that's happened and what's coming.

I pause at my bedroom door. I take a deep breath and tap softly. "Olivia? Can I come in?" No answer from her, do I open the door? It feels like an invasion of privacy. Is she putting up a brave front, suffering in silence? Quietly, I turn the knob. She's there curled as small as she could make herself in the center of my bed, her ebony hair fanned out behind her. I retrieve a blanket from my closet, gently covering her, for now she can sleep. I remove her phone from her hand, as I lift it, the screen lights up, Greg's contact information is on the screen.

What has she done? I resist the urge to wake her. Whatever it is, it can't be undone, she needs the rest. Setting her phone on the bedside table, I leave as soundlessly as I entered.

In the library, Steven and I pour over the file that Markus had given me. Every shred of information that he was able to dig up is here, newspaper clippings, police reports, hospital intake forms, and photographs. I burn Greg's face into my memory, when Olivia gets up, I'll check with her to be sure he still looks the same. Her and I have a lot to discuss, most importantly, why she had Greg's contact information up on her phone. I think I have an idea what she's thinking, it'll take some convincing to make her realize that she's wrong.

As we scour the information, learning all we can about Greg Daniels, Markus's name lights up my screen. "Tell me you know something Markus." An address would suffice right now, I'd be happy to show up personally.

"He's back in New York, but he was here. I'm still looking into the name he used but he flew in Thursday night and left Friday morning. Once you gave me a timeline of events, I was able to narrow my search. Originally, it was my belief that to stay under the radar he would drive, neither train or bus would get him here and back in time, if he plans on returning to work. I found him in the security feed from the airport. It takes time to verify all the passengers as soon as I get the alias, I'll let you know. Additionally, I haven't been able to determine who made the calls to you, I do know, the first one originated here in Vegas, the second came from New York." I listen, making notes, more information to work off. "My assumption, he has probably been in contact with someone here, he flew in, met them in person, probably paid them off and left instructions of what he wants, that's who contacted you first. When you didn't agree to his demands, this Daniels guy called himself, he used personal information to intimidate you. He knows what he's doing, I can almost guarantee that I won't get anything on the phones, he's smart enough to use burners." He flew in and flew out, while Markus works on piecing it all together, we can work on finding his contact here and how they came to be acquainted.

"Good work Markus, keep me updated regularly. I want you to get someone on the cameras around Olivia's address. If there's cameras on the buildings, I want the footage. If not, I want the footage from the streets and the surrounding areas. Someone was in her apartment last night, and someone got ahold of Nick today, I want to know who this bastard is." I give all the information to Steven, he can add it to the timeline he's working on.

Olivia didn't know the person that attacked her, we know for sure that Greg wasn't in the city at the time, he also wasn't here for Nick's attack. He's covering his tracks, but he's coming for her. Her piercing scream pulls me from my thoughts.

Chapter 21

Olivia

Falling... Hitting each stair, all the way down. I don't know if I lost consciousness, I only know pain. My left side is on fire, my right shoulder is burning. I can only draw shallow breaths, I must have lost control of my bladder, it's warm and wet between my legs. My head is pounding, I attempt to move, the front door only 10 steps away, but the pain is excruciating. Then his boots in front of my face, "You stupid bitch, you listen closely, you tripped on the top stair and fell, I came home to find you lying here, that's all that you'll say. You can't remember anything else, do you hear me Rae? Say you hear me, or so help me God, I'll leave you here to bleed out and call the ambulance after you're dead." It isn't the dream that wakes me, it's the scream that comes from my lips. Disoriented and confused, I don't recognize my surroundings, when the door slams open, I scramble off the bed, only to find myself in a corner. As I put together my thoughts, Ian stands in the doorway, I collapse, I have no strength to stand. Just as he did last night, he approaches me slowly, hands outstretched, I want him to just get here. I want him to make me feel the way he did last night. I want the security he has to offer, right now, I need that from him.

I can't speak, I can't tell him what I need, with all that I have left, I reach for him. It's all the prompting that he needs, he sinks to the floor beside me, opens his arms, and I bury myself there, breathing him in, and I wait, wait for the horror to subside. Again, I start with the grounding techniques, but I find them unnecessary. His presence drives away the anxiety, his warmth soothes me, his arms around me is all I need to feel, to bring me back. He doesn't grow impatient, he doesn't try to speak, without saying anything, he calms me.

The rumbling of my stomach breaks the moment, "We should get you something to eat." His words barely above a whisper, still he doesn't move and neither do I. It isn't my stomach that eventually gets us moving, it's the pins in needles in my legs and my feet, as well as my bladder.

"Thank you, that doesn't happen much anymore but with all that's happened, I guess it was inevitable." Part of what makes me feel so at ease with him is that he doesn't push, he doesn't expect explanations, doesn't demand to know anything. "I was having a nightmare, but it was something real, something that happened. When I woke up, I forgot where I was, I didn't recognize anything." It's so easy to tell him, the words come without any hesitation, without any shame.

"You don't have to thank me, I'm glad that I can be here. Let's go see if we can find some food. If you're ready to hear it, I have some information." I don't know if I'm ready, but I want to know all there is, most of all if Nick has had any improvement.

"Tell me." So long as Nick is ok, I can handle anything else he might have to say.

"Food first, we both need to eat. Decide what you'd like, and I'll send Steven down to get it." Steven is still here? I would've thought that all of them would be at the hospital.

Staring in the mirror, my eyes, red and puffy, my face splotchy all over, there is no hiding the tears I cried when I laid down or the ones that roused me from my sleep. I splash cool water on my face, soothing the irritation in my eyes.

Ian is waiting for me when I open the bathroom door, his eyes search mine, but I don't know what he's looking for.

"Can I have some soup? I don't think my stomach can handle much more than that." It will also help with the chill that I'm feeling.

I don't care what kind of soup and he doesn't ask. He disappears in another room briefly, when he returns Steven is with him. I can't look at Steven, I feel guilty for what happened to Nick. I'm afraid if I look at him, I will see accusation in his eyes, and that would be too much.

When the elevator slides closed Ian comes to sit with me on the couch, he doesn't try to put any distance between us, sparing me from having to try to get closer to him. "I checked on you while you were sleeping, I put a blanket over you and put your phone on the nightstand. I wasn't prying, but your phone opened when I lifted it, I couldn't help but see that Greg was up on the screen, I need to know Olivia, did you contact him?" I hear the strain in his voice, it's hard for him to maintain his composure.

"I wanted to, but I'm too much of a coward. I wanted to because if I give him what he wants then all of this will end, no one else will be hurt." Or worse.

"Except you. You must promise me that you won't ever make that call Olivia. I know what you're thinking, I know you feel responsible for what happened to Nick, it's easier said than done, but you need to stop thinking that way. Nick knows the risks involved in this line of work, this isn't your fault. Put the blame where it belongs, on the person that did this." He can't understand, as much as he wants to and as hard as he'll try, he can't. "If you make that call Olivia, then all of this is for nothing. Nick will take a beating, he'll put his life on the line, and he will die to protect a client, because he knows the work he does makes a difference. He chooses this life, he chooses to impact the world by helping one person at a time. Don't take that away from him or any of the others." Can I live with that on my conscience? "Just consider what I'm saying."

"What information have you gotten?" I don't make the promise he asked for, I don't want to be the person that makes a promise that I don't know that I can keep, everything he said makes me feel better about it all but still, I don't know that I can promise that yet.

The elevator doors open, Steven carrying a large tray and a paper sack.

"Where you want it boss?" He looks so out of place carrying that tray, he looks like he belongs on the football field, he lacks the poise and coordination to make serving a career, I can't help but giggle at the sight.

"You ought to think about changing jobs Steve, serving looks good on you." The good-natured razzing makes Steven blush, he only snorts in response, setting the tray on the island. With the paper sack in his hand he returns to wherever he was hiding before Ian sent him for our meals.

Ian silently lays out our lunch, or maybe it's dinner, hell I don't even know what time it is. I hope that he'll start to fill me in with whatever he's learned, to ask again will reveal the desperation I feel.

As if he's reading my mind again, "We'll talk while we eat, tomato bisque and grilled cheese. You eat, I'll talk. Don't think that I missed that you didn't agree to not make that call." I didn't think he would, but at least he isn't pressuring me or using that as leverage to tell me what he knows.

The smell of the soup sets the rumbling of my stomach off again, basil and oregano combined with tomatoes to make this thick, rich goodness. I wait for him to take his seat before I dig in, but my patience is waning.

"Eat." The grilled cheese sandwiches are cut into strips, each one perfect to dip and savor in conjunction with the bisque, the flavor exploding with each bite. I'm not just hungry, I'm ravenous, once I begin, I can't stop.

Ian watches me devour what's in front of me, while slowly eating his own, still not saying anything. The longer he takes to start the more apprehensive I get.

"Greg flew into Vegas Thursday night, he flew under an alias. He left Friday morning. We know he wasn't in town when you were attacked." My spoon clatters in my bowl, warm soup splashes on the counter, he was that close? My stomach turns, I make a concerted effort to not vomit.

"How do you know? I mean, are you sure it was him? Why would he fly in and fly out in just a matter of hours?" It's a minimum of 5 hours inflight. With the TSA restrictions and security, how is it possible to fly under an alias?

"We have video footage, I've had someone working on this since the flowers arrived for you, his reports are credible." He continues to eat, watching me, I've lost my appetite, my guess, he knew I would and that's why he waited so long before telling me anything.

If he can pop in and out like that, what's to stop him from doing it again? From showing up anytime, anywhere? It was so much simpler before I filed for divorce. I was safe, I was hidden, I was broke as hell, and on the verge of homelessness. Another thought occurs to me, Rachel and Alex are engaged, they are going to want to move in together, this understanding had escaped me in the excitement of the moment, in the happiness for my friends. Reminding myself that I'm being selfish, their engagement is awesome, but where do I go from here?

I excuse myself from our meal, I need space, I need to clear my head. In the bathroom I sit on the edge of the tub and contemplate what happens now. Angry with myself with not seeing this before. The notion of calling Greg floats through my thoughts again. If I call him and surrender, concede to go back, will it make the punishment for my transgressions any less? As more situations arise, calling him is quickly becoming the only solution to all of them. Earlier as I lay there, after typing in his number, entering each digit one at a time, trying to gain the courage to make the call, when his name appeared onscreen all my fortitude was lost, I couldn't bring myself to press the call button.

I feel him before he speaks, I feel his presence, I know he's there without him saying anything at all. "Olivia?" His deep tenor resonates outside the door that separates us. I can't hide in here forever, but I don't want to face him with the thoughts that I have, he is so intuitive, he'll know.

"Give me a few minutes." I know he's gone, I feel it, still confused about this connection between us, we hardly know each other, but it feels like I've known him forever. I lock away all thoughts of Greg, concentrating on the façade that I'll present, I use to be good at this, I put on plenty to make life easier, because as long as I pretended everything was just the way that Greg expected it, my life was much easier.

"That's great news! Thanks for the update, make sure he has whatever he needs." I assume Ian's being updated on Nick's condition, sounds as though he's doing well, relief floods through me. I'm not sure my psyche could've withstood any other outcome.

While he finishes up his call, I stare out the window. The sun is hanging low in the sky, I can see the neon lights starting to glow downtown. I look down on the city that has grown to be my home, disappointed in the knowledge that it's no longer my refuge, despondent that it's no longer my safe haven.

"A couple more hours and you're in for a treat, this view is something during the day but at night it's astounding." I can hear the relief in his voice, he was more worried than he had let on. "Nick's doing well, they're having a hard time keeping him in bed now. He's pretty banged up and he has a little swelling in his brain, they're certain that's why he was unconscious so long, his body did what it needed to do, but he'll make a full recovery." The air around him is lighter, the weight of his friend's health has been lifted.

"Will I be able to see him? I'd like to thank him and apologize. He wouldn't have been hurt if he wasn't tasked with my security." It's the least that I can do.

"I'll set something up, he'll be glad to see you, right up until you apologize, that'll probably offend him. You didn't do this, the team has some great leads they're pursuing. we'll find whoever's responsible for this." He moves closer to me, I feel the heat of his skin, try as I might, I can't stop myself from closing the gap between us, the security that I felt being in Vegas has shifted to just being near him.

"There's a few more things I need to tell you. I spoke with Alex, I couldn't let him come home and be surprised by all of this, and I needed to know how to proceed with the detectives." My anxiety triggers again, I hadn't considered the police reports, they never crossed my mind. "He won't tell Rachel until they get home, but he had to know Olivia. Instead of going to your apartment, he'll take Rachel to his place." Of course! I never thought about them going back to our place. At least Rachel gets to enjoy the rest of her stay, so long as Alex isn't working the rest of their time there.

"Are the police waiting to speak with me?" I know they are, a man was found beaten in his car while working a security detail for me, this just keeps getting worse. Needing his comfort, I put my arms around him, it's all the persuasion he needs to wrap me in his embrace.

Chapter 22

Ian

It was a long, restless night, together we watched the sunset and marveled at the beauty created in the sky. After it had gotten dark, the city lit up in neon, Vegas is thought to be the brightest city on earth, the lights can be seen from space. Watching her it was as if it was her first time to see it, in a sense it was, seeing it from this vantage point is much different than seeing it from the ground. The neon capital of the world. It's part of the culture, part of the identity of Vegas, the neon lights are forever immortalized in the words of Elvis, "turning night into daytime." Through her I saw it for the first time again, recognizing the beauty that I'm privileged enough to see every day, realizing that I've come to take it for granted.

Seeing how much she appreciated the view below, I took her up to the roof. We laid on a lounger and looked at the stars, we couldn't see as many as we could've if we got away from the lights of the city, but I was able to point out Ursa Major, the Big Dipper, and Leo. She was fascinated with the stories of the constellations, telling me they were reminiscent of when her mother had taken her out to the lake several times, telling her the same stories. Living in New York City, the smog and the lights obscure them, moving to Vegas didn't open the skies much for her.

Those were the good parts, those were the moments that were effortless. As the night went on, it was full of revelations and difficult moments. She stopped holding me at arm's reach, she brought me in, she couldn't carry the burden alone anymore. Lying there on the roof of the Lost Cities a storm began deep within me, she revealed parts of the hell she had been living for so many years, how it had gotten away from her and snowballed until she was isolated and had nowhere to turn. As I listened, I recognized so many similarities to what I had witnessed as a child, I felt the same hopelessness. I remembered the fear I felt as a child, but now it is fury that is building,

I kept it hidden from her, not wanting her to stop, not wanting her to close herself off again.

In between she would drift off into a fitful sleep, I would doze off with her, pulling her tightly against me, trying to ward off the demons that invaded her dreams. It didn't take long before she was thrashing around, trying to escape the boogeyman that held her hostage. Then we would start again, I called her name softly, reassured her she was safe, and we would settle back in. She would speak of the nightmare but really it was the past coming back to haunt her, each memory as horrifying and painful as the last.

Right before dawn, I was awakened again, not by screams, not by terror, but cries of anguish, that cut down to my soul. It wasn't the tears, but what she kept repeating, "I didn't kill our son, you did. I couldn't save him from you, kill me too, just kill me too." My heart shattered for her. I felt powerless while she worked through her grief, not saying anything, just allowing her to release all that she's kept buried, all that she's hidden. How could Markus miss this? Why wasn't there anything in his report about the death of a child?

"That was the last time. That's when I left, he came home in a foul mood, and I had spent the day wallowing in depression. He started yelling about the house being a mess, that I hadn't started dinner, and rolled into how I had let myself go, that being pregnant didn't give me an excuse to be lazy." My anger mounts again, but I pull her closer, she stays silent long enough that I think she's fallen back to sleep. "I got mad, I don't even remember what I said, but he hit me, one punch was all it took to drop me, he grabbed me by the hair and started to drag me to the stairs, I didn't want to go back in the closet, that's where he would put me, he said it was so that I had plenty of quiet time without any distractions to think about the lesson he was trying to teach me. He would handcuff me and leave me there for hours, sometimes all day, but this time I wasn't going to let him, I fought him all the way up the stairs, finally at the top I kicked out at him and connected, then he pushed me down the stairs." Trying to control my rage as she told me this was a task, I was unsure I could manage, but I had to, this was about her and what she needed. "I hit every stair, the pain was so intense I couldn't think clearly, I thought that I had lost control of my bladder, that's what I believed. He told me what to say to the medics, he made me say it to him, if I didn't, he said he would let me bleed out and call them after I was dead."

She didn't remember the medics arriving, nor getting to the hospital. She suffered multiple broken bones, her nose, left clavicle, 8 ribs, both her ulna and radius in her left arm, her lung had collapsed, and she miscarried her son at five and half months. It was after she came to that he told her that she had killed their son. The son of a bitch told her it was her fault because she was weak, told her that she had failed their child and him for not protecting him better, because that was her only job. It was then that she knew that she had to get away. She had no plan, no idea where she would go, what she would do, she just knew she had to get away. The day after she was released from the hospital, he got called into work, he mistakenly believed that she was too weak to escape, she took full advantage of what I believe would have been her only chance.

67 hours on a greyhound bus, her body beaten and broken, she needed a break, she needed something to eat and wanted a comfortable place to sleep. She found her way into the King's Ransom. Rachel saw her immediately, saw her struggling to juggle her suitcase with her broken arm, bruises covering her face, struggling to breath and she went to help her. Olivia credits Rachel with saving her life, she can't see that she saved herself. Rachel did an admirable thing, taking Olivia in the way she did, giving her a place to live, hardly knowing anything about her. Rachel gave her the hand up that she needed, but someday I will make Olivia see that she saved herself, she didn't need anyone else for that.

As the sun started to rise, she couldn't speak anymore, exhaustion had overtaken her once again. I carried her back down to my apartment and set her in my bed, and after the night we just shared, I didn't hesitate to lay beside her and envelope her in my arms. Finally, she was still, at last she slept peacefully. I on the other hand lay awake, trying to wrap my head around all that she'd told me, the woman beside me is a warrior. I will do everything in my power to ensure that she never has to face those horrors again. When I find him, he will pay for every mark upon her skin, for every bruise upon her heart, and every cut he put upon her soul.

I stay with her, not wanting to disturb the sleep that she so desperately needs. I stay with her because this feels right. I stay with her because there is nowhere else I want to be, there is nothing else that I want to be doing. Until yesterday, this place was just a place, it held no memories to speak of, it was just rooms at the top of a building, an extension of my office, my escape. With her here, it feels like more, like she was what was missing. I have never known a woman so intimately, even in all the years that I shared with Vivian, I never knew her like this, she never bared her soul to me.

I notice the change in her breathing before she starts to stir. Today will be a long hard day, Alex will need to talk with her, Rachel will want to talk with her, and I'm sure the detectives will be expecting to have a sit down as well.

"Good morning, Olivia." I speak quietly in case she isn't quite awake yet.

"It's morning, I can't say that it's good, I feel like I've been hit by a train. I'm really sorry about last night." It's barely a whisper. "I didn't mean to unload on you like that, once it started coming out, I just couldn't stop it." I squeeze a little tighter.

"Don't ever apologize for that, no one should have to carry that alone. I may not be able to carry it for you, but I'll make damn sure you don't ever bear that burden by yourself again." And I will walk through broken glass to keep her from ever having to live that life again.

Steven and Ryan had switched sometime in the night, Ryan is sifting through the file and all the notes, adding his own where needed. A tray of breakfast laid out on the breakfast bar, the newspapers beside it.

The Vegas Voice

Breaking News

It appears the most eligible bachelor in Las Vegas, Ian Alessandro may now be off the market. Sorry ladies, we know, our hearts are broken too.

Just over a week ago we reported that Mr. Alessandro had begun the process of withdrawing from his share in Ragtime Rhythm, just as his ex-wife and business partner was hospitalized. Our reporters may have dug up the reasoning behind his unexpected exit yesterday.

Pictured below, Mr. Alessandro and a mystery woman are leaving an apartment in the early morning hours, a tip from a reader led us to the address, Mr. Alessandro did in fact spend the night. Also included are photos of their visit to the Whiskey Wrangler, while they left as quickly as they arrived, you can't deny the chemistry between them.

Who is the mystery woman that has made Mr. Alessandro turn his back on his previous wife and a business that he started?

As new details emerge, we will keep you up to date.

If you have any information, tips, or leads, contact us at: thevegasvoice.com.

Fucking vultures! As if my personal life or business decisions are any of anyone's business! I had missed the article about my pulling out of Ragtime, I have no question who tipped them off on that, or why. In Lawrence's mind, I'm sure he believed that bad publicity might sway my decision. Even if I had seen it, it wouldn't have changed anything.

I can count on one hand those that knew that I went to Olivia's apartment, and there's only one name that stands out. As plans have changed, it's time to bring him in for a conversation, I want answers and I think he has them.

Olivia approaches, hair still wet from the shower, eyes red and swollen, yet still beautiful. "You might want to read this, you aren't mentioned by name, but it won't be long." I feel her anger as she reads the article quickly.

"How did they know, Ian?" Her voiced strained.

"We both know the common denominator, the attack, now this. Only a few people knew that I went to your apartment." I have failed her again. I couldn't keep her safe in her home and now her face is out for all to see.

"It's Brett, isn't it? Damnit! Why?" I wait for her to blame me, she has every right to do so. I sent him there, I hired him, I trusted that he would do the right thing, though I didn't trust him.

"We're going to find out. Alex and Rachel should be here in the next hour, Alex moved up their flight. We're going to all have a Pow Wow and make sure we all are up to speed, we'll come up with the best way to approach this." I'll put a couple of the guys on finding Brett, make sure we know where he is before I try to call him in. I won't give him the chance to miss that meeting.

My phone rings disrupting out conversation. "Markus? What do you have?" I hope he was able to track down the numbers from yesterday.

"I was able to pull the number that called you that originated from New York, that same number called Ragtime on July 22, since then there've been numerous calls from different New York numbers, all calls originating in New York, all calls last between 30 seconds to a minute and half. Prior to the 22nd, not a single call originating from there, nor from a number there." Brett had been working the Ragtime prior to the security detail, and no one would question him using the phone there even when not on duty. We've got the bastard.

Chapter 23

Olivia

"Rachel!!" As soon as I see her step out of the elevator, I run to give her a hug. It's hard to believe she's only been gone a couple of days, so much has happened, so much has changed. Starting with her, engagement looks good on her, she is vibrant, and I can feel her elation.

"Hello doll! I leave you for two days and all hell breaks loose." I can't help but laugh, we built up so much dread about what could happen, she was prepared for anything, of course it all happened after she left. "All kidding aside, you okay?" I don't want to talk about me, not yet, I want her to tell me again, I want to share in her euphoria.

"I'm fine, you first!" It's all the coaxing she needs, she tells me again about all they had done over the weekend, romantic dinners, breakfast in bed, Alex chimes in when he feels she's leaving something out. No sign of the stress that he'd been under on Friday morning, he too is excited and jubilant. Everything feels right, I let their happiness overtake me. I set aside all the chaos and feed off their energy and it feels good. Ian catches my eye, giving me a wink and the half-smile, I adore, he feels it too.

"Have you been to the hospital?" As Rachel winds down, Alex changes the subject.

"Not yet, I've been getting updates, I thought if Olivia was up for it, we would go today." Ian looks at me questioningly.

"Yes, please." I do want to see Nick, at the very least I owe him a thank you, I'll see if I think he'll be offended with an apology.

"Good, we stopped on the way from the airport, I strongly suggest that both of you stay away from there. Olivia, Nick didn't divulge the true reason he was there, none of the guys have said anything to the detectives, I think we can keep you out of this, but after that article in the Vegas Voice, if you two show up there, you will be questioned." I am surprised to say the least,

I've been preparing myself for it all to come out, preparing to be accused of lying, preparing for no one to believe me.

I'd called to talk to the District Attorney, Derek Long , I'd asked him to meet me, he initially agreed, but then asked what I wanted to talk about, I didn't want to say too much over the phone, so I said personal issues between us. He changed his mind and wouldn't meet. That alone I might have been able to forgive, but he told Greg that I called, told him that I had requested a meeting. Greg put me in the hospital that night.

"Can't he get in trouble for that?" As much as I don't want to talk to the detectives, I'd rather not let Nick face consequences trying to cover for me.

"It's possible but unlikely, if we contradict his story, then, yes, most certainly." Alex is nonchalant about it all, he's an attorney. Damnit Nick! How is it that I found all these amazing people?

"I'd still like to see him." Not so much that I'll risk going down there and having his whole story fall apart, but I would like to.

"I think he's being released tomorrow. I'll make sure you get to talk to him. Rachel will be staying with me for the time being, Ollie, you're welcome to join us, or the safehouse is ready if you'd like to go there." Did Ian talk to Alex and tell him I needed to leave?

"Or, Olivia, you're welcome to continue staying here. If you're comfortable with it, that's the option I would prefer." Relief floods through me, Ian makes me feel safe, he sets me at ease. "This is the safest place to be, no one can get up here." Does he prefer I stay here because there's less risk for me, or less risk for his team?

"I don't want to be any trouble, I've probably caused enough upheaval in your life, Alex, you and Rachel need some time alone, I can go to the safehouse, I'm sure it will be fine." That's not what I want at all, but suddenly, I'm uncomfortable being here, I feel as if I'm a burden. I'm questioning everything that's happened between us. Greg's voice in the back of my mind laughing at me for thinking that there's something more happening.

"You don't want to stay here?" His eyes perplexed. "I can't make you stay, and I won't try, but I'd really like you to stay with me." Greg's voice chimes in, *only because you've become his obligation.* "Olivia, please stay?" I don't care why, I can't fathom staying in the safehouse alone.

"Alright, as long as you don't mind, and I won't be in your way." I'll just keep to myself and try not to be a bother.

"Thank you. Alex, I need to show you what we've put together so far, Markus called with more information right before you got here. I want your thoughts and see what your ideas are." While they talk about that I can talk to Rachel alone.

For an hour I've talked nonstop, filling her in on all that's happened while she's been gone. Quietly she sat by and didn't say a word, she nodded when necessary, held my hand, wiped my tears, and just let me get it all out. I didn't hold anything back, I explained my bewilderment of what's happening between Ian and I, my thoughts to call Greg and just go back to avoid all of this, to keep anyone else from getting hurt, my fears, the nightmares. I laid it all out, to her credit she never tried to interject, even when I could see she had to bite her tongue, she didn't.

"Are you ready? Cause I gots lots to say Doll." I know that it isn't all going to be pleasant, but I nod anyway. One of the things I love about her most, is that she will tell me exactly what she thinks. "Calling Greg? Are you fucking serious? You better lose that thought, right here, right now. I don't care what happens, you do not ever make that call. All of this will be for nothing if you call him, and you can bet your ass that he will kill you this time. Don't. Even.

Think. About. It. You got me?" She waits for
me to agree. "You are worth protecting, you
deserve more than what he did to you,
more than what he will do to you if he ever
gets his hands on you again."

"It's easy for you to say Rach, people
aren't getting hurt because of you." She
can't understand the guilt that I feel.

"You're right, it's easy for me to say,
not because people aren't getting hurt
because of me, it's easy for me to say
because I know you deserve it. No one
should ever have to live the way you did, no
one should ever be treated like that by
anyone, least of all by someone that claims
to love them. So yes, it is easy for me to say.
As soon as you start believing that you're
worth it, the easier it will be for you to
accept, Doll." She pauses, giving me the
opportunity to argue, but I know better.

"And you need to get his voice out
of your head. Ian asked you to stay with him
because he wants you here, no one has
asked him, no one is making him, Doll, can't
you see the way he looks at you? I don't

know what kind of magic you spun on him, but he is into you. Do you know that aside from his housekeeper and now me, you're the only woman that's been up here?" I had no idea.

"Alex filled me in on what he could on the plane ride, he thinks Ian's falling for you, hard. So, tell the Greg that's in your head to fuck right off. He may not have known what he had with you, or been able to see how amazing you are, but the same can't be said about the smart, successful, good-looking guy in the other room, because he really seems to worship you. What the hell were you thinking saying you would stay at the safe house?" I wait for her to keep going, but she waits for me to respond.

"I thought he only asked out of obligation, or maybe because he was worried that if I stayed somewhere else, more people would get hurt." Before Rachel could respond, his deep tenor speaks behind me.

"If I did something that made you feel that way Olivia, I apologize, that was not my intention. I want you to stay here because no matter how much I trust my men, I know that I can protect you better, I know that you're safer here with me. I want you to stay here with me because I don't want to miss a single moment with you. I want to be with you when you laugh, I want to hold you if you cry, I want you to feel safe and protected. I want to be the one to protect you, because I value you." The heat rises in my cheeks, I feel his eyes burn though I can't see them, a grin plays on Rachel's lips and she mouths "Told you." I feel the honesty in his words, but I don't understand the genuine affection that he seems to feel for me and have a hard time believing it.

"I'm sorry." I don't know what else to say.

"You have nothing to apologize for, please know that I would not have asked you to stay if I didn't feel the way that I do." I still can't turn around to face him, Alex comes around to stand near Rachel, he breaks the silence.

"Everyone talking about their feelings makes me feel all warm and fuzzy inside." Ah, leave it to Alex, to ruin a moment, though I feel like he might have rescued me. "Anyway, ladies, there's another subject we must all discuss. Thursday is the annual Battling Back fundraiser dinner, black tie, an orchestra, silent auction. Ian and I need to be in attendance, it's up to us to get these people to open their wallets... I mean their hearts." He chuckles at his own joke. I grow more apprehensive as he speaks.

"I think what Alex is trying to say is, would you ladies care to accompany us?" A rock settles in the pit of my stomach, while butterflies join the mix as well. Is he asking me on a date? I don't think now is the best time. My crazy husband, the person he sent that beat up Nick, oh and let's not forget, I didn't pack formal wear when I left New York, I probably didn't own anything that would be suitable anyway.

"I'm not sure that's a good idea." I just turned him down, what the hell is wrong with me?

"Olivia, I know what you're thinking, everything will be fine, there will be plenty of security, we know Greg is back in New York, we are almost certain that Brett is his accomplice, and we intend on dealing with him this week, there is nothing to worry about." Well he almost knows what I'm thinking, he missed one little detail.

"Well Alex sure as hell isn't going with anyone else, Ollie, you'll be with all of us, please? We'll have fun!" Her excitement does nothing for the hesitation I feel. She has a closet full of things she can wear, while I have some money left, there's no room in my budget for something like that.

"I'll think about it." Desert Sands is supposed to be calling me in for another interview this week, if I know I have an income, I might be able to buy a dress.

Chapter 24

Ian

We all sat down and had lunch that Ryan went down to get for us. As nice as it would have been to get out of the apartment, I have no doubt there are reporters milling around looking for an opportunity to get more pictures. While I can't stop them from uncovering Olivia's identity, I can hinder their efforts.

We strayed from the negative conversation during lunch, focusing on the upcoming nuptials, Alex sat back and nodded in agreement to everything Rachel said, throwing in, "anything you want baby," every so often for good measure. Olivia was enthralled with the ideas Rachel threw out, I couldn't help but watch her. Something new is weighing on her mind, she smiles in all the right places and gets excited at the right times, but it doesn't reach her eyes. I know that she's happy for them, so what is it besides the obvious that is bothering her?

Wanting to do something that's just for her, to give her an escape from the reality of the last couple weeks, I text the head housekeeper, Alice, I have an idea, it's low key and our privacy will be upheld, but it will get her out in the fresh air and hopefully out of her own head.

"What's on your mind?" Alex and Rachel have gone, Olivia has been quiet, lost in her own thoughts.

"I don't think I could pick out just one thought." Vague, at best. I have watched her the last several days, I have seen her upset, somber, angry, fearful, when she felt helpless and defeated, this is new, there's something I'm missing.

"Try, just one thought." A hint is all I need, maybe I can help, maybe I can't, but I won't know until she sheds some light on whatever it is that's bothering her.

"It's silly and selfish, I don't know why the thought never occurred to me prior to this." She pauses, sorting it out in her own mind before she speaks it aloud. "I feel like I've lost my place in Las Vegas, don't get me wrong, I am so happy for Alex and Rachel, but I realized, I need to get my stuff together. They are going to want to live together, and rightly so. I can't afford the apartment alone, I don't think I can live alone yet." She's torn between being happy for her friends and her fear, who wouldn't be, with all that's transpired as of late.

"You know that things won't always be this way, all of this is temporary, you are a strong, capable woman, right now there is chaos, but it will all soon be resolved. We will make sure of that." Rachel isn't going to leave her right now, Alex wouldn't be able to drag her away, not that he would try or want to. Olivia has won him over, he cares for her and will stop at nothing to keep her safe.

"I can't ask them to put their lives and their plans on hold because my life is a wreck. I can't stand in the way of them moving forward in their lives because my past keeps coming back to haunt me." It's admirable that she is more concerned with their happiness than with what she has going on herself.

"It doesn't make you selfish and you won't have to ask for anything, neither one of them are going to desert you in this, for that matter neither will I. I know that this has gone on for so long for you but consider that it was just two weeks ago that this process started to end it all. I promise you this, this will all work out." She may not be able to see it right now, but all of us are invested in this. No matter what happens, she won't be alone.

She curls up in the chair by the window, no matter what I say, she has to come to the realization on her own. Her mind knows what I said is true, she just needs to believe it. Before I could follow her my phone rings, mom's face lighting the screen.

"Mama! Are you well?" Alex gives me hell for calling her that, but it's who she is, who she's always been.

"Ian, I'm good, tell me of what's happening with you yesterday, is everything alright?" Olivia had briefly glanced at me when I answered the phone but has gone back to looking down on the city.

"It's all fine Ma, no need to worry." Maybe not fine, but under control and nothing she needs to worry about.

"Who is the woman with you in the papers, Ian?" Of course, she's seen the local trash rag.

"She's a friend, there's a lot that I can't say right now ma, I promise as soon as I can elaborate, I will." She doesn't push, she knows if I could discuss things with her I would, I always have. Though she isn't satisfied with my answer, she respects it enough to let the subject drop. Because I had been so short yesterday, I guide her into easy conversation, life in Italy, Nonie and Poppi. Once I got her started, it was an easy conversation, she could go on and on telling me of the beauty of her homeland, the excursions that she has taken with her parents, the art museums, the culture.

"I want to show you where we come from Ian, when can you visit?" She knows it can't be until after the Whiskey is done, but she has waited longer than what she had thought she would have to when she first left. I watch Olivia from across the room and wonder if she would like to visit Italy.

"I promise ma, as soon as the club is finished and up and running, I will come visit." I will have to make it a priority, it's been too long since we've seen each other.

After an hour, there wasn't anything left for us to talk about, our conversation dwindled, the silences grew longer, but I waited for her, I waited until she was ready for the call to end. Olivia still by the window, watching as the day turned to dusk, lost in her own thoughts.

"I love you Ian, whatever it is that's happening, please be careful." One day I will tell her, but not today, not until it's finished. I wish there was something I could say that would ease her worry.

"I will mama, I love you. Give my love to Nonie and Poppi." When the line went dead, my heart grew heavy, it really has been too long since I've seen her.

"It's sweet that you still call her mama." My face flushes, a grown man, still calling his mother, mama, Alex razzes me every time he hears me say it.

"It's the only name that fits, I've tried mom, and mother, and neither of them seem right." Both seem completely foreign, she will always be mama.

"Will you tell me more about her?" Her eyes never leaving the view of the city.

"Her name is Bellezza, after she finished high school, Nonie and Poppi had gotten her a trip around Italy to see the art museums and galleries, she wanted to go to school for art. She met my father in Rome, a whirlwind romance, she fell head over heels. My grandparents disowned her when she married him, she immigrated to the US, ready to build a life with the man that she loved, she worked hard and got her citizenship. Not long after she got pregnant with me, my father ran out on her. A young woman in a strange country, pregnant and alone. I don't know how she did it, but she did. It took a lot of years before she called my grandparents, it was a difficult call for her to make. She has a lot of pride, to have to swallow that pride, it wasn't easy for her, but their reunion was the best thing for her, she had missed them so much. She was able to swallow her pride and apologize, but she couldn't bring herself to ask if she could go home, she struggled for years to support me on her own, then she took in Alex and it only got harder. She never let that show, she told us both what blessings we were on her life and no matter the challenges, she said they made us all stronger." As I spoke, she turned her gaze to me.

"I love her name. She sounds like an amazing woman." I know she is thinking of her own mother.

"It means beauty. Never has there been a more fitting name." My mother is beautiful, and like Olivia, my mother's inner beauty shines through and amplifies her outer beauty.

"I've been curious, do you speak Italian? You've said things to me in Italian, but I wasn't sure if you actually speak the language or if you just know the words to charm the ladies." The sparkle in her eye and the small smile on her lips is a welcome change to moments ago.

"I wouldn't say just the words to charm the ladies, I do understand it, I don't use it enough to speak." Mama was adamant that I speak English, but she spoke to me in Italian. If I would use it more, I could be fluent, but who would I speak to besides my mother and my grandparents? "How would you feel about getting out of here for a while? I'd like to show you something." Curiosity burns in her eyes, not apprehension, not anxiety, just curiosity.

"I'd like that." I send a quick text to be sure that things are ready, when I receive the response, we head to the parking garage.

She stops in front of the Bentley, why wouldn't she? It's all that we've been in, with my hand on the small of her back I lead her to the truck, the Bentley won't make it where I want to take her.

The silence between us is easy as I pull out of the garage, heading away from town, away from the traffic, the noise, the lights. Away from the people, the man that had attacked her, the same man or maybe someone different that attacked Nick. Away from it all, just her and I, in this moment, leaving it all behind.

The screen on the stereo displays "Under Your Scars" by Godsmack. I had seen it previously but hadn't been able to hear the words, but the title has me intrigued, so I turn up the sound.

If there ever was a perfect song for a situation, this would be the one for ours, it seems to speak to all that I feel. Glancing at Olivia, she too seems mesmerized by the lyrics. Tonight, will be a perfect evening, there will be no one or no thing that will be able to take this moment from us.

Chapter 25

Olivia

I'm glad he turned up that song, it spoke to me like no other piece of music has, even if I am taking it too literal. I'm sure the artist didn't create that song with physical scars in mind, but I can relate to the words because of mine, and because of all these feelings and emotions that I have for Ian. Right now, as we get further away from town, the darkness overtaking us, on this road there is no other traffic, the lights of the city are getting further and further behind us. I don't know where we're going, I don't care, because as we travel each mile, the lighter I feel, all the worry, all the fear, I'm leaving it in the city. Here with him, wherever we are going, I'm not vulnerable, I'm not afraid.

"I don't want to go to the banquet because I don't have anything to wear." I don't know what made me say that right now. The silence was peaceful, comfortable. I've been worried what he thought of my hesitation to go, I don't want him to think it's because I'm afraid, because I don't want him to feel that I'm afraid he can't protect me.

"Really? It's that simple?" He chuckles softly, "I've considered all the reasons you have to not want to go, I have to say, that one never crossed my mind." He glances at me, I see the blue in his eyes, the lights of the dash giving off just enough illumination.

"That's it, I didn't think to bring evening wear with me when I left, but the more that I think about it, if the Desert Sands calls me for another interview like they said, then I might be able to swing buying a dress, if I can, I'd really like to go with you." A look crosses his face at the mention of the Desert Sands, one that I can't discern.

"You aren't worried about the press? The gossip they'll start? I don't want to change your mind, but the Vegas Voice has no love for me, whatever they publish will be nasty." I hadn't considered the press.

"It won't take them long to get my name, once they do, it won't matter. I've had my face plastered across papers for a long time, I've been the victim and been given sympathy, but I've also been a victim and received their ire. The hateful things they said when Trinity caught fire, I'm no stranger to bad press. So, yeah, it's just a dress that's stopping me." Hearing it out loud, to him, I'm sure it seems like such a small matter, that's the difference between us, the cost of a dress is just a drop in the ocean to him, to me, it could mean the difference between paying my bills a little longer or not.

"With all that's happened, you're still going to interview there?" Like I have a choice in the matter, regardless of what's happening in my life, I have to be able to pay rent and utilities, I can't expect Rachel to pick up the slack for me, and I sure as hell won't take anything more from the foundation or from Alex.

"When I decided to pursue the divorce, I knew what it meant, and the whole point of going through with it is so that I can move on with my life, I can't hide forever." I'm tired of hiding, I escaped the hell that I lived in only to find myself locked away from the world.

His lips purse as if he is biting back a reply, I wonder what it is he wants to say, but I'm afraid of what it will be, so I don't ask.

Ian turns off the highway, onto a well-traveled dirt road, there is no moon to brighten our path, just the lights of the truck. It's eerie how dark it has gotten, surrounded by a sea of black. My curiosity is growing, my interest piqued, intrigued by what he could be showing me out here.

He stops at the top, turns off the motor and the lights, the darkness presses down on us, there isn't a whisper, far off in the distance I can see the lights of the city. In the stillness, I find a peace that's been missing in my life.

The break in the darkness when Ian opens his door hurts my eyes, startling me. "Come on, there's so much to see.

He opens the back door of the truck. I hadn't noticed all the blankets and pillows piled up in the seat. Ian moves them to the bed. The warm breeze brushes my skin, I watch as he spreads out the blankets and arranges the pillows. "What is all this?" I can't refrain any longer.

"You'll see." The boyish half grin plays on his lips. "Jump up here." He stands on the tailgate, hand outstretched to help me up. I crawl clumsily, joining him, no sooner have I gotten in, he lays down on the makeshift bed he's created. "Just lay back, tell me what you see."

The view is astounding, I haven't seen this many stars since I went to the lake with my mom while I was still in high school. This moment gives me hope that it will all be ok. Right now, everything seems right, I feel free, encompassed by the beauty of the night. The stars raining down on me. Laying here with him, a man that seems to know exactly what to do. A man that's protective, supportive, understanding. Relief washes over me. "This is amazing!"

Just as he did last night, he points out the constellations, and the planets that are visible. Boldly, I move closer to him, he stretches out his arm, allowing me to snuggle in. I feel the heat between us, drawing me in, my fascination of the stars shifts to his face, his lips. I can't help but to lean in, softly pressing my lips to his, his hand cups my face, slowly he deepens our kiss, his other hand caressing my back. It's sensual, seductive, I have no thought of what will happen next, I am lost in him.

Disappointment courses through me when he ends the kiss as gently as it started. "Thank you, Olivia." His words barely audible.

"For what?" Confused as to what I could have done to deserve gratitude.

"For that, for what I hope to be the first kiss of many, for trusting me." I strain to hear his words. I revel in what they mean.

Greg's voice sounds off in my head, *"Don't get yourself all worked up Rae, it doesn't mean what you think it does, he's just trying to talk your pants off."* I push the sound away, whatever this is, it won't be ruined by him.

"I'd like to buy you a dress for the banquet." I sit up suddenly, I wasn't expecting that. "You don't have to answer now, just think about it." He looks away, switching his focus from me back to the stars.

"Thank you, for this, for bringing me here, it's easy to forget how beautiful the stars are when they are lost to the lights. And thank you for not demanding anything of me." I can't imagine a more perfect night. Wanting to use this opportunity to get to know him, to get inside his head, I ask, "If you could do anything in the world, right now, what would it be?" It's a question my mother used to pose to me.

"I'm doing it. This is it, I'm here with you, I couldn't ask for anything more." While I reel at his answer, he opens a cooler that's beside him, pulls out a bottle of champagne, offering me a glass. What do I say to that, how am I supposed to respond to that? "Well, since you're already doing that, what would be your next choice?" My mind tries to comprehend the meaning of his words.

"My next choice, I guess would be to take some time off, go spend some time with my mom in Italy, I haven't seen her since she left." To have the chance to see my mom would be top on my list as well.

"Then you should go, life is too short, there will always be something happening that makes it easy to say, as soon as I finish this or that I'll go, you don't realize that you might miss your chance." My mom and I had so many plans, trips we wanted to take, shows we wanted to see, I can't ever get those back.

"You're right, but until the new club is up and running, I need to be here." He doesn't understand, time waits for no one.

"You and I both know that there isn't anything that you can't handle by phone or by email, or Alex can take care of, so what's really holding you back." Mom always told me, you could really learn about a person by asking that one question, that question opens the door to what a person wants most in life, that question will lead you to learn what drives them and gives you a peek into their wishes.

I expect his question when he asks me the same, but my answer isn't the response that I prepared. "To go back in time, back to when my mother was alive, to years ago, when I felt comfortable in my own skin, back to when I had self-confidence, to a time when I knew who I was, knew where I was going in life." Mom's game only works if you're honest but that wasn't where I meant to go with it.

"In just a matter of days you have regained so much of those things. I have watched as you have warred with yourself to take control again, you will get back there, Olivia." He doesn't mention my mother, it's not in him to deliver the news that I already know, there is no going back, each of us can only move forward.

"My second answer, I would go see The Phantom of the Opera. My mom and I had planned on going to San Francisco, we were going to go in December, every year there's a place that puts it on, even though she can't go with me, I still want to go." We had been getting ready to start buying tickets and making reservations, we were just waiting for the right time.

"You had it on the TV Friday night, when I got to the door, I recognized the music. My mother took me when I was in high school." Another parallel between us.

"I told her that I hated opera, she bought me a CD, the music was so moving, heartbreakingly beautiful. Our plan was to explore the west coast, just her and I. We were so off track with each other before she died, I was keeping secrets from her, I had never done that, I don't know why I kept it from her. I was scared, scared of what would happen to her if she confronted Greg, I was ashamed, I wanted to handle it on my own. In doing so, I pushed her away, I hurt her a lot." Regret surges through me, I'd give anything to go back.

He doesn't say anything, he knows there are no words to take away what I feel, I know that she forgave me, as well as I know that she loved me, but she didn't deserve the way that I treated her, if I could just go back and tell her how sorry I am. Ian pulls me into him. I find solace in his touch, we lay there and watch as the stars move across the sky.

Chapter 26

Ian

She didn't cry, and the tension that I felt when I first pulled her into me dissipated quickly, we lay quietly, each of us considering the revelations of our answers. Knowing that I can't take away her pain but wishing that I could all the same. In the distance a coyote yips, the breeze picks up around us. Both of us content to stay, neither ready to give up the tranquility we've found.

The responsibilities back in the city can't be forgotten for long, begrudgingly we pack up to leave, Olivia, pulls me away from my thoughts, "Thank you Ian, for all of this." She raises her hands and spins in a circle.

"This wasn't me, as much as I'd like to take credit." I wink at her.

"Maybe you didn't create it, but you shared with me something spectacular, thank you." The smile on her face is enough, already I'm thinking what I can do next to make her smile like that again.

Our trip down the mountain seems to take half the time as the way up. She reaches across the console, interlacing her fingers with mine. Aside from the moment of melancholy, this night could not have been more perfect, tonight we were alone in the universe. I need to remember to send Alice flowers, she pulled this all off flawlessly. Once again, going above and beyond what her responsibilities are.

She falls asleep before we are off the mountain, while she sleeps, I consider the things that need to be done. Brett is top priority, I want a conversation with him above all else. I will need to check in with the Superintendent at the Whiskey, get Olivia and Nick together, make sure that all is on track for the banquet on Thursday, and finish preparing my speech. Stephanie can clear my calendar for the week, I'll work from home. It's not a habit I want to create but under the circumstances, it seems like the best course of action.

I let my mind wander, I meant what I'd said, there was nowhere else that I wanted to be than with her. I give my thoughts the freedom to explore the possibilities of what that means. I have never met anyone so resilient. She longs to go back and regain her self-confidence, she fails to see that she gains a little more each day. Statistically speaking, an abused woman will go back to her abuser on average seven times, no matter the atrocities that they endure. Every day she fights to ensure that she doesn't ever have to go back.

What I see when I look at Olivia, courage, tenacity, strength. She is a Phoenix, she has burned and now she is rising from the ashes, beautiful in this new beginning. I am awed by her, and I wish that she could see herself through my eyes.

When Vivian and I first split, I didn't think I would ever find another woman that I would be willing to try to build a life with again. I have spent these years working tirelessly on building my business, Olivia walks into my life and I can't see a future without her. I want to spend the rest of my life seeing her smile every day, doing whatever it takes to make that happen. I want to take her to see Phantom of the Opera, just so that I can watch her take it all in for the first time. I want to take the trip to Italy to see my mother, but I want Olivia by my side when I go, I want to show her the vineyards, explore and experience Tuscany together.

I always loved Vee, but I never felt for her what I feel now for Olivia. Maybe Lawrence is right, maybe I didn't love Vee the way that I should have. Because what her and I had pales in comparison to what I feel right now, for a woman that I met only two weeks ago.

Olivia stirs in the seat beside me as we pull into the garage, I hate to wake her when she's sleeping so soundly but it can't be avoided. "We're home Bellissima." The words roll off my tongue, would she make this her home with me? I know I'm taking things too fast, I can't inundate her with the ramblings of my mind.

Mack is waiting in the garage when we pull in. "We got trouble Ian." Alex's silver Mercedes pulls in next to my truck.

What the hell is going on? "We've been trying to call you for hours, at least ten explosions have gone off at the Whiskey." All the air deflates from my lungs. I left my phone at home, I didn't want any distractions or interruptions. Olivia stands beside me, trying to take in what Mack has said. What could have exploded?

"Ian, we need to get down there, Markus has been there since the first call came in." The enormity of the situation lines Alex's face, Rachel stands beside him.

"Was anyone hurt?" That's what's most important, if everyone is ok, everything else can be fixed, it will just set us back.

"No one was there, the job site was empty, but reports from Markus indicate that the damage is substantive." What is substantive? I'm relieved that no one has been injured. I feel a tremble that shudders through Olivia and put my arm around her shoulders.

"Mack, you take the ladies upstairs and stay with them, Alex, I'll meet you there." I know that whatever happened out there, it isn't good. I can tell just by the look on Alex's face, but I won't allow my thoughts to take over before I can judge for myself.

"Olivia, will you be alright here? I have to get a handle on this." This isn't how I intended to end our evening, I'd prefer not to leave her but considering what happened at Trinity, I don't think it's wise to take her with me. I don't know how long I'll be, I'm sure there will be questions to answer, reports that will need to be made, it will be another long night.

"Go, we'll be fine." She's putting on a strong front, but I see in her eyes how upsetting this is, they've changed from the normal caramel color, to a dark coffee. I see the questions swimming, and the unsurety if this is an accident or intentional.

"I'll be back as soon as I can." Rachel hovers near, when my arm drops from Olivia's shoulders, hers replaces it.

Pulling into the dirt lot, I wasn't prepared. The building that would house the bar and the restaurant were still ablaze, a good portion of the stadium, reduced to rubble. Firefighters, law enforcement, the fucking bomb squad, what I can only assume is federal agents, what the hell happened here? Markus is milling around with them, I suspect gathering as much information as he can. The press back behind barricades, calling my name, hollering questions. *"Mr. Alessandro, where is Olivia Daniels?"* We knew it wouldn't take long for them to figure out who she is. I ignore the reporter.

"Mr. Alessandro, we're going to need you to back up, the area hasn't been secured. Until we're certain there won't be another explosion, you'll need to clear the area." My mind races with the possibilities of what could have happened. *"Mr. Alessandro, are you aware that Olivia Daniels owned a bar in Manhattan that was destroyed by arson?"* Once they knew her name, there was a wealth of information for them to feed off of.

"What else could be left to explode? Whatever flammable materials must have ignited by now." Soot is smudged on the man's face, his sweat leaving trails through the black. *"Mr. Alessandro, has Olivia Daniels shared her marital status with you?"* And so, the circus begins, I'm equipped to handle whatever they may throw my way, will Olivia be able to withstand the pressure and the accusations? Some of the press isn't interested in the story before them, they are looking for the gossip.

"That's all secondary blasts, it's not official but the initial detonations were explosives sir, someone did this intentionally." Alex has joined me, we stare in disbelief at the destruction of all we've been working on for months. This is more than a setback, this will be a complete rebuild.

It's hard not to wonder if this has something to do with Greg, the timing, the threat yesterday, but I don't want to be focused on just one possibility. I have my own enemies, but right now the only one that makes sense is Greg.

"Her husband is a psycho, how the hell did he accomplish this?" Alex's thoughts follow suit with mine.

"I think it's imperative that we talk to Brett, sooner, rather than later, he's going to be the key." My voice even and calm, I haven't wrapped my head around what is happening. After all these years of planning, waiting for the right time, all of it is gone. As if to solidify the point, another explosion on the far side of the stadium goes off, the force of the blast rocking me and Alex back on our heels.

"Sir, I need you to clear the area, there's nothing you can do here right now, go home, we'll be in touch." New flames build at the last explosion point. Maybe it's because I know that Olivia is at home, or maybe it's because the scene before me is making me physically ill, either way, I agree with the Chief. Tomorrow there will be more answers, until then, I can't watch.

Rachel and Olivia are huddled on the couch together when Alex and I get off the elevator. Rachel runs to Alex, and Olivia to me. There is no hesitation when she throws herself into my arms, she hugs me tight and I bury my face in her hair, the smell of strawberries fills my nostrils. With everything wrong happening outside, this feels right, she feels like home.

Alex claps me on the back, him and Rachel get back on the elevator, Olivia and I still standing, wrapped up in each other.

"I'm so sorry Ian, I never would have thought that this would happen, I don't know what else I can say." I hear the quiver in her voice, she's taking responsibility for what she had no control of.

"This isn't you, I don't want another apology, you didn't do this. We don't know who did, so don't carry this one Olivia." I can't imagine what she feels or what she's thinking, it doesn't matter if this is Greg, it's not on her.

"How can you say that? Yesterday, the phone call, you know as well as I do, if it weren't for me, none of this would be happening!" She's pulled away from me, looking in my eyes, speaking with conviction. My arms still wrapped around her waist, I lean into her and rest my forehead on hers.

"Regardless of the circumstance, YOU didn't do this. Even if it is him, he made the choice. Don't take responsibility for things that he does Olivia, you can't control him, nor his actions. Tomorrow, we will get some answers, then we'll go from there, but it's not on you." Her body tenses, she's poised to make another argument. "I really just want to lie down with you in my arms and try to get some sleep."

Her body relaxes and she lets out the breath she intended to use to protest, without another word, she leads me back to the bedroom. While she's in the bathroom, I use the closet, I change out of my jeans into basketball shorts and a clean t shirt, not ideal as I normally sleep in my underwear, but preferable to the suit I wore to sleep in on Friday and the jeans I slept in last night.

She is a vision when she emerges, her hair free from the ponytail, loose down her back, her face clean and fresh, still damp from being freshly washed, natural, exquisite. Wearing shorts and a tank top, a puckered red scar peeking out around the strap of her shirt.

"Do you want to talk about it? I know it's not the same, but I can empathize." She's timid in her question. As much as I know that she can relate, I don't, for now, I want to shut out the outside world, not consider what tomorrow will bring. But I know that even if we don't talk about the Whiskey, she needs to know the press have identified her. We are about to be front page of every gossip rag there is.

"There's something I need to tell you Olivia, the press was swarmed down there, they know who you are, they've been digging." Her expression doesn't change.

"We knew they would, none of that matters, the press is going to say whatever gets them the most sales, they aren't interested in the truth, only what sells. What's happening to the Whiskey, that's what is important." It's not the reaction I was expecting, granted we expected them to find out, I just thought she would take it harder when it happened.

"Are you ready for the gossip that I'm sure has already started? Tomorrow's publications will be much different than today, one of the questions I heard was about Trinity, while I'd like to believe that's the worst, I have a long history with the press, they won't be kind." Her expression doesn't change, she nods in agreement. With all the articles that I read, I know she's no stranger to negative press either.

Chapter 27

Olivia

Tomorrow, it will all be on display for Las Vegas, anonymity will be over. Somehow, I managed to tie myself to the most recognizable person in the city. I didn't consider the ramifications, not that I had a choice anyway, and most certainly not that I would change it.

He interrupts my thoughts, "Can I ask you a question?" He waits for my assent before continuing, "Will you tell me about this?" His finger barely brushes the puckered red scar that's exposed by my choice of attire. The memories of the night that happened come forefront, Ian misunderstands my hesitation. "I apologize, I shouldn't have asked." His voice full of regret.

"Greg and I went to a ball for his office, he was gunning for promotion." His body stiffens next to me. "We spent the evening rubbing elbows with the district attorney, the mayor, senators, congressmen. It wasn't a good night for me,

I was exhausted, I was sore, the night before I had slept handcuffed in a closet for some transgression that I can't recall." I feel Ian's heartbeat quicken against me. "I was ready to go home, that angered Greg, he told me to sit and wait for him, we would leave when he said." I knew I was in for another long night, he would be sure I fully understood his displeasure. "While I sat at the bar sipping a glass of wine, some guy sat a few stools down, I knew better than to engage him, but I didn't know what other option I had when he started talking to me." To not speak to one of Greg's colleagues would be rude. "It was small talk, nothing interesting, Greg saw us speaking and made his way over. The tension that rolled off him was daunting, I knew that he was unhappy. Through gritted teeth, he told me we were leaving, with only a curt nod to the man that was talking to me." His displeasure was obvious, I questioned if there was something that I could have done different, even now I wonder if there was any way I could have handled the situation that would have changed the outcome.

"If it's too painful, you don't have to go on Olivia, I don't know what possessed me to ask." It's relieving to talk about it, I'm learning that hiding it all away is slowly eating away at me.

"We rode home in silence, I knew from previous experiences that the silence indicated he was seething, fully aware that anything I said would only make it worse, I stayed quiet. I couldn't do anything to prevent what was about to happen, but I could ensure that I didn't make it worse. At home I went straight to our room, he sat in his chair, still not saying anything. I let myself believe that I might have let my imagination run away with me, that perhaps I had misread him. It wasn't until a little later that I learned how wrong I was. I drifted to sleep, letting the comfort of our bed take me away, I woke being punched in the ribs, he called me a whore, told me that I had humiliated him in front of everyone. He got nose to nose with me and screamed the vilest things. He pulled me out of bed by my hair, he kicked me over and over again, then he told me to get up, no sooner had I stood that he pushed me back on the bed, looking up at him, I had never seen him look more menacing than that moment, his face obscured by shadow, a cigar hanging out of his mouth." Up until that night, I knew that Greg was depraved, I knew that he was evil. "It was like looking at the devil himself, he ripped my clothes off of me, told me how hideous I was, that I should be grateful that he still wants me as damaged as I was, and then he forced himself on me, making it as painful as he could, while looking down on me with a maniacal grin. When he was done, he put his cigar out right here, as a reminder that I had hurt his heart. A hurt that he would carry with him the rest of his life, that it was only fitting that I have something as well." I feel the anger vibrating off Ian, I felt the same from Greg on many occasions. The difference, Ian's anger doesn't set me on edge, it doesn't instigate fear, his anger isn't directed at me and I'm proud of myself that I can distinguish that now, there was a time when I couldn't.

"Jesus, Olivia, I know that the things you've told me the last few days barely scratch the surface of what you've been through, I can't express how sorry I am that you had to suffer the way that you have." My mother's words echo, *we all play the cards we're dealt.* I let it all happen, I let it go on, I know that what he did isn't right and that no one should ever go through what I did, but I still have to accept my responsibility as well. If I hadn't excused his behavior early on, if I hadn't accepted it, maybe things would have been different. I won't ever know. I played the cards I was dealt when I should have turned them in and drawn a new hand.

"Thank you for asking, I've always feared the questions, I've spent a lot of time trying to forget all of it, frustrated that I can't. Telling it out loud is freeing, because in locking it away, I've been locking away part of myself as well." It wasn't my intention to tell him in such detail, I never imagined I would ever tell anyone all of it. His demeanor, the gentleness, his calm, just pulls the words out of me.

"You are an enigma, you don't see the strength that you possess, the determination, you don't realize the fortitude that you exhibit, not just in what you survived, but in the way that you carry on now. The courage that it took to expose yourself in filing for divorce, most people can't understand that, but I do, you are an inspiration, just being who you are. You are the epitome of Invictus." He doesn't know that he has just given me the most meaningful compliment of my life.

As I drift off to sleep, I recall William Ernest Henley's poem that got me through the hardest of days:

Out of the night that covers me,

Black as the pit from pole to pole,

I thank whatever gods may be,

For my unconquerable soul.

In the fell clutch of circumstance,

I have not winced nor cried aloud.

Under the bludgeoning's of chance,

My head is bloody, but unbowed.

Beyond this place of wrath and tears,

Looms but the Horror of the shade,

And yet the menace of the years

Finds, and shall find, me unafraid.

It matters not how straight the gate,

How charged with punishments the scroll,

I am the master of my fate:

I am the captain of my soul.

Waking up this morning I was aware of what would be in the papers, what I didn't count on were the feelings that would immerge seeing the devastation at the Whiskey. I skimmed through the articles, the reputable news sites focused on the story at hand. The pictures were graphic and brought forward the memories of standing in front of Trinity while it burned, my heart aches for the man sitting across from me.

It's been a quiet morning, he didn't say anything when he got up this morning. He kissed the top of my head before he showered and dressed, back in a three-piece suit to handle the obligations that he will face today. As I look at him, I'm torn, freshly shaven, hair tamed and in place, he looks like he belongs on the cover of GQ, but yesterday, in his baggy jeans and t-shirt, tousled hair and scruff on his face, he looked every bit as good. I laugh out loud at the absurdity of my thoughts.

Ian looks up from the paper he's reading, the boyish half grin playing on his lips, "What could possibly be funny?" Heat rises to my cheeks, I've given myself away.

"I can't decide if you're more handsome today, all cleaned up and spit shined, or yesterday when you were dressed down. It's a serious dilemma that I intend spending the rest of the day finding the conclusion to." The grin that I love so much expands, his laugh fills the room and my heart, in light of everything, him being able to laugh, lightens the dread that I feel for the day ahead.

"I can hardly wait to hear the arguments, if I think of anything that may aid in your research, I'll text you." The playful banter is fun, the opposite of the way my life once was. Greg would have been angry that I wasn't taking the situation at hand seriously, he would have been lost in his own feelings and would have lashed out that I was being unsympathetic. I push the thought aside, I can't compare these two men, they are as different as night and day, and frankly it's insulting to Ian, even if it's in my own head.

"Are you sure you don't want me to go?" I don't really want to see firsthand, but he has been with me every second of this weekend, available to lean on, pulling me through the most difficult moments I've had to face since coming to Vegas. How can I not offer him the same support?

"As much as I appreciate the offer, this will be a long day, full of meetings, questions and sifting through the rubble to find answers, you don't want to watch all of that." I don't, but I will. "I don't want you to watch all of it, Rachel has to work this evening, but Alex said she's going to come see you for a while." Maybe she can help me to make sense of all of this, I'm confused by the feelings I have about Ian, distressed at the lack of fear that I have for the things happening around me, and dismayed that Greg is responsible for the devastation at the Whiskey. "Are you ready to see what the Vegas Voice is reporting?" He hadn't handed that one over yet of course not.

The Vegas Voice

Breaking News

A series of 17 explosions at the Whiskey Wrangler last night rocked the surrounding community. While the source of the explosions is unknown, an anonymous source within the fire department has said that the blasts were intentional. Ian Alessandro, casino mogul and owner of the Whiskey Wrangler arrived at the scene three hours after the first blast was reported. Neither him nor his representatives would give a statement.

The mystery woman Mr. Alessandro was with on Saturday we have confirmed as Olivia Daniels, the wife of New York City Assistant District Attorney Gregory Daniels, and owner of an establishment in Manhattan that was destroyed by arson nearly four years ago. Coincidental?

We reached out to Assistant DA Daniels, his wife Olivia, recently filed for divorce, he states, "I'm going to fight the divorce, I just want my wife back. We've had some rough times and I haven't been the best husband, I just want her to give me the chance to make things right between us. I hope whoever this guy is will step aside so that I can put my family back together." Mr. Alessandro stands between the attorney that puts the bad guys away and his wife.

"Son of a bitch, they just made me the most hated woman in the country, and you the villain. Greg's inferred that I left him to be with you. If that was the case, shouldn't he be suspect number one? Why don't they make that implication?" I wasn't expecting a quote from Greg, I expected Trinity to come up, I expected the divorce, but Greg spoke with them, he's playing the victim, he's not only going after me, but after Ian. If nothing else, at least we know, he's going to contest the divorce. What does that mean? What happens now?

Chapter 28

Ian

It's only the beginning, I can imagine the accusations they will throw out next, right now they are leading with implications, leading people to form an opinion without any context to the facts. Because he's in New York, and we're here, because leading the city to believe that I am reaping Karma for engaging with a woman that's married, will sell more papers. Because no one wants to believe that a man in such a position of authority could do anything wrong, and to make that implication without evidence would be suicide for their publication.

"It's not the first time I've been the villain, it won't be the last." I was the villain in my divorce as well, Vee spoke to anyone who would listen, made the divorce all my fault, her affairs, her drug use, she took no responsibility and all of them conveniently forgot those things. I was the villain for initiating the divorce and leaving Vivian alone with little to show from our marriage.

"Markus and Alex are meeting me downstairs. Markus will brief us with the information he's attained, I'll have to meet with law enforcement as well. Ryan is in the library, if you need anything, let him know, or send me a text." As much as I'd rather stay here with her, I don't want to hold any of the meetings here. Markus made me aware that not only will I be meeting with local law enforcement but also the ATF and homeland security, there isn't any question that some kind of explosives were used. Alex and I will need to determine how to get to the bottom of this without involving Olivia.

"How are you handling all of this so calmly? When I lost Trinity, I was a wreck. I was angry, frustrated, sad, disappointed, a random act committed by a stranger. You just lost a dream that you've been building for years, you know who did it and you know why, yet you aren't blaming me, you're still able to smile, you're about to go downstairs as if it's just another day in the office." If Greg is behind this it still isn't her fault, how could I hold her responsible for the actions of a deranged man trying to get to her.

"I can't change what happened, I only have control of how I react to the situation and how I proceed. I am angry, honestly, I'm furious, but I must put that aside in order to get to the bottom of things, anger will only warp my perception. Additionally, there's a lot to be grateful for, no one was injured, the jobsite was vacant. If it is Greg, then the opportunity presents itself to press charges in Nevada, to see him go to prison without you ever having to return to New York. It's just a place, it can be rebuilt, you're safe, that's what's important." Part of Olivia's reasoning for not filing charges against Greg is her fear of returning to New York, Nevada can't pick it up, unless he does something to her here. Right now, until we can prove he was on that plane, he's never stepped foot in Nevada.

She searches my eyes trying to understand. We stand face to face, one step and I could wrap my arms around her, but I don't, instead I reach for her hand and bring it to my lips. Not the parting kiss that I want, but the one I think she needs. As I turn to the elevator she pulls me back, pulling me into her, her lips searching for mine, different from last night, this kiss is demanding and urgent, one hand on my neck pulling me in, the other holding around my waist, reluctantly she softens the press of her mouth to mine.

"Text me if I can help." She releases her hold on me, I leave her with a kiss on her forehead.

Alex and I meet up in the reception area outside my office, Stephanie informs us that Markus is waiting inside. I turn my thoughts of Olivia to the matters at hand. "Markus, what do we know?" He looks tired, I would imagine, he spent the night at the Whiskey, when all of this is over, I owe the man a nice vacation.

"Whoever is responsible for this knew what they were doing and had access to dynamite. It's not official yet, but I was able to ascertain information from the bomb squad." Is that the reason that Greg made the trip out here, did he need to get in contact with a supplier? Try as I might, it's difficult to not zero in on him. "I've got some guys working on surveillance cameras in the area, as well as traffic cams. Local police, as well as the ATF, DHS, and FBI are doing the same, but we won't have access to their reports, nor will they share information in an ongoing investigation." The Vegas Voice may have done us a favor, unintentionally they have made Greg a suspect with their article.

"Have you gotten any new information regarding Greg Daniels? Who he was in contact with while he was here?" Markus shakes his head, he updates Alex with the information he's already given me.

"In my opinion, he couldn't make this happen in that amount of time, even if he's been talking to someone over the phone, this takes time to plan, the dynamite was strategically placed to cause the most damage, whoever did this knew exactly where to put it for complete demolition." Greg has a lot of connections, access to a database that would give him the intel, he's the only one that makes sense, I disagree with Markus on this one.

"So, what are your thoughts Markus? Do you have any theories we should be exploring?" Alex is doing what I should be, he's looking for other possibilities, not fixating on Greg.

"I'm looking into it, as soon as I get the confirmation, I will let you know, until then, I don't want to cast undue suspicion." I could argue, but I respect a man that researches the facts before making accusations that could be damaging to someone's reputation.

Stephanie's voice comes over the intercom, "Mr. Alessandro, Special Agent Miller and some associates are here to see you." Alex opens the office door, inviting them in.

"I'm Special Agent Tom Miller, ATF, this is Special Agent Harold Watkins, DHS, and this is Federal Agent Bonnie Harris, FBI. We will be heading up the case at the Whiskey Wrangler." Alex and Markus introduce themselves, I've worked with Alex long enough to keep my mouth shut until he says otherwise.

"Mr. Alessandro, we were called in because of the nature of the incident last night at the Whiskey Wrangler. At approximately 11:30 pm, numerous incendiary devices as well as explosive devices were detonated, at this time we have agents still sifting through the scene. Can you tell us where you were prior to 11:30 pm?" Special Agent Miller sits across from me, Agents Watkins and Harris stand close by. Alex nods at me to answer the question.

"If you are asking if I blew up my stadium and set my bar on fire, the answer is no, I took a friend to Gass Peak last night for stargazing, we left about 8:30 and didn't return until around 2:30 this morning." Alex confirms my return time, questioning Agent

Miller on specifics, looking for details that could assist us in our own investigation and being stonewalled with every question, Markus taking notes at the back of the room.

"Do you have anyone in mind that you suspect Mr. Alessandro, anyone you've had issues with recently?" The only person I believe capable of this is Greg, the dilemma is leading them in that direction without involving Olivia. "We understand there was a tense moment at the hospital between you and your ex father in law, Lawrence Michaels, would you care to elaborate on that?" How the hell did they dig that up so quickly, do they think that Lawrence could have done this.

"All of the interactions I have with Lawrence are tense, he holds me responsible for his daughter's actions, but I don't think that he would do something like this." Lawrence doesn't have the know-how or the stomach.

"We are just exploring all leads that have been presented so far. What can you tell us about Gregory Daniels?" Is he inadvertently implying they have reason to suspect Lawrence? Besides Vivian, I think they have it covered who I've pissed off most recently.

"I don't know him personally, but a friend is currently seeking a divorce from him." Now we're getting somewhere, I am ninety-nine percent sure that Greg is responsible for this. He has the knowledge, and he has the influence and the tools to seek out those that would be capable of carrying this out in his absence. Try as I might to be open-minded, I keep circling back to him.

"I think that answers our questions for now, if you think of anything else that is pertinent, call me. For now, the site is off limits until our investigation is complete." I've been barred from the Whiskey, Agents Miller, Watkins, and Harris shake hands with Alex and I before they depart.

My phone vibrates in my pocket, hoping it might be Olivia, I reach for it, as I pull it from my pocket a folded, lined sheet of paper comes out with it landing on my desk. My mother's face is on the screen, no doubt she has gotten word of all that's transpired. I respond to her with a text message, promising to call her back later.

Markus announces his exit, one of his guys is looking for assistance, and Alex needing to get back to his office follows behind him, when anything new comes up we'll meet again. Sitting back in my chair, I try to make the connections between the few things the Agents had said, unable to concentrate, I call my mother so that she doesn't have to worry any further.

"Mama! All is well, no one has been hurt." As soon as she answers, I respond to the questions that I know she will ask.

"Ian, what happened?" I give her the information that I have but keep from her who I suspect is the culprit. "Does this have something to do with the article in the Vegas Voice yesterday, the phone call on Saturday? Are you seeing a woman that's married?" My mother tries not to pry, but under these circumstances she isn't able to refrain from asking.

"Mama, I promise, when the time is right and I'm able, I will tell you all that I can, at this time though, you're just going to have to be satisfied that I'm alright and so is Alex." I hate that she will continue to worry, but there isn't anything that I can do about it. I tell her that I love her and end the call.

I still need to find Brett, and get him in here, I call Flynn looking for an update, he's been looking for him since Saturday, so far Brett's been a ghost.

I unfold the paper I found in my pocket. Surprised by what it contains.

Open My Heart

My heart has traveled down a road,

That tears my soul in two

With many dreams that were shattered,

And love that was untrue

Now I stand alone,

With a wall around my heart

Fearing that every man,

Will tear my world apart

One can only take so much,

Before they live in fear

The eyes can only cry so much,

Before there's no more tears

So, if you want my heart,

I'm afraid you'll have to fight

Show me that you love me,

And hold me very tight

For now, that is the only way

To unlock my heart's gate

Though it may take some time,

My love is worth the wait

When I learn to trust again

When I know your love is true

I'll open up my heart,

And tell you, I love you

A glimpse inside her mind, a window to her heart. She is trying to tell me how she feels, to say the things that she's unable to articulate any other way.

Chapter 29

Olivia

I've studied the pictures on the mantle and watched as the world went by 56 stories below me, my nerves fried wondering if he found what I slipped in his jacket this morning, questioning my rash decision to give it to him, especially now. I haven't heard from him, I don't know if he's found it, or could he have lost it, or if he read it and doesn't know how to let me down easy. Ugh... I should have done it differently. Last night, after he started to softly snore, I was still keyed up, my mind wouldn't shut off. My notebook was on the bedside table, the words came so easily, a quick scribble by the light of my phone. This morning, I had transferred the words, so they were legible, the idea to slip it into his pocket wasn't thought out, I just acted on impulse.

"Ollie?" Ryan interrupts my thoughts, "there's a delivery on its way up, would you like me to get it?" Funny that he has fallen into the nickname given to me by

Rachel, he doesn't follow the lead of his boss using my given name, Ian is still the only one that uses it. Is he asking me to take a delivery for Ian or just giving me some notice that someone will be arriving?

"I can get it Ryan, thanks for the heads up." It's only moments after he returned to the library that I hear the elevator.

"Ms. Mason, these are for you." She doesn't use my married name, I cringed internally as soon as I heard Ms. She's thin, and older, a Lost Cities Floral nametag on her shirt, her hair pulled tight into a bun, and hands me an enormous vase, overflowing with purple irises, gardenias, and tiger lilies. She didn't wait for a response before getting on the elevator again. I know these are from Ian, he remembered, the silly 100 questions game we played, my favorite flower was one of his questions. I pull the card with my name written in neat, elegant script,

Forever is how long I'll wait for the key that unlocks your heart's gate.

~*Ian*~

He found it, I let out a sigh of relief, not just that he found it, but his reaction. It was completely out of character for me to share my writing, but I felt compelled to give him that piece, he was the inspiration, additionally, it explains how I feel. There is something between us, a connection that I can't explain, it's been so easy to tell him things that until now I have kept hidden. I've felt no shame, nor embarrassment.

Rachel arrives as I sit at the breakfast bar, inhaling the scent of the irises, feeling the softness of the petals, lost in the confusion of what's happening between Ian and me.

"Hey Doll! I thought you didn't like flowers." Until now, not really, flowers, roses in specific were a non-apology, the first couple times Greg sent them, I believed in the message, but it didn't take long to realize they were only meant to smooth things over. I grew to hate the smell, each delivery was a reminder, and message, sorry, not sorry.

"Well, I guess it depends on where they come from, because these, these I like a lot." I feel the heat rise to my cheeks. Even with all that's happened, I'm giddy, I haven't been giddy in so many years, I don't think I got giddy when Greg and I were dating. To be honest, Greg and I had a good time in the beginning, we didn't have a lot in common, but back then we were both willing to compromise. Our dating just progressed, there was never a swoon moment, we progressed and after dating for two years, it just seemed like the next step. He was never romantic, not that it was entirely his fault, I worked nights, we stopped dating and just fell into a routine, before his parents were killed, I was content.

"Spill it! How have you so effortlessly taken Vegas's most eligible bachelor off the market?" After reading the card from Ian she's all but jumping out of her seat, I'm hoping she can explain it to me, because I have no idea what the hell is happening, I just don't want it to stop.

Last night I didn't go into detail, both of us were in shock, we both worried while Alex and Ian went to the Whiskey. Neither of us knew what to expect, or if something would happen to them while they were there.

When I get her up to date with all that's happened between us, she says, "He's a smart man, he sees through you like I do, he sees in here." She points to my heart. When I start to shake my head, she stops me, "Stop it Ollie, you are an intelligent, kind, beautiful woman. You saddled yourself with a shitty human being that didn't value you for who you are. Now his voice is stuck in your head and he's fucking wrong! You can't see past the things he made you believe and the scars that he left on you. I'm going to tell you again, and I will keep telling you until you realize it's true, YOU ARE AMAZING! Everyone around you sees it, you're the only one with doubts." I wasn't always this way, it really wasn't even that long ago, compliments didn't make me avert my eyes, I didn't question the motives behind them.

"Do you think I'm foolish?" All the wreckage that I'm causing in his life, if I wasn't so selfish, if I didn't crave that security that he instills in me, I would walk away from him, because he deserves better than what's happening to him right now. "Maybe he does feel something toward me, but how long will that last before he says I'm not worth it, Greg just bombed his lifelong dream." I couldn't blame him if he did, if he walked off the elevator right now and told me to get out, I would go and not hold any ill feelings toward him.

"He would never say that, his lifelong dream has been postponed, we don't know that Greg did this, Alex told me the agents they met with questioned Ian about his ex-father in law, he said that him and Ian had some tension between them at the hospital when his ex-wife overdosed on heroin." It dawns on me how little we have talked about him, he's answered all my questions, told me about his mother, hell I even met his ex-wife, but he changed the subject away from her as soon as we got in the car.

"We all know that Greg is behind this, the calls that he got when he took me to see the Whiskey prove it." Before she can reply the elevator opens, I look expecting to see Ian but instead it's a woman holding dress bags.

"Ms. Mason? My name is Myra, Mr. Alessandro asked me to bring these up to you, there are three different sizes, he asked that you try them on." How does Ian live like this? Anyone can just walk into his place anytime? "I can help you if you like, if the size is a bit off, we can tailor it to fit." What has he done?

Her white hair framed around her face, still surprised by not only her visit but what she has in her hands, I forget my manners, fortunately, Rachel jumps off her seat to help the woman.

Ryan pops out from around the corner, "Sorry Ollie, I meant to let you know that someone else was arriving, I just got wrapped up in the report I'm working on." He looks like a kid that's about to be reprimanded for doing something wrong.

"Thanks, it's fine." At least someone was forewarned of her arrival. I can't hold it against him, he has enough on his plate without acting like a butler to announce the arrival of guests, I could almost bet, that isn't in his job description.

While Myra holds two of the bags, Rachel has relieved her of one, "Oh Ollie, this is so beautiful!" She's unzipped the bag, but she hasn't turned so that I can see what's in it. "It's perfect!" It's the same color as the irises, deep, the color of royalty, the top is fitted and sleeveless, made of satin or silk, adorned with crystals making it sparkle. Though there aren't any sleeves, he considered my scars, the edges of the sleeve would stop at the top of my arm, covering most. The dress is long and flows, freely moving. I've never seen anything like it, I can't imagine how much something like this would cost. As I finger the material, I can't help but look for a price tag. I didn't agree that he could buy me a dress.

"Let's go! Myra, we'll be right back." Rachel turns me in the direction of the bedroom, pushing me forward, relieves Myra of the other two bags and follows me down the hall.

With all that he has going on right now, he took the time to stop in not one but two different shops to send me gifts, he isn't like anyone that I've ever met. His calm demeanor, his concern of how I feel rather than how he feels, his generosity but most of all, just how easy it is to be around him, to talk to him.

"Ollie, come back from lala land, try this on doll!" Rachel's words pull me back from my thoughts. She's holding one of the dresses up, the back unzipped, ready for me to step into. I'm not ashamed in front of Rachel, she's seen the scars before, accidentally, but she's seen them. When she walked into the bathroom that day, I heard her gasp before she apologized and closed the door. When I emerged a few minutes later, her eyes were rimmed with red, still glossy from tears that she'd shed but she never asked, never expected an explanation, and most importantly she never pitied me. She just waited, it was several weeks later that I told her, I will never forget the horrified look in her eyes. She never asked a question, she was just content with what I told her. Now she knows most of it but not because she pried, only because I let her in, a little at a time. I pull my t-shirt over my head and take off my jeans. Rachel holds the dress as I step into it, she chose the largest of the three.

She meets my eyes in the mirror as she zips up the back, stopping below my shoulder blades, it fits well through the waist, hiding the belly that I've developed but there is no way it will close up top. "Wait here, I'll be right back." She bounces out of the room. It's more beautiful than I could have imagined, the high neck, fitted bodice and the skirt that flows below my waist, I turn side to side, the dress swirls around my legs and feet. The scars on my back would be hidden, only a few of the smaller ones would be visible on my arms.

Rachel returns with a tape, she measures around my chest, measures the gap in the zipper, taking the time to note the numbers on the palm of her hand. "She can let it out up here, I think there's enough room, we don't want to go up a size because you will lose the fit down here and it's perfect! You're beautiful Doll!" She gathers my hair off my neck, pulling it into a messy bun on top of my head. "Look at you!" She squeals.

"I don't know if I can afford this Rachel." I know he said he wanted to buy me a dress, but I don't want him to, he's done so much for me already, this is just too much.

"You know as well as I do, Ian sent this as a gift, swallow your pride, say thank you, and do him the honor of walking into that banquet as his date for the evening." She doesn't mince words, she usually doesn't. I struggle with what she says, is it my pride holding me back?

I touch the jewels sewn into the dress around the neckline, feel the softness of the skirt, I feel beautiful, I can picture Ian and I walking in, him in a tux and me in this dress, it excites me, makes me hopeful, can I set aside my pride? Rachel's right, he didn't send this up expecting me to buy it, the price tags have been removed on all of them, was that at his request?

"Ok." It's all that I can get out, so much is jumbled in my head, I can't make a coherent sentence.

Rachel takes the dresses back to Myra while I redress, I look at my reflection and wonder how this is all possible? How did I get so lucky to find these people?

Chapter 30

Ian

Since going to the office was unavoidable today, I decide to handle all the business that I can before going back upstairs. On my way to a department manager meeting, I glimpsed the vase of flowers, I hesitated before I went in, but it seemed to be the best way to let her know that I got her note. On the way back I stopped in Flair, after seeing the dress in the window, envisioning how ravishing Olivia would look in it, I thought I would take her lack of response as her assent to let me buy her a dress for the banquet.

As I return calls and clear my schedule for the rest of the week, I keep glancing at my cell, waiting for her to message. Nerves tighten my stomach, I'm suddenly unsure if I made the right choice, wondering if I might be pushing her too hard, too fast. Because of her poem I grew confident, that confidence may have led me to overstep.

My thoughts are interrupted by Markus coming through the door. I signal for him to wait, as the conference call I'm on wraps up.

"What do you know of Lawrence's military career?" Markus wastes no time as soon as I replace the receiver in the cradle.

"I don't know much, just that he served in the army for 8 years, why?" It's not a topic he entertained, and certainly not one that he brought up.

"I got a hold of some video, his car has been in the vicinity of the Whiskey for the last week. When I pulled up his record, he was a munitions specialist, the training that he has makes him prime suspect in my book. He's furious with you over the divorce and rehab and Ms. Michael's problems, I don't believe it's a coincidence that his car has been nearby for an entire week prior to last night's events." Is Lawrence really the one responsible for this? Is he really that blinded with hatred?

"Additionally, I got a line on one of the phone numbers that called you and a couple of the calls to the Ragtime, it's a payphone used by inmates of Woodbourne prison, in New York. It's an unlisted number and because it's within the prison, it took some time to sort out." None of this makes any sense. Don't inmates have to call collect?

"How is an inmate calling me? Do you know who?" It's asking a lot, but Markus doesn't usually fail to deliver.

"I'm working on it, and I'm trying to piece together how it all fits. When I know more, you will." He leaves before I can say anything else. More pieces to add to the puzzle, the problem is, none of them seem to work together. My positivity that Greg is responsible for the Whiskey is waning, but I'm still not counting him out, just considering the possibility that Lawrence may be Greg's contact, perhaps they struck a deal to work together to strike at Olivia and I at the same time?

It seems the more information we get the more tangled the web we fall into. With nothing else left to do in the office, I make my exit. Still unsure what to expect at home, but knowing that's where I need to be, to face whatever consequences for my actions that there may be, and to pass on this new information to Ryan so he can add to what he's working on. I'm nervous, like a kid standing on the doorstep of his first date as I ride up the elevator. It's not rejection that I'm concerned about, it's how I may have made Olivia feel, that I may have pushed too hard and pushed her away.

When the elevator doors open, all doubt fades away, her face lights up and her smile brightens the room. Before I've made it two steps out of the elevator, she has me locked in her embrace, her face nuzzling my neck, my nerves subside, the uneasiness melts away.

"Thank you for the flowers... And thank you for the dress. How did you remember my favorites?" How could I forget? I burned every answer to memory.

"The little things are important, I try to treat them as such, I wanted you to know that I was thinking of you today, you were all I could think of today. When I saw that dress, I could see you in it, like it was made just for you." I would have rather stayed home with her today but finding that dress was worth venturing out.

"After some alterations I'll have to agree with you, Myra said she will have it back tomorrow. Thank you again, it's beautiful." Perhaps Olivia and I will go out tomorrow and find whatever else she may need for Thursday.

We fall into easy conversation, her day with Rachel, the dress, the flowers. I pull ingredients out of the fridge, I intend to wow her with my cooking skills. Mama made sure that I knew how to cook, she said that one of nicest things you can do for a woman is to give her the night off with a home cooked meal.

Olivia joins me in the kitchen, following my lead, anticipating what needs done next, working by my side. When she stopped speaking, we kept moving together, embracing the quiet, moving together in our own little dance.

It isn't long before she asks about the Whiskey, if I had any information. I tell her about the interview with the feds, the meeting with Markus, his thoughts and even the thoughts I've been entertaining. The possibility that Greg found out who I am and sought out Lawrence, both getting what they want, Greg to get to Olivia and Lawrence to get at me.

"Let's have a change of pace, you know all about me, some things that I've never told anyone, tell me about you. You've talked a bit about your mother and Alex, but what about you?" I haven't really thought about it, probably because I'd rather hear about her than talk about myself.

"I was born here. I've spent my whole life in Vegas. I met Vivian in high school, I fell in love with her the moment I saw her." I don't spend a lot of time giving her the details of Vee, not that I want to keep it from her, but isn't it a rule to not talk about your ex? Hell, I don't know how this works. "I bought this casino with my winnings, it was on the verge of shutting down and being boarded up, little by little, year by year, I just kept adding and improving, then started venturing into clubs and other casinos." It's strange to talk about myself, it's not easy to tell her without sounding like a braggart. I don't want to come off that way, I know that I got lucky, I've been sure to keep that in mind as my businesses grew, as well as remembering where I came from. Knowing that without the luck and the support of those around me, especially mama and Vee, none of this would have been possible.

"What happened to you and Vivian? It sounds like you guys were really in love." She asks quietly, unsure if she should.

"We were, but sometimes love isn't enough. It's my fault really, she's an only child, as we dated in high school, I was able to give her all she needed, attention mostly. She spent her whole life with her mother and father doting on her, throughout school, I did the same. It was just ingrained in her to be the center of everything, back then I agreed, she was the center of my world. As business started to progress, although she was still the center of my world, and everything I did was to create a better life for her, for us, I had other obligations that needed my attention as well. When I couldn't give her the time and attention she was used to, she suffered. I tried to dial back how much I was working, I made time to surprise her with lunches and weekend getaways, but the business was always going to take time away from her." I haven't really told anyone this, I haven't wanted to look at the part that I've played in my divorce.

"I don't think it's your fault, I understand that's what she was accustomed to, but we all grow up and realize that the world doesn't revolve around any one person. We all have to go out and make the best that we can, and if we want a good life, we have to be willing to work for it." I imagine Olivia can see both sides of it, she grew up as an only child, her mother devoting herself to her, helping her to start Trinity, but then Olivia saw what it takes to create a successful business, she threw herself into her work and created what she wanted for herself.

"Yes and no, for Vee it happened overnight, she had no adjustment period, one day it was her and I and the next, I was in business and had to be there to make it work. She tried to adapt, that's how Ragtime came about, she thought if she had something she could focus on, something to throw herself into... so I opened the Jazz club for her. In that club she found what she was looking for, men would fawn over her, and then she found the drugs. The drugs gave her the euphoria she was looking for, she got to be the center of her own world. So, in part, I am responsible, if I had done things different, loved her more, paid closer attention, and caught her sooner." I will take responsibility for my failures, but I know that she has her own and I can't and won't take those from her.

"We are all responsible for our own happiness, if we count on others to make us happy then we will never have it. I think that's why she turned to the drugs, she couldn't make herself happy, but she found it in the drugs. You still love her, I can see it in your eyes, especially when you were talking about the beginning. If you can still hold love for someone that did the things that she did to you, you loved her enough." I do still love her, not who she is now, but I will always love her for who she was and for what we had. I learned a lot from her, I learned from the mistakes that I made with her, and I learned what kind of person that I want to be because of her.

"Are you hungry? It's ready." It's simple but delicious, just like mama taught me.

"I'm impressed Mr. Alessandro, chicken fettuccine alfredo, salad, and perfectly toasted bread, I've never met a man that could cook." This is only the beginning Ms. Mason, it's only the beginning.

Chapter 31

Olivia

It's the best chicken alfredo that I've ever had! Creamy, perfectly seasoned, and melt in my mouth, he didn't just cook for me, he created a masterpiece.

While we eat, he tells me of his childhood with Alex, how they worked through the trauma of watching Alex's mother be killed by his father, and his father being killed by police. Both feeling like they failed Patricia. Alex denying grief for the death of his father but eventually learning that regardless of what his father had done, Alex loved him. He had to learn to process emotions that most adults don't know what to do with.

They pulled each other through it all. Even before the adoption, they were brothers, and because they went through that together, they understood each other on a level that no one ever could. Each of them offering a hand up to the other, until they climbed out together.

I marvel at the reverence Ian has for his mother, how hard she worked to provide them both with a good life, never giving up on either of them. He openly admits that there were plenty of times that a lesser woman would have thrown in the towel. When one or both of them were acting out, shoplifting, graffiti, vandalism, but the more they acted out, the more love she showed them, until they understood that what happened wasn't their fault. They couldn't have stopped it, there was nothing that two ten-year-old little boys could have done.

"That's how I learned that anger will only lead me in the wrong direction, because of that day, I learned who I didn't want to be." I feel my eyes swimming in my tears, I can't imagine what they felt.

"A lot of kids wouldn't be able to move beyond that, the anger, the fear, the grief, they would hold onto it and let it destroy them." I saw it a lot in New York, seeing kids on the street, and stories that Greg would tell me about cases that he worked on.

"In part it was Alex and I, but more than that, it was my mother never giving up on us. It was the love she had for us and the love we had for each other and for her. Then we became determined, we set our goals high, and we used our situation to propel us into a better life. For Alex, his mother was a motivating factor. He was driven to make her proud, to not let her death destroy him, but to elevate him into a man that she would be proud of." It reflects in him, he is a good man, honorable, and eager to make a difference, one life at a time. Right now, he's making a difference in mine, him and Ian, the foundation, it's what will save me from a similar fate. There is no doubt that if I stayed with Greg, he would have eventually killed me.

The elevator doors open, Nick and Mack emerge, Nick with two black eyes and stitches that start at his forehead and travel back across his bald head, but still a bright smile and laughter in his eyes.

"Oh! Nick!" I scramble to greet him, once in front of him, I don't know what to do, I want to hug him, but I'm afraid I might hurt him, so I stop in front of him, he opens his arms to me and I go in gently. "I'm so sorry, Nick." It's all I manage to say, before he stops me.

"Ollie, there won't be any of that, unless you're the one that beaned me on the head with a pipe, I don't want an apology from you." I didn't get the details of what happened, it makes me sad and it makes me angry to learn he'd been beaten with a pipe. I hear the offense in his tone, just as Ian said.

"What I mean is, I'm sorry this happened to you. Is that better?" I don't want to offend him, I just want him to know that I hate that this happened, even more, I hate that it's because of me that it did happen.

Mack makes his greetings but leaves us to check in with Ryan, see what he's been working on and get any updates. Nick sits on the sofa, his movements slow and deliberate, pain showing as he eases himself down.

"Thank you, thank you for protecting me, not just from whoever did this to you, but also for protecting me from what I would have had to face if you had told them why you were there." It seems so small, just words, but I feel them deep, the gratitude I have I can't express. "What did you tell them?" I know that the other guys waited for his lead, that meant not answering questions until Nick came to.

"I know what we're protecting you against Ollie, all of us do, if you were ready for people to know, you would tell your story. It's my job to protect you and that means protecting your secrets too, so I told them I was meeting someone to buy a stereo, and I got robbed." That won't hold up for long, it won't be hard to find that there isn't anything to support his story. "Fletcher is fairly good with a computer, he created an ad with a fake account, made it look like it was posted last week and even put some comments from me and emails back and forth. Mack told them he was driving by and saw someone being jumped, and they ran off when he stopped his car and he got out." They made their lie come together, all risking the possibility of facing charges if they are found out.

"I don't know what to say." My mind circles around all that these men have done for me, what they are willing to risk for a stranger.

"We all think a lot of you Ollie, none of us want to see anything happen to you. We know the things that can happen doing this kind of job, so don't say nothing." Ian runs his hand up and down my back, he leans in and whispers, "I tried to warn you." I turn my head to look at him, his half grin playing on his lips and he shrugs his shoulders.

Ian and Nick fall into easy conversation, sports, books, music, and I try to wrap my head around Nick's nonchalance, his attitude that being beaten is just another day at the office.

As the conversation winds down, the lulls grow longer, Nick asks Ian about new information surfacing and how it's all related, "Let's go check it out, the guys have been building a timeline, trying to fit it all together." Nick is slow to get up but manages on his own, Ian holds his hand out to me, inviting me to join them.

I haven't been in the library since it became a makeshift security office, different monitors set up, Ian's portion of the parking garage, the elevator that comes to the apartment, and the elevator entrances. Even though that's all that I can see, I imagine they can access any camera they want through the system.

A dry erase board has a timeline of events and another has different names with possible motives. Greg, Brett, Lawrence, and Vivian are listed here, a couple of New York phone numbers, one attached to Woodbourne Prison.

A thought crosses my mind, going back to when Ian got all the information about Greg, what led Ian to find me on the floor of my apartment after I'd been attacked. Greg got in deep with the Russian mob. He's tied to them, a few deals between them, favors, meaning he's acquainted with Angus Kelley, the man that killed my mom. What if Angus made the call from Woodbourne? That's where he went after his sentencing. He has the connections to make it happen, but what would be the purpose? And why would he make multiple calls to Ragtime?

Mack, Ryan, Nick, and Ian talk amongst themselves while I look at all the information before me, trying to see a connection. Considering Lawrence's military experience and his anger at Ian, it could be him, but something doesn't feel right about that. Lawrence has been angry with Ian since the divorce, why wait until now to do anything? Lawrence seems like a distraction. It all circles back to Greg, he has the motive, he knows that Ian has been helping me, he has access to information to find someone in the area with knowledge to pull this off, but does he have the means to make someone do it?

My thoughts circle back to Angus Kelley, the things that Ian told me about Greg, things that occurred before she was killed. I need to sit down, it never occurred to me until now, is it possible that my mom's accident wasn't an accident? Did Greg make it happen? My knees buckle, I collapse into the leather armchair. I had considered previously that the mob may have killed my mom to send a message to Greg. My mind has taken a darker turn, did Greg employ the mob and have my mom killed? Ian looks up and comes to me, kneeling beside me, "Olivia, are you alright?" His eyes questioning, darkening with concern.

"Angus Kelley, he's in Woodbourne Prison." Ian makes the connection instantly, Nick, Mack, and Ryan don't understand the meaning, "He killed my mother, he's the enforcer for the mob, what if my mom's death wasn't an accident? What if Greg used his relationship with the mob to make it happen, to isolate me more? And now he's using the mob to get through you to me." How did I not put this together? I can see this is something he has already considered, it's not a new thought.

"I had already wondered that myself, but there are nearly a thousand prisoners housed in Woodbourne. We don't know for sure that the call even came from there, that number could have been spoofed, what would be the point of Angus Kelley calling? He's in prison." He may be able to explain it away, but I feel it, it's all connected, and it all leads back to me.

I hear the hushed tones that Nick is making in the phone, he picked up the phone as soon as I explained Angus Kelley. Mack is on his cell phone talking with someone else and Ryan is typing furiously on the keyboard. Ian may be downplaying it, but I think I just gave them a lead to work off.

"He's up for parole soon, they're counting on you figuring it out, Greg is sending a message. Angus Kelley is notorious, the crimes he's been accused of, but he's so good they can't prove anything, he walks away." He pled guilty to the vehicular manslaughter charge, he took his sentence, admitted he was texting at the time and didn't see her. Why would he plead guilty to that? He has walked away scot free from open murder, why take the rap on this one? I need to know what Ian uncovered. I want to know it all.

"It doesn't make any sense Olivia, the call from that number came through as an unknown caller, he said he was a friend of my mother's and owed it to her to give me a warning. The guys will check it out and see if it's even plausible. We can see if we can dig up more about your mother's accident as well." A new wave of guilt comes over me, my refusal to leave Greg, to keep what was happening from my mom, the possibility that it truly is my fault that she died.

I need time to think, I need to be alone, I feel like I am going to crawl out of my skin. Once I'm sure that my legs will carry me, I go into the bedroom. I can't sort out my mind with the murmured phone conversations and the incessant clicking of the keyboard. I can't wrap my head around my epiphany with Ian telling me to wait until we have more information. Even if I'm wrong about the phone call, I know in my heart that Greg had something to do with my mother's death, and now I know how he did it.

Chapter 32

Ian

I don't try to follow her, as much as I want to, I can see she needs some time to herself. I had already considered her logic, Greg had some shady dealings with the mob, it stands to reason that he is responsible for the death of her mother. In turn, Olivia will hold herself responsible, it will take more than just me to convince her otherwise.

I pull Markus's report from my file cabinet and turn it over to Ryan, he can investigate it, it's possible it's all connected, if it is, they will need all we have.

After twenty minutes, I leave them to do what they do, I need to check on Olivia. I gave her as much time as I could, but I don't want to wait too long.

"Can I come in?" I knock softly. After a moment it opens, she stands before me, barely keeping herself together, I see the signs, her tells. She breathes deep and holds it for a moment, then releases, she's trying to keep herself under control. Her eyes aren't red from crying, but I see the quiver in her shoulders. Every part of me wants to reach for her, but I wait, I don't want to push her. It's a fine line to walk, with her history it's hard to tell what I should do from moment to moment. Sometimes she is vulnerable and wants me to hold her, sometimes she's vulnerable and needs me to keep back, I have to wait for her cue, no matter what I want, it isn't about me, it's about what she needs.

I don't have to wait long, she crosses the threshold, closing the gap between us, wrapping her arms around my waist and I envelop her in mine. Wanting to have some privacy, I drop my left arm and pull her into my right side and walk her back into the bedroom, closing the door behind us. We settle in the chaise lounge by the window, overlooking the city, dusk is settling in, the neon's starting to glow.

"I know I don't have proof yet, but he killed my mom. He killed her because of me, because of the influence she had, because I almost filed for divorce, because she would always be there for me and would always be an escape, he stole her from me." Thankfully, she's putting the blame where it belongs, but I know that she will feel some guilt at some point, even if it isn't right now.

"I think you're right. Markus didn't dig that up originally, but he wasn't looking for that, all the guys are looking into it all now. We will find out the truth, you need that." I try to put myself in her position, I would want to know, I can't fathom what she's feeling right now.

"I got my mother killed, Ian, she would still be alive if I had never married Greg, or if I had left the first time he hit me, or even the second. She could still be here if I had talked to her or gone through with the divorce when I first saw an attorney." The what if's and could haves. There are a hundred scenarios that she will play back, and all of them will come back to if she had done something different.

"No, if any of this is true, the blame still resides with Greg and Angus Kelley. You don't know that he would have let you go even after the first time, or the second, you don't know what would have happened if you would have filed the papers. You can't take the blame for the actions of others, you didn't do this." She must come to understand that on her own, it won't matter how many times I say it, she needs to see it for herself, but I will say it over and over until she does.

I hear the wheels turning in her head, she is content to just sit here with me, I won't fill the silence with words. I am here so she knows she isn't alone, if she needs to cry, or talk, I'm here for whatever she needs.

After several nights of little sleep, we both drift off. Despite the circumstances or the events that have happened, we both sleep soundly, peacefully.

It's still dark when I wake, Olivia is still snoring softly. Without waking her I rise from the chaise, looking at the city below me, the neon's lighting up the streets. The city that never sleeps, traffic has thinned but is still heavy, people milling around, taking in the sites, the Eiffel Tower, the Colosseum, the Big Apple, so many sites from around the world all displayed along the strip. Traveling to Vegas you also enjoy, New York City, Paris, Rome, Venice.

Exhaustion has overtaken Olivia, she sleeps undisturbed by her thoughts, uninterrupted by nightmares. I wish I could give her the experience that the tourists are enjoying, the carefree, wonder of the city. One day I will, when all the mysteries have been solved, when the devil is no longer knocking on her door, I will take her out on the town, show her what Vegas is really like.

I leave her to rest, I've slept all that I will. With any luck the guys will have answers for the questions that continue to multiply.

Nick is still here, him and Mack combing through all the information that we have. I would tell Nick to go home but he wouldn't listen, he's now more deeply invested in this because now it's personal.

"Hey boss, that call definitely originated in Woodbourne, we're working on confirmation of who made the call, but we know it came from the prison. We have a list of inmates, we're cross referencing names, we started with Angus Kelley, right now it looks like Ollie may be right." Is Greg using him as an intimidation tactic? If that were the case, wouldn't they want us to know it was him that called? Use his name as a threat.

"I want Markus working on Angus Kelley, I want his whole history. I want to know every crime he's been accused of, under suspicion for, and I want to know if he has any kind of relationship with Gregory Daniels." Perhaps if we can see how it all connects, we can unravel it all.

"Markus called, Lawrence has been arrested. He was picked up on a federal warrant, the feds are interrogating him now. He set up the blasts at the Whiskey." I underestimated his anger. Now knowing his experience, it doesn't surprise me. The question remains, how is it all tied together?

"Has Lawrence received any calls from New York, anything that might tie him and Greg together?" My life is well publicized, Greg sees the turmoil between Lawrence and I, he has access to find out that Lawrence is capable, is this a two birds with one stone situation? Lawrence gets his revenge on me, while Greg utilizes it to get to Olivia?

"We haven't looked into it yet, we've been tracking down this phone number." I look over new notes, new names, none of which I know, my irritation growing.

It won't do any good to hover, these guys are professionals. They know what they're doing, what needs to be done. If I start interrupting their process, I will only slow things down.

Leaving them to their research, I go back to the bedroom. Olivia is still sleeping but she's become restless, I slide in behind her on the chaise, hoping that she will get back to peaceful sleep.

I smooth her hair, kiss the top of her head, and settle in, watching the lights in the city below. All the while trying to piece it all together in my mind. Brett is still MIA, I'm confident that he plays a part in all of this. If the feds picked up Lawrence, and the guys are confident that he is behind the Whiskey, does Vivian also play a part in this? Was she aware of what her father was planning? Then there's Greg, are they all tied together, or do we have separate attacks going on? The questions circle in my thoughts, never getting anywhere, no answers emerging, just more questions with no answers.

The sun begins its rise, the light in the room changes, Olivia, starts to stir, it's the first good night's sleep she's had in days, "Good morning." Her voice is groggy.

"How do you know that I'm awake?" I haven't moved in hours. I had no reason to.

"Once again, I could sense it." Just as I can with her.

"How did you sleep?" If she slept half as good as I did, she will be in good shape.

"Better than I have in a long time." She hesitates, but I wait, "You know the other night when you told me the things that you uncovered about Greg?" I respond only with a nod. "I couldn't listen to it all then, I want to know the rest, I want to know because if I can piece it all together, then I might be able to offer insight. Even though Angus's name came up in your report, the prison he's in, you guys didn't put it all together. So maybe if I know what you found out, I can add context to it, and we can come up with some answers." I have no doubt the guys would have made the connection, but I don't need to tell her that. She helped us see it sooner, that's all that matters.

"I will tell you anything you want to know. After breakfast, you can read the report, it's your story Olivia, I won't ever hide it from you." Initially, I felt like I invaded her privacy, and I had, it worked out that I had, but I won't ever do that to her again, and I will never keep information from her.

In the kitchen, again we move together in a rhythm, a choreographed dance that we never learned, that just comes naturally. Together we prepare omelets, when the first two are done, she delivers them to the library, surprising Nick and Mack who are still piecing together the information that we have, when she returns ours are done and on the breakfast bar. A fresh cup of coffee in front of hers.

"Did you sleep well, Ian? That lounger couldn't have been comfortable for you." I didn't think it would be but surprisingly it was comfortable. I slept better there with her than I had in my own bed for years.

"Actually, I was quite comfortable. After we talk and you read Markus's report, how would you feel about going downstairs? I believe you still need shoes and we can pick up your dress." It would be nice to get out for a bit, even if it's just downstairs. It's a mini city, shops, eateries, games, movies.

"I haven't seen the latest gossip rag, is it safe down there?" Today, there isn't anything, perhaps the feds picked up Lawrence after deadline. So far, they haven't gotten any other information on Olivia yet.

"It will be, I don't think the press will be looking for us in the shops, on the floor, or in the restaurants, maybe but not in the shops." Again, I'm struck by her resilience, she still isn't letting anything being thrown at her stop her.

"Let's do that after breakfast, I will read through it all and we can talk after." Each of us finish our breakfast in silence, content to just be in each other's presence, each lost in our own thoughts, mine curious of what hers are.

Chapter 33

Olivia

Now more than ever, I wish I could talk to my mom, to hear her words of wisdom, to let her see that I'm safe. That I made it far from Greg and that I have all these wonderful people surrounding me and helping me through. I want to ask her if she blames me for her death, does she hold me responsible? Because right now, I hold myself responsible. No matter what Ian says, I let it happen. He is right in that I can't know the outcome if I had left. What would he have done if I had filed for divorce? Would he have killed us both? Just me? So many questions without any answers. I know that I can't dwell, in my heart I know that mom doesn't blame me, I also know that I have to bring myself out of that train of thought, I just don't know how.

"Penny for your thoughts?" Ian's voice breaks through my thoughts.

"Just trying to think it all through, trying to understand if it's all tied together, if it's separate, there's so much happening right now." My thought, perhaps Greg used Lawrence and it's all tied together somehow.

"We'll figure it all out, we know that the feds have Lawrence, so we can eliminate the Whiskey from the thoughts of what you are holding yourself responsible for. Lawrence had a grudge against me, he did that to me, not because of you." He emphasizes himself. He doesn't question whether Lawrence worked with Greg, just takes it at face value that it revolves around him. Myself, I'm not so sure.

"I'm going to go shower, then we can go whenever you're ready." I should stay and help clean up, but my mind won't stop, and though I know that Ian is trying to be helpful, he is distracting me from the bigger picture.

His shower is bigger than our bathroom at home, all marble tile and shower heads on each wall, totaling four spraying from the wall and a large one hanging from the ceiling, all of the fixtures beautiful in brass. The heat of the water soothes my nerves, I stand soaking it all in, trying to organize my thoughts, though finding it impossible. So much has happened, so much is still happening, where does it end for me and begin for Ian? Or are they intertwined? Round and round I go, not finding any conclusions, still missing too much information. Hopefully, I will find something in the report from Markus, or maybe they will find Brett and he can give us some insight.

Shoe shopping hadn't been on my list of things to do. As a matter of fact, I had forgotten the dress as well, but I think both of us could use a bit of a distraction. I know that Thursday is an important night for the foundation, Ian, and Alex. It's important to me as well, the foundation has benefitted me so much. What they do through the foundation is so critical that Thursday needs to be a priority for me.

I dress quickly avoiding my reflection in the mirror, not wanting to see the scars, the imperfections, but once I'm dressed, I look carefully at myself, I see subtle changes in my appearance. The dark circles aren't so prominent, my eyes are lighter, not as shadowed as they were, I don't look as tired as I did, it's nothing dramatic, just enough that I notice. Perhaps, the life I was living was part of my appearance, and perhaps, being happier than I've been in so long, even with all the events that are unfolding, are contributing factors.

Ian greets me with a smile when I reappear at the breakfast bar, he is just finishing up with the cleanup, the kitchen sparkling like it hadn't been used. "Olivia, you look refreshed and radiant, do you feel better?" I blush at his compliment, I don't know how to respond, but the heat rises to my cheeks and I can't meet his gaze.

"Thank you, I do. I would have cleaned up, I just needed a minute." Not that it helped, but I thought it would.

"It's done, I'll get ready and we can go." He stands in front of me, making no effort to walk away. I hesitate for just a moment and then I lean in. I've come to crave his touch, to depend on it to ground me, to offer me comfort, he doesn't disappoint, wrapping his arms around me, and all else just fades away. Breathing him in, feeling his warmth, everything is pushed from my mind, except this moment. He squeezes tighter for just a moment, then brushes his lips across my forehead and lets me go.

The void that comes over me when he walks away makes me feel empty, am I developing an unhealthy dependency on him? A therapist would probably say yes, but I don't care, I don't think it's him, I think it's the way he makes me feel.

My thoughts are interrupted by Ryan, "Boss, you have to see this! Oh! Sorry Ollie, I thought Ian was out here." Nick and Mack must have gone while I was in the shower, Ryan taking their place.

"He went to shower, what is it? Do you have something?" He hesitates in his response, unsure if I should be included in whatever it is, he has for Ian. "It's ok Ryan, he'll be out soon." My curiosity is overwhelming, but if it isn't my business, I don't need to see whatever it is.

"I'm sorry Ollie, I just think that Ian should probably see it first." That only adds to my curiosity, fortunately, I don't have long to wait. Ian comes striding down the hall, his hair still wet from his shower, the scruff on his chin still intact, his eyes burning blue, without a hint of the gray shining through. "Boss, you need to come look at what Fletcher just sent over." I hadn't seen much of Steven or Jay, leading me to believe that Fletcher, Nick, Mack, and Ryan made up the core of Ian's security for the foundation.

Ian waits for me at the door to the library, his hand outstretched. Whatever it is that Ryan wants to show him, Ian is making it clear that he would like for me to see as well.

Ryan turns his laptop to face Ian and myself, an email filling the screen titled, I found him. My stomach rolls, unsure who it is he found, as Ian scrolls down the page, images fill the screen. I recognize Brett but it takes a moment to place who he is with, standing in front of a house, his arms wrapped around a woman, it's Vivian. Ian doesn't say anything, just scrolls through the images, scrutinizing each one.

"Tell him to pick him up, bring him to my office, let's see what he has to tell us." He seems unfazed that Brett is with his ex-wife and it's apparent that they are intimate, his mannerism and tone is just business.

He looks at me, "Are you ready?" I want to ask if he's ok, but it's a stupid question, how could he be ok?

"If you are." I'd rather wait until we're alone, maybe he doesn't want Ryan to see that the pictures affected him.

He wraps his arm around my shoulder and leads me to the elevator, I can feel his anger radiating off of him. I begin to doubt the things that he's said to me, how can he feel the way he says about me, if he's this upset about Vivian being with Brett? "Ian, we can do this later if you want, you kind of just got sucker punched." He obviously has other things to work on right now.

"I'd rather go with you than sit around and wait." He isn't quite as warm as he was before his shower, but he doesn't seem cold toward me either. "It was a shock, I wasn't prepared to see that, but don't misunderstand, it has nothing to do with the fact that they're together, it makes me now question the motives of the things that have happened." I'm not following what he's saying. "Lawrence is the one that set explosives on the Whiskey, Brett allowed someone into your apartment to harm you, seeing them together now makes me wonder, was Brett contacted by Greg or does my ex-wife have a part in that as well as the Whiskey?" The thought had never crossed my mind, she said in the parking lot that she knew that Ian was seeing someone, but how could she have known it was me? Security had just started, and I didn't really know Ian aside from the interview until that night when he found me.

"But how? You and I hadn't had any contact before I was attacked except the interview. It can't be her, this still has something to do with Greg." The elevator doors open, instead of finding us on the main floor, this floor has shops lined all the way down the corridor.

"Perhaps, we will see, let's move past this for now. Fletcher will bring him down and we can get some answers, all the speculation is only going to drive us crazy and not really help to formulate answers." He's right, and admittedly, I feel better knowing that his anger was only due to the thought that his ex-wife may be involved, not that she may be in a relationship with Brett.

"One last question, where are Stephen and Jay?" It isn't any of my business, but they both took care of me too, I can't help wanting to know about them.

Ian laughs, the warmth coming back, "Not what I expected, but I'll take it. Can you keep a secret?" His blue eyes dance with amusement, waiting for me to reply.

"You know I can." My curiosity raised further by his question.

"Alex would kill me if he knew, but I have them keeping an eye on Alex and Rachel. I felt like they needed someone watching their backs, rather than send either of them back to regular security, they are keeping watch on them from afar." It had never occurred to me that they would also be targets.

I stand up on my toes and brush my lips across his cheek, the stubble tickling my lips, "Thank you." He responds only with the half grin that is my favorite.

His arm around my shoulders he walks with me down the corridor, showing me the different shops, a candy store, athletic wear, casual wear, a trinket store, a kid's toy store, it's a shopping mall. At the end I see a marque, displaying movies that are playing. He stops in front of a shop called Flair, inside I see formal gowns and suits, I recognize Myra sitting behind the counter. Ian pulls open the glass door and greets her.

"Myra! You've met Olivia." She smiles at him warmly, "You know I have, and your dress is ready my dear, would you like to try it on now?" She grasps my hand and gives it a squeeze.

"Yes, thank you. It will make it easier to find shoes as well." My excitement brims, the dress is so beautiful, like nothing I've ever had before. In light of all the chaos going on around us, this is something light, to prepare us for something fun.

Myra hangs my dress in the fitting room, she offers to stay outside the door to help with the zipper, I almost accept before I remind myself of the scars that I'd rather she not see. "Thank you, I will call for Ian, but I appreciate it." As I pull off my shirt and jeans, it's hard not to notice the extra fat around the middle. The things I had avoided in the mirror earlier are front and center now, I become self-conscious of Ian zipping up my dress. It's silly because I know he has already seen the scars, but a different thought has filled my mind. What is happening between us? How will we go forward? Is he going to want more than what's been happening? Of course he will, am I ready for that? I know that he's seen my scars, but to see me naked, could I bare myself to him? The walls around me are too close, it feels like they are pressing in on me. I sit on the chair in the corner, taking a deep breath and holding it, I need to calm down. How the hell did trying on a dress come to this?

"Olivia?" Ian taps lightly on the door. "Do you need help?" Ugh, now I've been in here long enough worrying about something that I shouldn't, long enough to make him question.

"Just a sec." I quickly step into the dress, zipping it up as far as I can on my own before opening the door. I smile as best as I can, but it doesn't feel right, I can't imagine how it looks. I see the questions in his eyes, but I turn away from him, giving him access to zip me up the rest of the way.

As he zips me up, he leans in and whispers, "What happened?" He's too in tune with me, he reads me better than anyone. I keep my head down, I don't want to meet his eyes in the mirror, not until my embarrassment subsides, but he doesn't let it go. Once my dress is zipped, he turns me toward him, using his fingers to lift my chin gently, "Olivia, what happened?" I am pulled into his gaze, though I feel humiliated by thoughts I couldn't control, just his gaze and the softness in his voice set me at ease.

"I don't want to talk about it here, can I tell you later?" And I suppose that I will, it seems that I can't keep anything from him. Maybe if he let it go, we would both forget and I wouldn't say anything, but I know he won't forget.

"You look stunning..." Another whisper, it gives me chills, and boosts my self-esteem, ever so much, even with the self-doubt that's still fresh in my mind.

Chapter 34

Ian

I know she's keeping something from me, but I can push it aside for now and just take in this moment. The dress looks even better than I could have imagined, the tight bodice, high neck, the shoulders coming down far enough that most of the scars are hidden, those left visible won't be noticed by anyone. The regal dark purple, the color of royalty, she looks like the queen that she deserves to be, perfectly jeweled with the crystals in the bodice. Breathtaking.

"Look." I turn her back to the mirror, stepping back so that she can get the full effect, the long flowing dress, the sparkle of the gems. "You are enchanting." Color rises to her cheeks, her eyes break contact with mine, my hope is that one day she can see herself as she truly is.

"Thank you, it is beautiful."

I notice she isn't speaking of herself, "No, you make the dress beautiful." Sensing her discomfort, I let the subject drop.

Myra joins us, carrying several boxes of shoes, "I wasn't sure what you would like, so I picked different styles for you to choose from, I guessed you at a size 9." She lays them out on the bench and opens each box, revealing flats, pumps, heels, some with straps, some silver with jewels, others plain, several pair of black.

Olivia fingers the strap of a pair of silver, jeweled heels, about 3 inches high, she hesitates before moving on to a pair of flats, her eyes wandering back to the heels before pulling the flats from the box and trying them on. She gazes in the mirror at her reflection, her eyes looking back at the heels again.

"Try these ones." I hand her the silver heels, I don't understand her hesitation, but it's obvious to me that these are the ones that she wants. She takes them from me and slips them on, standing before the mirror, they are the perfect complement to her dress, she stands taller, straighter. I step in closer to her, "I think they are perfect." She meets my eyes in the mirror, slowly nodding her head.

While she is in the dressing room, I receive a message from Fletcher, he is waiting in my office with Brett, now we can get some answers.

I take the dress from Olivia when she emerges from the dressing room, Myra has already taken her shoes to the front. "Fletcher is in my office, I need to head over there." Before I can go on, Rachel appears.

"Ah damn, I missed it, I wanted to see." Clearly, she is disappointed she didn't arrive sooner. While her and Olivia greet each other, I arrange with Myra to have the dress and shoes brought up.

"As I was saying, Brett is in my office with Fletcher, I need to head to my office, Olivia, would you like to go? Or perhaps, would you and Rachel like to enjoy some time at the spa on me?" I won't stop her from going, if that's what she wants, but my preference is not to have her anywhere near him.

"What about me Ian, I'd like to go, I could strong arm him for you, helps to make people a little more honest when their arm is on the verge of being broke." Rachel flashes a bright smile at me.

"Um... will you just tell me about it, I don't think I want to see him, and since my shoes are open toed, I think a pedicure is probably a must." I make the call to set them up in the spa, anything either of them want, billed to me personally.

I turn to leave them at the spa, but Olivia stops me. "Thank you, I just can't face him right now." I nod, place a kiss on her forehead and leave her with Rachel.

Fletcher standing near the door, Ryan sitting in the chair next to Brett, none of them speaking. Brett has beads of sweat running down his temples, he should be nervous.

Taking my seat behind my desk, I consider my words, "Tell me about Friday." Carefully, I rein in my anger, losing control now, will only impede progress.

"A flower delivery was made, and then I went home." His voice barely above a whisper.

"We can do this easy, and you can walk out of here, or we can do this hard and you won't." I don't often make threats, and never make them with violence, but he is going to understand that he's going to tell me what I want to know.

"Why don't you ask your ex-wife." His shoulders slump, his tone, defeated. "She's the one that asked me to let the guy in, I did it for her and now she's screwing me around." His voice rises with anger.

"Vivian asked you to do this?" Not believing what I heard, and honestly, surprised at how easy he's willing to give up the information.

"Yeah, we've been hooking up for a while, then it tapered off, as soon as I got pulled for babysitting duty, she starts calling again. She said to call her if the opportunity presented itself that I could get someone in the apartment." The pieces still aren't fitting together, how is Vivian involved in this. "I did what she asked, I knew you guys would put it together, so I've been laying low, the she calls me again today, got all up on me, asking for information, as soon as she found out I didn't have the answers she was looking for she told me to piss off." That explains why he's not trying to hide it.

"Who was the guy?" Still trying to put together how Vee is involved, Fletcher is on his phone, probably passing on information, Ryan making notes as Brett speaks.

"I don't know, big guy, bald, white, tattoos, he has a cobra tattooed on his head, brass knuckles on his neck." He may not know him, but I do, Ed Carson, one of

Vee's dealers. He got picked up the first time she overdosed.

"Let him go, make sure he has all his shit, and explain to him how imperative it is that he not step foot on any of my properties again." I direct my comments to Fletcher, he can keep an eye on him. "You might consider a new career path, I intend to make it well known that you think with your dick, with no thought of the harm that could come to the clients." I'd like nothing more than to take him out so he could experience what happened to Olivia because of him, but I have bigger fish to fry, he'll get what's coming to him, just not now.

Fletcher takes him out, I call Markus, "Add Vivian's phone records to your search, let's see who she's been talking to, we just got information that she staged the incident at the apartment." I don't wait for an answer before I hang up.

"I'll head back to the spa boss, Grace is there now, I'll hang out until Ollie heads back upstairs." Steven or Jay should be there as well, how either of them are blending in is yet to be determined.

"Tell Grace thanks, and also tell her she'll be brought into rotation." She came through in a pinch, I know what she's capable of and I know that she's trustworthy. I won't make the same mistake that I did with Brett.

"Mr. Alessandro, Special Agent Miller is on line one." Stephanie comes over the intercom.

I give a nod to Ryan as he leaves, "This is Ian." Hoping that Miller can fill in some pieces to this ever-growing puzzle.

"Lawrence Michaels has admitted to setting the explosives at the Whiskey Wrangler, he has given a full statement. He worked alone and has been setting it up for over a week, this was a personal grudge against you. As we have found no evidence of this being domestic terrorism, local authorities will be taking over the investigation and prosecution from here." I don't ask questions, I'll be able to get more

information from local authorities than
what the feds will give me.

"Thank you for the update." Markus
will start pressing his contacts, he will find
out if there is more to this than just
Lawrence's personal grudge. My priority
right now is Vivian, Lawrence can't do any
more harm sitting in jail.

The question now, is Vee working
with her father in an effort to get back at
me, or is Vee working with someone else
and brought her father into the fray? If
there wasn't a question of the New York
phone numbers, I would say that all of this
has been an attack on me, but there is no
explanation for the calls from New York
except for Greg, bringing me back to the
point, Greg may have capitalized on the
turmoil between Vee and me.

Chapter 35

Olivia

It should have been a perfect girl's day. Rachel and I had facials, manicures, pedicures, waxes, and our hair cut, colored, and styled. Rachel prodded me for information of what's been happening with Ian and I, but she gave up when I wouldn't embellish on anything. My thoughts were in Ian's office. Wondering what was happening in there, regretting my decision to not go, I should have been there, at least I wouldn't be wondering.

When she couldn't distract me with Ian, Rachel tried a different tactic, trying to draw me in with the ideas she has for her wedding. I tried to be involved, I tried to be excited, but in all honesty, I don't even know what her ideas are. To give her credit, she isn't holding it against me, I'm sure she understands, she knows what's happening, who they're talking to. I hope that I can make it up to her.

Steven and Ryan stand nearby while Rachel and I say our good-byes, I apologize again for being so distant. Rachel being Rachel won't hear it, "I love you Ollie, we have plenty of time to plan the wedding and really, you don't have to tell me what's happening with Ian, I see it with my own eyes." She hugs me again and tells me to thank Ian for her, she doesn't have an issue with him paying for today, but I'm feeling guilty for it.

Ryan steps in beside me as I walk down the corridor but remains quiet. I'm tempted to ask him, but I don't, I'd rather hear it from Ian.

Ian is waiting for me when I step off the elevator, taking me in his arms, and a brush of his lips across my forehead, "You look beautiful." Barely above a whisper. Ryan went on to the library, leaving us alone.

"Tell me." Spoken so quietly I'm not sure he hears me. My anxiety rising, even his presence isn't distracting me like it has in the past.

"He said it was Vivian that asked him, so it could be another attack on me, all

of this could just be centered around me."
He doesn't believe that there's no
conviction in his words.

"It could be, but that doesn't explain
the flowers on my doorstep, nor does it
explain the phone calls from New York." His
reaction or lack thereof, I know that he's
already considered what I've said.

"Agreed, Markus is working on
Vivian's phone records now, the guys are
still working the call from the prison, and
we're also checking to see if Vivian and
Lawrence were working together. We have
to let them find the answers." It's so
frustrating, the waiting, the not knowing.
The longer that we wait the more complex
it all gets.

Ian releases me and pours us each a
glass of wine, after handing me mine, he
clinks my glass, "To another step that brings
us closer." Is he talking about what's going
on around us? Or is he talking about us?
The lines of everything are so blurred.

He busies himself in the kitchen,
throwing together something for us to eat,

and gives me more detail of what Brett said and the feds regarding the Whiskey. Nothing that jumps out at me as an explanation, but I can't say that it makes me feel any better to know that I'm not the only one with a crazy ex. It's somehow connected, all of it, but how?

When he's exhausted all of his hypothesis, many of them the same as mine, after we've gone in the same circles, asking the what if's, and maybe's, we agree, until we get more information, we just don't know anything really. Going over it again and again, is just growing tiresome.

"Thank you for the spa day, Rachel said to tell you thanks as well. I will pay you back." I don't want to be showered with gifts, every step I make seems to be a step backward. I'm not comparing Ian to Greg, or my relationship with Greg to whatever is happening right now with Ian, but the fact remains that when I left Greg it was so that I could get away from the abuse and stand on my own two feet, to take care of myself again, to not ever be put in the position of needing someone again. Until now, I've done most of that, I paid my share of the rent, the utilities, the groceries, Rachel has taken care of me in other ways, and I was dependent on her for things as well but that's different, this is me giving up control again.

I can't not notice the hurt in his eyes, I wish he wouldn't take it personally, it has little to do with him and everything to do with me, I hope that he can understand that. "If you'd like." He recovers, smoothing his features.

"I would, I do appreciate the gesture, please don't get me wrong, you have already done so much. All of this Ian, taking care of me, being there for me, the flowers, the dress, the shoes, the night under the stars, a day at the spa, all of it is so thoughtful, so generous. Just try to understand that I want to know that I can take care of myself, I need to prove that to myself." I can't fall into a pattern of being taken care of. Some things have been out of my control, but I have to take charge and do what I can for myself, for my own sanity.

"I know you do, just know that I don't offer these things expecting anything in return. Accepting a gift doesn't make you reliant on me, or anyone else, you can pay me back if you choose, but I did those things because I wanted to. Because you deserve to be appreciated, because I like to see the glimmer in your eyes." I know he's not keeping a tally, he isn't noting a scoreboard, none of these things will be held over my head and used as leverage, still, it's what I want to do for me.

We fall into silence, each of us lost to our own thoughts, nibbling on the meat, cheese, and veggies that he had set out between us. It's the first uncomfortable anything that's passed between us.

I lose my appetite. I feel guilty for making him feel bad, but I stand my ground, even if it makes me feel like shit.

Ian notices me pushing the food around my plate, turning his stool to me, he reaches for my hand, I can't bring my eyes up to his, "Olivia, please don't retreat. I understand, you are entitled to feel the way you feel, you don't owe me an explanation, and you shouldn't feel bad for stating your feelings. I apologize, next time, I will do my best to accept your feelings more gracefully." His mama did a good job in raising him, if I hadn't experienced this for myself, I would have never believed that men like him existed.

"You are an enigma, thank you for understanding, thank you for what you've done. I can't express how much I appreciate just being here with you or the way you make me feel." He doesn't respond with words, he leans in, resting his forehead on mine, the connection between us restored, the uneasiness departed, a moment of intimacy that communicates what words can't.

Nick came in to relieve Ryan while Ian and I were cleaning up the light dinner we had shared, he passed through quickly with a nod and a smile. I would have liked to have talked to him, check on how he's feeling. I still don't think he should be back working yet but don't think much would keep him away.

Ian brings the bottle of wine with us, settling in to watch Las Vegas glow, dimming the lights and turning on music to play softly in the background. Under different circumstances, this would be the perfect way to wrap up a day with someone that you love. Whoa! Where the hell did that come from?

My thoughts are interrupted by Ian as he quietly sings the chorus of the song that plays. The deep tenor of his voice resonating all the way through me, sends chills up my spine. Making me forget the thoughts that I had, bringing me into this moment, singing the words that belong to someone else, making me believe that though the words don't belong to him, they were written just for us. Shinedown fades away and all I can hear is Ian.

I let myself believe that he isn't just singing the song, that he's telling me how he feels, I let myself hope that he feels the same for me as I feel for him. The realization of the feelings that I have for him sets in, I'm falling in love with him.

Chapter 36

Ian

I will follow her anywhere, I was set in my path, prepared to focus on my business, I wasn't wanting to get tangled up with anyone. Life had been so messy with Vivian at the end, it had soured my idea of love. Building the Whiskey while still building the other businesses up, I had plenty to keep me busy, enough to keep my mind occupied. But the moment she walked through Michelle's door, all that changed.

Everything about her, the flicker of fire in her, her resilience, her determination, her resolve. Again, I'm reminded of a Phoenix, she has burned to ashes and now she is rising again, stronger, and more beautiful than before.

"Would you like to go upstairs and look at the stars again?" Her eyes glimmer hopefully.

"I'd love to." Whatever it is that she wants to do, wherever she wants to go, I'll follow her.

The view doesn't compare to the other night, so many of the stars are lost in the brightness of the city, but still, up here we get a better view than if we were anywhere else in the city. As we settle into the lounger, she tells me of camping with her mother.

"My mom wasn't big on camping, but my dad was, so he compromised. He bought her a little cottage on Stoner Lake, it wasn't much, but there was power and indoor plumbing, two things mom didn't want to be without. We spent weekends and summers there when they were still together. When they divorced, mom was so angry, she was hurt, she fought him for the cottage, and she won. It was her way of paying him back for cheating on her." Some of her happiest and her saddest childhood memories were tied up in the cottage. "We hardly used it after the divorce, but mom took me up there a couple times, we would seek out the stars, I would tell her all my dreams. Those are the moments I treasure the most, just her and I, no distractions, it just felt like home." I can't fathom what she feels, how much it hurts to have lost her mother, or the feelings that are surfacing now with the ideas that maybe her death wasn't an accident.

"What happened to the cottage?" Did it get forgotten and sold after Olivia grew up?

"As far as I know, I still own it, but Greg did so much that I don't know. He could have sold it, or the IRS could have taken it for taxes, or maybe it's just there waiting to be remembered." It's a question that I could have answered with a little digging.

She goes quiet, introspective, lost in memories of her childhood. I get wrapped up in all that has brought us here, my investigation that led me to her, finding her battered, unconscious on the floor, the demolition of the Whiskey, I find that though I'm angry about that, I'm not as angry as I should be. Is that because it's part of what brought us to this moment? It's a place, when all the dust settles, I'll set it in motion again, but it's part of what brought me here, it showed me what I was missing in my life, who was missing from my life.

Olivia stirs beside me, turning herself to look at me, she leans in, our lips meet, gentle, tender, slow, building in passion and urgency, it's demanding. The heat between us rising, it's so unexpected, desire intensifying. Then she pulls away, though I still crave her, I don't try to pull her back in.

"Wow, um... sorry." She bites her lip, bowing her head, hiding behind her hair.

I touch her chin and lift her face, wanting her eyes to meet mine. "Don't apologize, that was incredible." It was unexpected, different from every other kiss we have shared. Even in the dark I can see the color form on her cheeks.

The vibration of my phone in my pocket interrupts the moment, Alex's name flashes across the screen, "Alex, how's it going?"

"I'm trying to reach Ollie, but you should probably be close by when I talk to her." I sit up straighter, knowing that he has something that's going to upset her.

"She's right here." Turning on the speaker phone, "Go ahead Alex, we're listening." Perhaps I should have given her some warning first, but it's obvious from the look on her face she knows.

"I've been in court all day, I got back to the office a few hours ago, Greg is contesting the divorce Ollie." Her breath comes out in a rush. "I called as soon as I came across the documents. From what I've gathered so far, he is asking for court mandated counseling, if that is denied, he is requesting that an audit be done on your finances, he doesn't think he should be held liable for all of the debt, which appears to be substantial. Additionally, he feels that he should be given half the insurance money on Trinity. Don't shoot the messenger but he says that you took his grandmothers ring, and he wants it back." Confusion washes over her face, and hopelessness.

"The judge can't force her to do counseling! If she wants a divorce, she can't be made to endure counseling." My anger rising, growing stronger the longer I have to see the despair that she feels.

"Calm down, I'm telling you what his response is, not what's going to happen. I know he's been talking to the press, I wanted you both to hear it from me, instead of reading it in the papers. We will fight all of this, except the ring Ollie, if you have the ring, we need to turn that over." She shakes her head back and forth, opening her mouth only to close it again.

"I don't have it Alex, I left it on the bedside table when I left, I didn't want it." So, either he has it and is going to use it as leverage, or he didn't find it and it got knocked off and is probably under the bed.

"Alright, I will subpoena the financials, start going over them, prepare yourself for the possibility that you may have to assume some of the debt, it's not likely but it's also not impossible. I'll see what I can do to get us on the docket." Olivia doesn't look reassured, her tension growing.

"Alex, make this happen quick, get it over and done, if she has to pay anything, see that it's handled." Olivia starts to protest, but I shake my head at her, she can pay it back if she wants to or if she feels the need, but Greg won't hold any debt over her, if I can do anything about it.

"I'll get on it first thing in the morning, right now, I'm going home to see my bride to be." The line goes silent, my phone reverting to the home screen.

"I won't let you pay whatever I might owe, I appreciate the gesture, but this goes back to what I said earlier, I want to know that I can take care of myself, if there's a debt to be paid, I will pay it. I don't want your money Ian." I'm not going to argue this with her, when the time comes, the check will be sent, she can be angry with me then. Or, perhaps, I can make her see the logic in paying it and being done.

I nod my head and stand, holding my hand out to her, the magic of the moment gone, the atmosphere between us now tense. She doesn't hesitate to join me,

I hope that we can salvage the rest of the evening without any bitterness between us.

Silently we walk back down the stairs, I can't help but wonder what's going through her mind. I understand why she feels the way she does, but why can't she see the complications that I'm trying to help her to avoid. She wouldn't be obligated to me in any way, she could consider it a loan and pay it back if she chose to, as long as she isn't in debt to him.

Back in the apartment, Olivia goes into the bedroom, she doesn't say she's going to bed, doesn't ask me to join her. Trying to give her the space that she needs, I stop in the library to check in with Nick. Stacks of papers are laid out before him, he's referencing on one stack and cross referencing on two others.

"Hey boss, need something?" Looking up from his work.

"Getting anywhere?" It's been a slow process, so many different avenues to explore.

"Slowly, it's not complete yet, but I feel confident enough to say that Angus Kelley was the caller from Woodbourne, there's a few in there that Ollie's ex locked up, but no other connections. The relationship with the mob and Kelley and Daniels is solid, there's been a lot of favors back and forth." I nod in agreement, the history with the mob and Olivia's husband, made it likely it was Kelley. "Markus is still trying to run down the other number, but he did find it in Vivian's personal phone records, we know that it wasn't Kelley calling her or the Ragtime." Movement at the door catches my eye, looking up, Olivia standing in the doorway, wrapped in my bathrobe, her hair wet, falling down her shoulders.

"Am I interrupting?" Sounding unsure of herself.

"Of course not, we were just finishing up. Would you like to hear what Nick has uncovered?" Trying to keep my promise to keep her involved. She shakes her head, learning that Greg is going to fight her on the divorce has been enough for the night.

"Goodnight Nick." He waves his hand at us, already immersed in the reports again.

Instead of turning to the living room, Olivia heads back to the bedroom again, while she still hasn't invited me to join her, I feel better about following her now than before. I close the door behind me, watching as she folds her long legs underneath her to sit on the bed.

"I know you don't understand my resolve in that I will pay my own way, it's okay that you don't, how can I explain it to you when I can't even explain it to myself? It's just the way that I feel, it's what I believe, it's what I think will be the most liberating, the most freeing. To make it through this and do as much as I can on my own, that's the best that I can describe it. You are the most generous person that I've ever met, I want you to know that I recognize that, and I appreciate who you are." She considers her words as she speaks them. I have joined her, sitting on the edge of the bed, not interrupting, trying to listen and hear what she's saying, rather than listening to respond to what she's saying.

"You don't have to justify the way that you feel." Kicking myself for making her feel the way that she does. I don't have to agree with her, she's a reasonable woman, she will weigh the options that she has and she will choose the one that she can live with, but also understand that she may have to count on others to help her through.

She rises to her knees and wraps her arms around me, drawing my lips into hers, this kiss much like the last in its urgency, it's intensity. I reciprocate, following her lead, only matching her, not pressing her for more. The shoulder of my robe slides down her arm, revealing bare skin underneath, I fight my urge to untie the belt. I want her more than anything else in the world, but I have to let her decide how far she wants this to go, let her guide me into what she wants.

I let my hands rest on her hips, hers holding onto my shoulders, she falls back on the bed, pulling me with her. Her fingers fumbling with the buttons of my shirt, I pull back from her, unsure of myself, hesitating only long enough for her to tell me, "I want this Ian, I want you." I pull my shirt over my head, tossing it to the floor, kissing up her jaw to behind her ear, she pulls her belt off, opening the robe, I'm mesmerized by her beauty, enraptured by this woman.

I run my finger from her navel in a straight line to her neck, watching her skin quiver at my touch. What I want is to devour her, but instead I slow things down, kissing her gently while she pushes my pants down my legs. Touching her softly, positioning myself above her, giving her every opportunity to stop, but instead she pulls me in.

The explosion between us was earth shattering, our bodies moved in rhythm, each of us anticipating the moves of the other. Lying here with her, our naked bodies intertwined, hearts pounding, a satisfied exhaustion. All of the tension from earlier forgotten, her head resting on my shoulder, a perfect moment in time.

Chapter 37

Olivia

All of my fears, all of my insecurities dissipated. I wanted Ian, I wanted to feel him inside me, I wanted to get lost in his arms. It wasn't an urge that I wanted to control, and he didn't disappoint, he followed my lead and only hesitated once. Lying with him now, my self-doubt hasn't resurfaced, I haven't scurried away to find something to hide the scars that adorn my body, I'm content, I'm satisfied and now, I just want to sleep wrapped up in this man.

I wake in the same position I fell asleep in, my head resting on Ian's shoulder, his fingers tracing up and down my arm, the sunlight filtering in through the windows. "Good morning." My confidence still holding over this morning, I'm not afraid of what he may be thinking of the naked body I've grown ashamed of, last night he worshiped every inch of me.

"Good morning Bellissima, how do you feel?" I blush just a little, and I can't stifle the giggle.

"I feel fantastic, I slept well, and woke up here with you, the day is off to a great start." I could do this for the rest of my life.

"Me as well, what I'm not looking forward to is getting up, unfortunately, that's going to have to happen sooner rather than later. Care to join me for a shower?" Two weeks ago, I might have balked at the suggestion.

"Absolutely!" Everything about him is perfect, what's more, he is perfect for me.

As the water cascades down upon us, and streams from every side, he kisses me tenderly, softly, before turning me away from him, I hear him fumbling with bottles before he takes up my hair, lathering shampoo into my scalp and down the ends, using his fingers to massage the shampoo in. I close my eyes and revel in the way that it feels. After rinsing the shampoo, he repeats the process with the conditioner, then moves on to my body, lathering soap from my head to my toes, pausing at my back. For a moment I want to turn away, I want to hide what he sees there, but I resist the urge, allowing him to take in what he knew was there but had only seen glimpses of. Before he continues, he kisses my shoulder.

I can't hide them away forever, but I never thought that I could let someone in like this. Anyone else, I probably wouldn't have been able to, but Ian is different, he seems to know just what to say, and how to react to every situation. He does so without causing fear or distrust.

"You are beautiful, and I only use beautiful for lack of a better word, because beautiful doesn't begin to describe you, Olivia." He looks intently in my eyes.

"Thank you." What else do I say to that?

Both of us dressed, ready for the day, though I don't know what is planned, I still need to call the Desert Sands. Roger had said he would call at the beginning of the week, it's Wednesday and I haven't heard from him. Ian has an empire to run, I don't know if he'll be running it from here or if he needs to go into the office.

"Should we cook breakfast or have something brought up?" As much as I like preparing a meal together, breakfast prepared by someone else sounds good.

"Can I get an omelet brought up?" I feel a bit guilty once I say the words, if I was home, I would have made myself something, I seem to be falling into this a bit more than I wanted.

"Anything you want." He leans in and kisses my forehead, my guilty thoughts forgotten as I follow him out of the bedroom.

Breakfast arrived, Ian and I sit at the breakfast bar, each reading a paper, both grateful there doesn't seem to be anything about either of us in the news, like a couple that's been together forever.

Ian lays down his paper, elbow rested on the bar, his hand rubbing the scruff on his chin, contemplating something. I set my paper aside, waiting for him to notice, not wanting to interrupt his thoughts.

"Last night was incredible." He looks at me, but its more than that, it's like he looks into my soul, I bow my head, I feel my cheeks flush and a grin that I can't control. He tips my chin, drawing my eyes back to his. "Incredible." He emphasizes.

It was all I wanted and didn't know. It was years of pent up passion that's gone unexpressed. "I thought so too." It isn't just what happened, it was incredible, also because of him. Could I have tossed aside my inhibitions with someone else? Probably not. Ian makes me feel safe and adored, he doesn't make me forget what I've been through, but he makes me feel strong enough to overcome it all, makes me see that my past doesn't have to define my future.

He raises my chin more, slowly leaning in, softly his lips touch mine. Tender, slow, sensual, gradually intensifying, desire floods through me, and then it's gone, Ian pulls back, "I have work to get done and a speech to write, with distractions like this, I won't accomplish either." The ache inside me deepens, flashbacks of last night adding to the heat of his kiss.

"Well, I'd hate to be the cause of the fall of an empire." I've taken up a lot of his time as of late, I'm sure he has fallen behind in things he should have been handling all along. I can sacrifice what I want so that he can attend to matters that need his attention.

He doesn't get far from me throughout the day, we say little but always remain close physically, close enough for a stolen touch, close enough to minimize my disappointment in the physical distance between us.

As he catches up with his work, I keep myself busy journaling, highlighting notes in the text that I might apply to other writings later. I've written little since I came to stay in his golden tower. I want to remember it all, not just the moments but the feelings. When I get to last night, I try to decipher how it came about, what changed that all of my fears did an about face?

The initial kiss started it, things within me stirred that had been silent for years, still I was apprehensive, still I was afraid, I just wasn't ready to take it further. Alex's phone call was a catalyst, hearing from him what I had feared from the beginning was becoming a reality. Realizing that my life is still on hold, that I'm still allowing Greg to rule my life, no longer directly but indirectly. Alex's call was only the beginning, it was Ian as well. The way that he conceded although he disagreed with me, not just last night but since I've met him, helping me to wield my own power in controlling my life. Making me recognize that I have that power.

As the day goes on there's no call from Alex with any update, I contemplate again calling the Desert Oasis but lose my nerve. With all that's happened, is right now the time to be out? I know that I would have security, but to mitigate the risk to myself and those around me, it seems to be a blessing that I haven't received a call yet.

"I've got something." Fletcher interrupts my thoughts. Ian stops typing, looking up at me, Fletcher joins us in the living room, "The unknown call you got, came from Edward Carson." I don't know the name, but Ian seems to recognize it.

Seeing my confusion, Ian explains, "He's Vivian's dealer, the one Brett let into your apartment." Fletcher has just tied Vivian and her dealer to Greg. I can't comprehend why she would do this, she didn't even know me, even if she's trying to get back at Ian, why use me? Prior to the attack I had only met him for the interview, she couldn't know what would happen between us, I didn't know things would progress the way that they have.

"Why?" I'm angry with myself for not being able to formulate a better question.

"This is about me. Think about it Olivia, Greg gets papers drawn up by Alex, does his research and finds Battling Back, it's not a far jump to assume that Alex is using the foundation to represent you. In that connection, he finds me, who better to employ to do his dirty work than my ex-wife, none of them could have known the relationship we've developed. In his mind she was a perfect candidate to get to you, in her mind, she could destroy the foundation to get at me." It's all so calculated, a reasonable explanation, but what kind of person would allow someone they don't know to be hurt just to get revenge on another.

"Markus still hasn't gotten anything on the New York number and the guys still haven't found Vivian, they've been looking for her since yesterday. Additionally, Greg submitted a request for a leave of absence, he didn't go into the office today." What does that mean? If Greg has someone here working on his behalf, why wouldn't he go back to work?

"I want to know where he is, keep looking for Vee, and her dealer, keep Brett on the radar as well, if you need to reach out to your network, do it. Aside from the obvious, have we figured out if Lawrence blew up the Whiskey at Vee's request?" Fletcher shakes his head, but I miss his response, my own ideas surfacing. It appears that it's all connected, we aren't being attacked separately, from multiple directions, it's one person orchestrating it all. It boils down to me. All that's transpired between us is a direct result from the first attack. What would Greg think if he knew that he had driven us together? That the attack that was intended to frighten me, had been instrumental in creating not only a fierce ally but also created this relationship that continues to build, growing stronger.

Fletcher returns to the library, Ian wraps me up in his arms, soothing me, calming me. "That's enough work for the day, I can finish my speech tomorrow." He doesn't release me, only squeezes a little tighter, resting his chin on the top of my head. "We've missed lunch, unless your opposed to it, let's let Fletcher and the guys work on the new revelations, you and I have an early dinner and talk about anything except our exes and what they're doing." Until we can stop them, what is there to discuss.

"That sounds like the perfect evening." We've spent time talking about other things, but so many of our conversations are overshadowed by the current events taking place, a night without sounds nice.

"I'll make dinner, we can turn on the TV, watch something mindless, put in a movie, whatever you want to do. I'm up for anything as long as it's with you and provided we lift the shroud that's been plaguing us and toss it aside." I don't want mindless, I don't want a movie that entertains us, I want engaging.

"We'll think on it and I'll help with dinner." I like the connection it brings, being in the kitchen together, being with him, doing the mundane things gives me a sense of being home. I consider what that means, home has always been a place, New York was home, but there is nothing left for me there. Vegas has never felt like home, just a safe space to reside, but here, not the apartment but with Ian, this feels like home. Can you find home in a person? Is that possible?

Ian sets the oven, and starts washing potatoes, I locate the foil and wrap as he sets them down. As I put them in the oven, he lays out steaks, seasoning them and setting aside, then together we build the salad, each of us focused on the tasks before us. Neither of us with much to say, both of us feeling the connection and communicating regardless of the lack of conversation. Both stealing glances, and each taking every opportunity to brush the others skin. It's communication on a deeper level, our hearts interacting, our souls connecting.

"Let's turn on some music and watch the city light up." It sounds like a relaxing end to the day, just him and I watching the world go by.

Chapter 38

Ian

Anything, so long as we don't have to rehash and try to piece together the puzzle that's thrown us together. I can't be dismissive of all that's transpired, without it, I wouldn't be here with her. She could have suggested anything, and I would have agreed, but music and the live show that is Las Vegas would have been my choice as well.

Dusk has already fallen, the lights growing brighter as night comes upon us. The music just barely loud enough to hear, a bottle of wine on the table, each of us with a glass. I'd told Fletcher we didn't want to be disturbed, we both need the break, to not be consumed by the chaos around us. Without all the rest of it, this right here I could see happening for the rest of my life.

"What made you decide to buy a casino? You told me about winning the poker tournament and how it came to be, but you never said why you chose a casino." Olivia breaks the silence.

"I'd spent my whole life around casinos. Maybe if I had grown up somewhere else, I would have chosen real estate or stocks, but here, casinos are the lifeblood of this city, I knew I could be successful and that's what I wanted. It wasn't that I dreamed of owning a casino or clubs, I dreamed of being successful, and I was determined to be successful enough to be able to take care of mama." The years that she spent working to take care of Alex and me, the sacrifices that she made, I wanted to pay it all back, Alex did too but his journey took him on a path that he wanted to honor his mom, hence how he ended up in law school.

"So, if you hadn't won the money and bought a casino, what would you have done? What did you want to be when you grew up?" I went to business school. I don't know if that was what I dreamed of growing up, but I knew that anything that I did with a business degree would only help to make me be a success.

"The only thing that I ever really wanted was just to be happy and to be able to take care of my mom. I had no set goal in mind, I was happy to follow wherever the road took me, as long as I could have those two things." Still listening, Olivia stands by the window, getting a further view. I set down my glass and join her, standing behind her, closing her in my arms. I had found success, and now I've found my happy, because even with all that's happening around us, I am happy.

She turns to face me. Wrapping her arms around my neck, the music in the background, we sway to the music, dancing in the living room, the rest of the world fades away.

She softly snores laying at my side, my fingers explore the naked skin of her back, feeling each scar, tracing them. When one ends, there's another to follow, the pain she has endured in this life.

Tonight, ended much like the last, our bodies joining in passion, lust, urgency, and need. Both of us wanting the physical connection to coincide with the emotional one we feel. Unlike last night, my mind won't shut off, it keeps trying to piece together the new information with the old. I'm not drawing conclusions, just circling the information. Expanding into how to keep her safe, how I can best protect her, how to keep her from suffering more scars at the hands of Greg. She can't stay hidden forever.

Once I got to sleep, I slept soundly, the smell of Olivia's strawberry shampoo soothing me, feeling her next to me, knowing she's safe. While she still sleeps peacefully, I run a checklist of what needs to be accomplished today, I need to finish my speech and I should probably check the ballroom is set. Cocktail hour begins at 5, followed by speeches from Alex and I, dinner, then the silent auction. It's a big night every year. Olivia has asked how we're able to do what we do with Battling Back, she will get to see for herself.

Her breathing changes and I know she is waking up, "Good morning Bellissima." She groans in protest. "It's going to be a good day, but there's a lot to get done." She lifts her head, gracing me with a brilliant smile, the smile that shines throughout her face, lighting up her eyes.

"Coffee first, then you can put me to work." No day can be started without coffee.

A routine has formed, we sit together at the breakfast bar, reading our newspapers, having coffee, having a quiet moment before we attack the day. Today will be different, we have a plan, today we have something to do other than watch the world go by and enjoy the time we have together.

First stop is the ballroom, set up to accommodate three hundred guests, a stage at the back of the room, sectioned off to the right of the stage is the pit for the orchestra, to the left is the bar. Thirty large tables with settings for ten at each, alternating black and red tablecloths, with bouquets of white lilies as the centerpieces. Along every wall there are tables and easels set up displaying the art, trips, services, and all the other things that have been donated that's up for bid in the silent auction. Every item will be bid upon, each will sell for more than the value, the guests that get out bid will still open their checkbook and give a cash donation. It's through these donations that we keep the foundation going. These donations pay for job training, clothing, housing, utilities. Alex, along with several other attorneys at his firm, work pro bono for the foundation. Security is handled through me, in addition to several apartments that I maintain specifically for foundation use, a steppingstone when housing is hard to find.

Olivia wanders through looking at the items up for bid, while I check in with the chef and the maître de, I watch her from afar while I am briefed. She pauses for a long moment, a piece of art that I can't make out from here, something that has caught her eye, I'm curious what has piqued her interest?

When I finish with the staff, I catch up to her, at the same spot she had paused before, she had wandered through and looked at each of the displays, then came back. She's drawn back to a realistic painting, simple, elegant, but a beautiful piece by a young talented artist that was once a client. Purple irises in a clear vase sitting on a rustic table in front of a window looking out to a green pasture.

"We should probably go get ready." She doesn't flinch in surprise, only nods her head.

"I knew you were there, and I knew you were going to say that." I step beside her, she laces her arm through mine and lays her head upon my shoulder.

"Is that how old couples know that the magic is gone, when there is no element of surprise left." The ring of her laugh fills the cavernous room.

"I do believe you still have plenty of surprises for me Mr. Alessandro." She winks before she turns her eyes from me.

While Olivia showers, I finish my speech, for the most part, my speech consists of numbers, statistics, with a few personal touches thrown in the mix. Alex's speech reminds the guests that anyone can be affected by domestic abuse, he draws them in with his own story, how profoundly domestic violence has impacted his life. This year we have a special guest, the artist behind the irises has asked to speak, she wants our guests to see a success within our non-profit, a testimony of what our foundation does, and how it helped her to get her life on track.

Olivia emerges from the bedroom a vision, her hair up in an elegant knot, make-up that I've rarely seen her wear, done simply, but perfect, the top of her dress loose because she needs help with the zipper, the bottom moving with every step she takes. She is perfect.

I zip her dress up the rest of the way, with my lips close to her ear, "Affascinante!" She turns her head to look at me.

"What does that mean? Is this ok?" Her nerves are working overtime.

"You are enchanting, ravishing, you look glorious." I need to expand my vocabulary, none of those words even begin to describe what I see. "Relax Olivia, you will be the most beautiful woman in the room, of that I have no doubt."

I take my leave to get myself ready, trying to hurry. I had let her go first because quite simply it just won't take long for me to get ready, a quick shave, a shower, my tuxedo will do the rest. I hurry in part because I don't want to leave her alone for too long, letting her anxiety build, but also because I'm excited to give her the gift I had delivered while we were gone.

She's calmer than I expected, sitting straight and still on her seat at the breakfast bar, her shoes tipped over beside the chair. "Mr. Alessandro, you look positively debonair, I knew you cleaned up nice, but this is over the top." A half grin plays on my lips.

Fumbling the gifts behind my back, I drop both boxes bringing them around to hand them to her. "Well this could have gone a lot smoother." Retrieving the gifts from the floor, I hand them to her. "Thank you, Olivia, please don't refuse this, it's just a couple things I wanted you to have for tonight." I can see her biting her tongue, I know she doesn't want to accept, but she's trying to do as I ask with grace.

Opening the larger of the two, she pulls a small silver clutch, crystals adorned to the fabric, it's not large enough to carry much, but a place for her phone and lip gloss. She opens the second before she says anything, I hold my breath that she won't refuse this one, teardrop diamond earrings and a small tennis bracelet, both of which will accent the crystals on her dress, without taking away from them.

"These are beautiful, this is too much Ian." She barely glances at me before looking back at the jewelry, fingering the bracelet.

"It's not too much, it's just enough." I take the tennis bracelet and put it on her right wrist, just as I thought, it's the perfect piece.

While she puts on the earrings I kneel, sliding on and buckling the straps of her shoes. "You look like a queen, absolutely regal." Offering my arm to her, "My lady." She slides her phone and lip gloss into the clutch, taking my arm, allowing me to escort her to the elevator.

Alex and Rachel were already seated when we arrived, Rachel and Olivia excited to see each other, huddled together to catch up on all that they've missed. Alex and I discuss the evening to come.

Guests continue to mill in, stopping first at the bar, prior to finding their seats. The orchestra plays, filling the room with peaceful music in the background. Leaving Rachel, Olivia, Alex, and I take our places on the stage. I will take the podium first, Maryanne will follow, then Alex.

The orchestra fades away when I approach the podium.

"Good evening ladies and gentlemen, thank you for joining us, coming out to support the victims of domestic violence. Each year we are inundated with victims, both male and female. Most of which have nowhere else to turn, they have no friends, they are estranged from their family..."

A piercing scream shatters the quiet, a yell for security from down the hall. Guests standing up to see what's going on, event security, as well as personal security racing to the far door. Looking at our table, Rachel is weaving through the crowd, Olivia is alone at our table. In her hand is her phone, the look of horror on her face, she meets my eyes, black streaks run down her cheeks, her makeup smeared by the tears falling. She pushes her way through the crowd, not running toward me, running from me. Confusion and chaos, as I try to get through to catch up to her.

My phone vibrates in my pocket, hoping that it might be her, I pull it out, a text message from an unknown number.

Now she knows and so do you.

Attached is picture, a birth certificate, my birth certificate, except the last name is wrong, and rather than the space next to father being empty, the name, Angus Riley Kelley. What the fuck is happening?

"Ian, we need to clear everyone out." Alex is trying to get my attention. "Ian, they just found three dead bodies in the

bathroom down the hall, one of them is
Vivian."

Fist of Rage

Book 2

Returned to Rage

Coming April 2021